Dear Zoe,
I hope you enjoy Charlotte
& Henry's story as much
as I do

Queen Pin

Jacquelyn Marker

JmK

Literary Wanderlust | Denver, Colorado

Queen Pin is a work of fiction. Names, characters, places, and incidents are the products of the author's imagination and have been used fictitiously. Any resemblance to actual events, locales, or persons, living or dead, is entirely coincidental.

Copyright © 2022 by Jacquelyn McBride

Published in the United States by Literary Wanderlust LLC, Denver, Colorado.

https//www.LiteraryWanderlust.com

ISBN Paperback: 978-1-942856-99-3
ISBN Digital: 978-1-956615-00-5

Cover design: Kylee Howels

Printed in the United States of America

1

Charlotte

Eyes are the windows to a person's soul. Medicine cabinets are the window to their habits.

Toothbrush, toothpaste.

Razor, shaving cream.

Hairbrush, pomade.

Jock-itch spray? Hmm, someone's got the fungus.

Condoms—ribbed, extra-large, economy-sized box, half empty.

Amoxicillin. Did the fungus get out of control, or is it syphilis?

The sound of crunching from the gravel driveway tells me my time is up. I slam the mirror to the cabinet shut and make a mad dash to the living room, cracking my elbow on the door jamb on my way out. "Son of a biscuit maker!" I cry out, cradling my elbow. I can hardly breathe from the searing pain running up my arm, and I kind of want to cry. Why do people call it the funny bone? There is nothing the least bit humorous about it.

The two-bedroom bungalow is charming with hand-me-down furniture and so many windows the seamless beauty of the ocean seeps into the tiny home. If it weren't for the seagulls squawking and the waves crashing onto the Miami coastline, I would think I was looking at a painting.

An oversized leather recliner with duct tape on the armrest sits in front of the TV. I take my position, my feet dangling over the edge of the seat, and I kind of feel like Goldilocks sitting in Papa Bear's chair. Kicking my legs and torquing my shoulders, I swivel so I'm facing the front door. I want to be the first thing he sees when he walks in.

I am giddy with excitement, like being at a surprise party, waiting impatiently for the moment the guest of honor arrives. Dousing my giddiness is the presence of something hard pressing against the back of my skull.

A familiar metallic click resonates in my ears.

It's a gun.

There's a gun to my head.

"Who are you?" asks a deep voice. There is no wavering, no give to his hard as steel tone.

Moving at the pace of a tortoise, I raise my arms in surrender, pain lancing down one elbow. "You don't know me."

"I figured that out already. Who are you?" he asks, his gun pressing harder against my scalp.

I squeeze my eyes shut and let out a sigh. This is not how it's supposed to go. The plan was for him to walk in the front door and find me sitting in his ratty chair. The shock of an intruder would stun him, keeping him from reacting quickly, and I would immediately have the upper hand.

"My name is Charlotte Sutton. And you're Brian Cain's big brother—Henry."

The pressure from the back of my head is gone, but the sting lingers. The leather of his holster creaks as he sheaths his gun.

He lets out an annoyed grunt, and I can hear his footsteps retreat, but I don't dare turn around. I put this whole situation in motion, and the first hiccup has me regretting every decision which led me to this house with this man.

"Can I get you something to drink, Charlotte?" he asks, the persona of a trained cop beginning to soften.

I turn the chair around in time to see the towering figure with dark hair walk into the kitchen. "Um, water would be nice."

Brian Cain is a beanpole of a man with chronic scraggly hair and a bad complexion. His brother, on the other hand . . . Wow.

When Henry walks out of the kitchen, my mouth runs dry, and my heart beats to a strange mix of West Side Story songs. There is no way the two men can be related. Henry is tall and muscular. So muscular, his biceps are stretching the seams of the sleeves of his policeman uniform. His dark hair is combed back with a slight pompadour which would look ridiculous on anyone else. On Henry Cain, this style adds to the magnetism that must have women fighting for his attention.

Henry pulls off the utility belt which contains his gun, handcuffs, and other tools a cop keeps handy, and walks over to where I'm sitting. He hands me a cold bottle of water, and my fingers brush against his. Shivers run from the tips of my fingers all the way down my spine. Whatever this is, I think he feels it too because he holds onto the bottle for a beat too long, then clears his throat and lets go. He sits on the couch across from me and cracks open a can of beer, then extends his long arms across the back of the sofa. "Did he rob your mother?"

"Excuse me?" I ask, momentarily forgetting why I'm here.

"Brian. Did he max out your credit cards?"

Right. "No and no."

"Are you pregnant?"

I laugh a little at the insane notion that Henry thinks I would ever sleep with a man like Brian. "Definitely not."

He nods and takes another sip of his beer. "I give. What'd he do this time?"

I sit forward on the edge of the recliner so my feet touch the ground and cross my ankles. No matter how hard I try to exude confidence, I feel like a child. Choosing to wear my red hair in pigtails doesn't help. Instead of Jessica Rabbit, I'm more like Pippi Longstocking. "Mr. Cain, I'm not here about your brother. Well, I am. But not exactly. I've never done this before. I'm not sure where to start."

"Start from the beginning."

"Yeah, that's a good idea. I lost someone close to me recently. My brother."

This is the first time I have spoken the words aloud and it feels wrong. I don't know how to live without my twin brother. It's like a part of me is missing.

Henry purses his lips, and his caramel eyes cast downward. "I'm sorry for your loss."

"Thank you. It's a long story, but what it boils down to is that I'm starting to question my own safety in my current situation."

"What makes you think you're not safe?" he asks, his dark eyebrows crinkling in the middle.

"My brother's death was . . ." I search for a word that won't raise too much suspicion in case this whole thing blows up in my face, "suspicious." That was not a better word, but the best I can come up with under pressure. "And I'm not sure I can trust the people who are being paid to protect me."

He nods and seems to think about it for a few, painstakingly long, seconds. He takes a couple more swigs of his beer and says, "You have people who protect you?"

"Yes."

"And you don't think they're effective?"

"Correct."

"I'm sorry, but what does this have to do with me?"

"Because I want to hire you. I need someone from the outside I can trust." I tell him.

"And how does Brian fit into all of this? Do you think he had something to do with your brother's death?"

I laugh and shake my head, disbelieving he would have such a low opinion of his brother. From what I know, Brian Cain will never be given the key to the city, but he's not a killer. "No, not at all. Maybe I'm not being very clear. Have you ever heard of the Scalise Family?"

Now it's his turn to laugh at me. "Of course I have," he mocks with a smirk.

"Good. Then you'll understand if I told you your brother is deep in debt to the family."

My words cause Henry's entire body to stiffen. "And I assume you represent the Scalise Family? At least in some capacity."

"In some capacity." The truth is I'm now the head of the world-recognized crime family, but this might not be the moment to mention that tiny detail.

"It seems to me this is a bigger problem for you than me. You say you fear for your life, or at least that's what I'm getting from it, so why not get a different job?"

If only I could. "Nothing in life is ever that simple, Mr. Cain. Besides, I'm not in a position to change jobs at the moment."

"And Brian's debt? What does that have to do with this?"

"I've made arrangements for your brother's debt to be wiped clean in exchange for you providing me with protection." There, I've laid it all out, excluding a few details, now I have to see if he'll bite.

Henry finishes his beer in three strong pulls then crushes the can in his fist. "You have the authority to make that arrangement? For my brother, I mean."

It should be the very least I can do. In truth, I have little say-so in any matters. If Henry Cain accepts, that will all change. "Absolutely."

"I have a job, Miss Sutton," he says, waving a strong arm along his uniform. "It is Miss, isn't it?"

My cheeks heat. I'm not very good at picking up when a man is hitting on me, and I'm not saying he is, but he might be. "That's correct, I'm not involved with anyone," I tell him, my voice small and shy.

"That doesn't matter to me," he says with no inflection. "I

wanted to know if there was a husband or boyfriend who could be at the root of your problems."

My heart deflates with embarrassment. "No. No boyfriend, no husband."

"Good. Now, as I was saying, I have a job. Are you expecting me to work for you exclusively? And for how long?"

It doesn't take a genius to figure out he's worried about money. There is a fair amount of research that goes into finding the right person to exploit. I had three potential contenders, but Henry Cain came out on top. He's twenty-seven with a steady work history. His age suggests a firm grasp on the complexities of life and the agility to handle the physical aspects of my proposal. A strong work history proves he's dedicated to his profession and to those he works for. He's also a police officer, so I know he can handle tense and dangerous situations. Such experience also means he's trained on using firearms, which is essential for obvious reasons. It also helps to know he has less than two hundred dollars in his savings account.

"This will need to be an exclusive arrangement for the next six weeks or so. But don't worry, Mr. Cain, you will be well compensated for your time."

He doesn't say anything, and I'm sitting here like a silly little fool. Minutes tick by on the Felix The Cat clock in the kitchen. It's been precisely 184 seconds since I propositioned him. Giving up, I stand and pull a folded piece of paper out of my purse and hand it to him. "I'll need your answer in the next forty-eight hours, or I'll need to look elsewhere. Call me when you decide. If it's a yes, I'll have my driver pick you up and drop you at my home." I sling my purse over my shoulder and pull open the front door.

I walk out and head down the sidewalk, pleased with myself. I had the last word and the upper hand. I turn onto the next block and hop into a rusty Ford pickup truck. If Henry Cain says yes, I can make my play to take over the family business.

—

Nothing about my plan has been easy. The variables are minimal, but the timing of every detail must be precise. My entire life is monitored. If there is no camera, there will be a bodyguard. My daily routine, weekly, and monthly schedules are planned to the Nth degree. I wouldn't be shocked to find my menstrual cycle is also monitored.

For the past week, I have been taking daily naps at two o'clock, trying to establish a new pattern for my day. During my "naps" I would observe the guards in the guard shack. I needed to determine their exact routine for switching shifts, the rest of the details would be done at night, cloaked in darkness.

Just before my nap today, I manually disabled the alarm system to allow me to climb out my bedroom window undetected. The in-house security cameras were set on a two-hour loop taped from two days prior. Change of guard gave me two minutes to scale from my bedroom and run the expanse of the compound and climb the wall to the other side undetected. I walked three blocks away and ordered an Uber to take me to a grocery store parking lot. I could only hope I would have a driver who could be bribed to let me borrow their car for an undetermined length of time. I didn't want to have witnesses to where I was going or any theory as to why. Luckily, my face is not as well publicized as my father's and brother's faces were.

The Uber driver was surprisingly anxious about letting me drive his truck for a vehicle with the entire passenger side held together with duct tape. I'm sure it didn't meet Uber regulations, but I paid the Nervous Nelly three hundred bucks for the opportunity. The truck shimmied the whole way to and from Henry Cain's house, I wasn't sure I was going to make it back to the Publix parking lot in one piece.

Getting back into the compound was a little less complicated. I ordered a pizza to be delivered to the Publix lot, bribed the delivery driver, and rode in the trunk to get back into the secured property of my family home. That required a few phone calls for clearance with the guards. Five hundred dollars later, and I'm now standing two stories below my bedroom window. I scaled the trellis on my way down, now I have to climb back to the top.

I hook my foot into a latch, then another, balancing my weight as I fumble through the vines. As I approach the second story, I spy one of the housekeepers dusting in my father's old study. My heart still aches from missing him. I don't have much time to consider the loss before the rail under one foot snaps, knocking me off balance. My body shifts, putting all my weight on the opposite leg. The threaded wood beneath my other foot breaks, and I find myself jolting down the trellis. My fingers slip through the greenery, and I can't grab hold of anything substantial.

"Oh," I chuff out as I hit the ground with a hard thud.

Amara, the cook, rushes out the front door. "Is everything okay?" she asks, stomping on the blooms in the flower bed to get to me.

"I'm fine," I tell her, pushing up off the ground. I dust the dirt from my knees and backside. "I was looking at the roses, and then a spider jumped out at me. It was a big one too," I tell her, using my thumb and index finger to indicate size.

She crinkles her nose, and I know she doesn't believe me. I hate lying to her, but I would prefer it been Amara who caught me over Ray.

"Right," she says, turning on her heel, and I follow her through the front door. "You missed your dinner with Ray. I saved a plate for you, it's in the warmer. Unless you would prefer pizza," she says, pointing to the pie I had ordered to get back into the compound.

Fudge-sticks. I completely forgot about my weekly dinner with Ray. "Did he say anything?"

Amara nods. "Yeah. I went up to your room to look for you, but you weren't there. I told him you hadn't been feeling well all week and asked to reschedule dinner with him for Friday night.

I hope that wasn't too presumptuous of me?"

I smile so wide with relief it could almost split my face. "That's absolutely perfect. Thank you," I tell Amara, dropping a light kiss on her cheek. "I don't know what I would do without you."

There is little doubt Ray will be furious, and I don't have a strategy yet to deal with that problem, but I'll figure it out when the time comes. Of course, this all hinges on the prospect that Henry Cain will accept my proposal.

Amara steps out of my embrace and runs her calloused working hands across my forehead, sweeping away the loose strands of my pigtails. Her lips form a delicate line of worry. "Me neither," she says as she pulls a plate out of the warming drawer and sets it on the island.

I hop onto the barstool. Literally, hop. I remember having to climb this seat when I was about five, then graduated to jumping when I was twelve, and I haven't grown an inch since. I will forever be doomed to hurdle my seat in the kitchen.

"Listen," she sighs, as I stab my fork into the salmon, "I don't know what's going on or what you're up to, but I don't want you to get hurt."

There's a small pang of regret when she says this. I've known Amara my whole life. She's been like a mother to me. In fact, she's been so much like a mother that my father never bothered to hire a nanny. Amara took me to dance lessons and mended my first broken heart. She drove Charlie to hockey practice and taught him how to be a gentleman.

"I know." I catch and squeeze her hand for reassurance. "I'm doing everything in my power to keep myself and everyone I love safe."

She shakes her head and raises an eyebrow, her disappointment obvious. "I guess that will have to be good enough."

I finish my dinner, and she takes my plate and heads to the sink to wash the dishes.

"Do you want me to do the dishes?" I offer.

She waves me off. "I got it. But thank you."

I let out an obnoxious yawn and stretch my arms in the air for good measure. "I'm so tired. I think I'm going to head upstairs and take a hot bath and go to bed."

We say our goodnights, and I bound up the stairs. When I arrive at the landing on the second floor, I peer down the hall and decide it's time to visit my father.

I walk the familiar corridor, taking my time, avoiding the points in the hardwood that creak. It brings back pleasant memories of me trying to sneak up on Daddy—I had spent months learning all the spots which might give me away.

I was six years old crouched down on my hands and knees, stealing into his office.

He was on the phone. "About the pony for Charlotte's birthday," he said to whoever was on the other side.

I was so excited that I got to hear about my big birthday plans and that he had no idea I was there. I could barely contain my giggles, I had to cover my mouth to smother my enjoyment.

"We need to cancel it," he said.

I learned so young that spying can yield disastrous, heartbreaking results.

"Charlie wants a T-Rex, and I don't think it's a good idea to have a pony and a T-Rex at the same party," he declared through the line.

Of course, Charlie would want a T-Rex for his birthday. "Daddy," I cried. Even at the age of make-believe and imaginary friends, I knew dinosaurs were extinct.

His handsome, smooth face broke into a wide grin as he opened his arms, inviting me.

I ran to him and hopped on his lap. He wrapped his arms around me, and I felt safe, cherished, and loved.

"Daddy," I said, snuggling into his chest.

"Yes, bug."

"Don't tell Charlie, but there aren't any T-Rexes anymore.

They all died a gajillion years ago."

He had laughed, and I can still feel the rumble of his chest beneath my cheek. "I won't, bug."

I wipe away the tear trailing down my cheek. My father was not a perfect man. He did things that could make one question his value for human life. To my father, lives were disposable and easily replaced. It was part of the job. As flawed a man as he was, there was a time when he was the perfect father. Some days, I wish I could travel back in time to when life was less complicated, and everyone was who they said they were.

However, it seems I can't travel time, which is why I need to do this. For my brother. For the family legacy. I hope I hear back from Henry Cain because, without him, I don't know that I will be able to pull this off.

2

Henry

"**W**hat the fuck did you do, you little pissant?" I bellow as I lunge through the front door of my parent's house. Brian's carrying a sandwich into the living room, and his eyes go wide as I rush toward him.

He falls flat on his ass, his plate crashing to the hardwood floor and tiny shards fly across the smooth surface. The touted unbreakable dishware after surviving three children has finally met its doom.

Brian raises both of his hands in surrender. "I didn't do shit! What the hell is your problem?" He scrambles to pick up the food and works to reassemble his sandwich.

"The Scalise Family? Really?"

"Fuck," he sighs as he pushes himself up from the floor, taking a bite of bologna. Brian isn't short. When he isn't hunched over in defeat, as he almost always is, he's just over six-foot. But I still have a good three inches on him. We're as opposite as brothers can be. Where he's lanky, I'm bulky. I have my own place; he still lives at home. I worked my ass off for everything I have, and Brian looks for get-rich-quick schemes. If they have a pulse, Brian will find a way to swindle them.

"Yeah, fuck," I agree, plopping down on Mom's couch.

He sits next to me. "It's not what you think."

"It never is. Remember when you were in high school, and you put itching powder in the jockstrap of every guy on the football team?"

Brian's eyes glaze over, and a small smile tilts his lips.

"They were ready to beat you to a bloody pulp until I convinced them it was an infectious case of jock-itch that spread through the locker room from poor hygiene." As an adult, I recently found out the load of crap I fed those teenagers was real. We recently had a rash of jock-itch swarm the police locker room. I spent two weeks scratching my junk and spraying it down before it went away. Now, I never change at work, always at home.

"I got you out of that mess and dozens more since, but this one? I'm not sure about this one." I can't keep saving his hide, and every part of me says it's time to let him deal with the fallout on his own. The one problem is he's managed to screw over one of the most notorious crime families on the eastern seaboard.

"I don't expect you to clean up my messes, you know." Brian takes the last bite of his sandwich. "I'm a man. I'm twenty-three years old, I can take care of myself," he says, breadcrumbs flying out of his mouth as he speaks.

I snort with laughter at his declaration. "You've done a great job so far."

He doesn't reply to that because he knows I'm right.

"How'd you find out?" Brian asks, bowing his head and twiddling his fingers.

"When I arrived home after work, there was a representative for the Scalise Family sitting in my living room." When I pulled up to the house, I noticed a beat-up F-10 parked down the street. Sure, it could have been someone visiting a neighbor, but my spidey senses were tingling. I parked a block away and walked up to the house, scoping out the perimeter. When I peeked into the bathroom window, I found a tiny woman digging around in my medicine cabinet. Who does that, seriously? People have a right to privacy, toothbrushes and ointments included. Once I was convinced the perp was alone, I parked my car in the driveway and revved my engine. I could have left my car and entered the house without giving away my position, but I wanted to be a dick. Announcing I was home would give the nosey fairy in my bathroom a false sense of control. It was a sick little thrill when I stepped through the patio door of my bedroom, walked with measured steps into the living room, and pressed the muzzle of my gun to the back of her head.

"Shit," he says, sounding surprised. "Listen, I'm sorry. I didn't mean for you to get dragged into this. I thought I had it all under control. Simon called and we made arrangements for me to pay back—"

I cut him off. "I don't want to know the details. I'm a fucking cop for Christ's sake."

"They didn't tell you?" Brian asks.

"No, and I'm glad they didn't."

"What did they want then?"

My mind floods with images of that adorable strawberry-blonde sitting in my recliner. Charlotte looked ridiculous, way too soft and small for the chair, and the attitude she brought with her. "They offered me a job. Said if I took it, they'd wipe your debt clean."

"You're not seriously considering it are you?"

"I don't have much choice, do I?"

"This could destroy your career. Don't let me ruin your life," he pleads.

"My career isn't as important as you, Brian. This isn't sleeping with the mayor's wife then stealing his car. This isn't about a few years in the pen. It's life or death."

"Dinner," Mom calls out to us.

There are some comforts of a childhood home that never get old. The smell of thirty years' worth of cooking baked into the peeling floral wallpaper. The creaks of the floorboards on the walk to the dining room. The site of a dinner table large enough to host the Queen of England. For the first time in a long time, I remember why I love it here so much.

"Come on," I say to Brian. "Let's go have a nice dinner with the folks." The topic of the Scalise's is over, and I know everything I need to. I've been mad as hell for the past two hours. A part of me wants to beat some sense into him, but Brian is my brother, and I have to protect him. I've said my piece, no point in dwelling on something that can't be changed.

In the dining room, Mom brings a platter with a butt roast trimmed with potatoes and carrots. "It's been too long, Henry. What made you decide to come home?" she asks as she sets down a basket of biscuits.

I knew she would be suspicious. I haven't been to Fort Lauderdale to visit my parents in almost six weeks. Brian had been shacked up with some woman in Miami until a week ago. I assumed once he left, he would take his troubles with him. I was wrong. "No particular reason. I simply missed your smiling face," I tell Mom, then tear off a bite of a biscuit.

She raises her eyebrow at me, and I know she doesn't buy it.

"Sit down and enjoy your dinner, Bev," Dad says, slopping potatoes and roast onto a plate for her. "Don't ask questions, just be glad he's here at all."

The first point goes to Dad. It's a double whammy, stand up for my defense, then guilt-trip me. "Thanks, Dad," I tell him, and as peeved as I am for him being so manipulative, I'm also grateful for the distraction. I take a bite of the roast and pass the platter around. "This is amazing. You've out done yourself."

Dad frowns at me. He does all the cooking; Mom does all the dishes. It's an arrangement that has kept their marriage strong and fair. As a Michelin-Star chef, my father is rarely enthusiastic about cooking at home. Nothing fancy, but always delicious.

"Brian, what was your high today?" Mom asks, pulling out the old game of highs and lows, where we tell the best parts of our day, but her version leaves out the lows.

"My high," Brian says, then plops a carrot in his mouth as he thinks it over. "I had a job interview."

I'm shocked as shit to hear that. Never thought Brian would go the honorable route.

"That's great," Mom says. "Where at?"

"It's nothing special, just the gas station down the street. It's walking distance," Brian says, shrugging his shoulder and pushing his food around on his plate.

"Hey, it's honest work. Don't play it off like it doesn't matter," Dad chimes in.

Mom nods, agreeing with Dad. "What about you, Henry? What was your high?"

"I met a girl," I say, trying to deflect any possible scent of deceit with the aid of Mom's kryptonite—my love life.

Beverly Cain can smell a lie from a mile away, probably from the years she spent as a homicide detective. If she grills me, I'm going to crack like a walnut. I could lie to St. Peter at the Pearly Gates if I had to, but my mom? I can't do it.

"Do tell," she says, her eyes wide with hope.

"Well, she's cute and sweet. You'd like her." I don't know how sweet someone like Charlotte Sutton can be. She did break into my house and blackmail me, so "sweet" isn't the best word to describe her, but it's the perfect way to convince Mom.

"I'm so excited," she says, clapping her hands. "When do I get to meet her?"

Never. I immediately regret bringing Charlotte into this conversation. Still, she has been on my mind from the second she left my house. "Calm down, Mom, I haven't even gotten the nerve to ask her out yet. What if she doesn't feel the same way about me?" I need to find a way out of this. Telling her about my love life is going to cause me grief. I'm in for late-night phone calls asking for updates on my progress with asking out the delectable little redhead.

"How can she not feel the same way?" Mom squeals, pinching my chin between her thumb and forefinger. "Look at that face. Besides, she must be pretty special if she's your high for the day."

In this case, Mom might be right. There is undoubtedly something special about Charlotte Sutton.

—

My choices are limited. Take the job and destroy my career. Do nothing and sentence my brother to death. I've run through a multitude of scenarios, and I can't find a way where it results in a win/win. The choice is clear. I sent a text to the saucy Miss Sutton late last night to let her know I'm accepting her offer. She replied within minutes with a short message telling me when I will be picked up.

A hundred questions roll around in my head. How is Charlotte Sutton associated with the Scalise Family? Why does she need protection? What happened to her brother? What service or expertise does she provide for the Scalise Family? Does the carpet match the drapes? Does she taste as sweet as she looks?

It's going to take an insurmountable effort to keep my libido in line when it comes to Charlotte. She's adorable and petite, but with enough curves to make a man pay attention, and I'll be damned if that isn't the exact type that makes my cock twitch. I need to keep my dick in my pants and stay focused. I'm a cop about to walk into the lion's den. I'll be privy to information that will keep me under the thumb of the Scalise Family for the rest of my life. Trying to sleep with Charlotte will complicate things.

An armored Hummer limousine pulls in front of my house. I'm not certain who Charlotte is, but if she's sent me a limo to take me to her, she's obviously a valued resource for the family.

It's the moment of truth. Stepping into that vehicle will change the entire course of my life. My job, my family, all of it is going to change. If I don't follow through, I may lose my brother, and his life is worth more than any plans I had for my future.

I sling a duffle bag over my shoulder and make my way to the limo. As I get in the car, I get a text from Mom. Since our discussion at dinner the other night, she's texted me thirty times. "Have you asked her yet?" "Where did you meet?" "Girls like flowers and pretty things." I roll my eyes when I read the most recent text. "The good ones don't stay single for long." I text her back, telling her I'm about to go in for my shift, and if I do ask Charlotte out, she will be the first to know. It's the most response I've given her yet. I've managed to ignore most of them, but she's chomping at the bit, and I have no one to blame but myself.

I send off a quick text to Brian and inform him that I accepted the job and to distract mom as much as possible. He replies with a thumbs-up emoji.

The driver weaves through light traffic as he takes us westward. I pull a thick file from my bag and take the time to review the information about the Scalise Family I had managed to find at the station. I had to be careful about how much info I accessed so I wouldn't raise any red flags. I put in a request for a leave of absence effective immediately. I told my captain and everyone at the station that my brother has been missing, and I was trying to find him and hoped to convince him to go to rehab. Brian may be a first-class loser, and I say that with all the love in the world, but he's never had an issue with drugs. However, everyone at the station knows I've had problems with Brian, and I'm pretty sure they all thought he was into drugs anyway. Their misconceptions were to my benefit, making this whole ruse easier to pull off. Except, heroin or meth is a more straightforward problem than this shit storm.

As to the Scalise Family, the basics I already know. John Scalise was the head of the family until thirteen years ago when he disappeared. His death has never been officially declared, but it's thought one of the other three crime families in the area may have ordered a hit.

The Scalise's have a reputation for selling black-market goods, but what they're selling and who they're selling it to is unknown. They're virtually untraceable, even their Italian lineage is unclear. Their influence is vast, and they have been connected to other networks across the globe. They're so cunning and careful they wouldn't even be on the radar if it wasn't for their association with other crime organizations.

What is known is that every single informant who came forward or was planted by various government agencies disappeared. No one knows if they were bribed, blackmailed, or met their doom and are now sleeping with the fishes.

Despite John Scalise's disappearance, the family continued to be successful in all their ventures. It's been rumored that with the seat at the head of the table open, John's second in command, Ray Thatch, filled in. However, that is where it gets interesting. Sometime late last year, the head of the family business changed. There's no concrete evidence—only rumors, and theories. As far as I can tell, no letter of the government can figure out who is running this network.

Charlotte Sutton's dossier was a little harder to get my hands on. She has no criminal record, no warrants, nothing in the realm of legal troubles. Her driving record is squeaky clean. She graduated high school through some sort of homeschooling program, with no indications of her ever attending college. More troubling is that I can't find a link between Charlotte and the Scalise organization. Other than a few official documents, the woman doesn't seem to exist. I wanted more information, but I couldn't rush the process and take the risk of sounding the alarms. The pressure was on, and the clock to respond was ticking down.

What I'm doing, who I'm getting in bed with, it's a big fucking deal. If I started snooping around the station too much, then went to work for Miss Sutton, there's no doubt my career would implode, and I could even end up doing time. The idea of bunking in a cell with someone I put behind bars has my blood running cold. Working for the Scalise Family could be a death sentence. Still, death by mobsters would be more humane than the inevitable torture I would receive behind bars.

We pass a sign as we drive into the Miami suburb of Coral Gables. I'm shocked to realize that Miss Sutton lives in such an expensive area of Miami. Fucking A-Rod has a house here.

A few minutes later, we pull up to a gate, and the driver talks into a speaker. The gate swings open, and we drive up to a stunning Spanish-style home with a tile roof and intricate tile work bordering each window. Even from my seat in the back of the limo, I can tell the house is massive.

The driver exits the car and comes around, but I open the door and hop out before he gets a chance. There's no way in hell I'm letting another man open a door for me. I nod to him, and he stares at me expectantly. It takes me a moment, but I think he's trying to hint that I should give him a tip.

"Thanks for the ride," I tell him, slapping him on the shoulder.

My heart pounds relentlessly as I ring the doorbell. I've never been a nervous kind of guy. I'm not sure if it's from reality sinking in or the woman I'll be protecting. When the door opens, I'm greeted by an older woman with dark hair pinned back in a tight bun, wearing a cliché housekeepers' uniform.

"Can I help you?" she asks, scanning me from head to toe.

"I'm here for Miss Sutton," I tell her, looking her in the eyes, letting her know I won't be intimidated.

The housekeeper's stare is just as fierce. "Charlotte isn't expecting company."

How the hell did the driver ever make it through the gate if we weren't expected?

The woman begins to close the door, and I thrust my hand against it, stopping her. "Wait a minute—"

"It's okay," a chirpy voice calls out behind her.

The housekeeper turns around, and I look past the annoyed woman. Charlotte is bounding down the stairs toward us. Her gorgeous red hair hangs loose and spills over her shoulders. The evening sun beaming through the windows cast a glow, giving her an ethereal presence. I've never used the word "ethereal" before, but there is no other word in the English language that can describe what I'm seeing.

The breath rushes out of my lungs as if I've been sacked by a lineman. Charlotte's beautiful green eyes sparkle with curiosity as she gives me a welcoming smile. A smile filled with such genuine enthusiasm that the entire reason I've come here seems impossible. There is no way anyone could want to hurt someone so innocent.

3

Charlotte

Amara had no clue I was expecting Henry or anyone for that matter. I didn't think it was a good idea to spread this information until I made my position clear. When Henry's driver buzzed the gate, I made sure I was in the security room adjacent to my father's office. My chauffeur bringing in an unvetted guest would raise a lot of questions, and I needed him to be able to get in without any trouble or suspicion. The last thing I want right now is for Ray to find out.

I make my way out of the security room and toward the stairs. The doorbell rings, and I know I need to get there before anyone else has the chance to answer the door. However, Amara beats me to it.

I dash down the steps, taking them two at a time, but as I come to the landing, I see Henry. His stance is firm, legs braced and one foot in the threshold as he pushes the door open with the palm of his hand, despite Amara's intentions of shutting him out.

Cheese and rice, he is a good-looking man. Everything about him screams masculinity. His stubbled jaw, the way his muscles fill in his T-shirt. His eyes, caramel, and . . . sweet? Yes, sweet because even though he looks tough on the outside, I can tell there's something soft and gentle about him.

"It's okay," I call out to Amara, trying to slow my pace, but my feet keep moving. I grab onto the railing, forcing the momentum to slow, but instead, my feet tangle with my legs, and I miss a step. Then another. One knee lands on the edge, and my head careens over my middle. Before I know it, I am rolling the rest of the way down the stairs until I land face-first onto the oriental rug of the entryway.

"Shit," I hear Henry mutter, followed by his bag sliding across the Travertine floors. "Are you okay?" He bends down and runs a hand from my head to my back to my—

"Yeah," I grunt as I roll over and force myself to sit up.

He lifts my chin and turns my face from side to side, looking me over, his brows crinkling with concern. "You're sure?"

"Yup, just a few bruises. Luckily, my pride took the brunt of it," I tell him, half-joking, half-serious.

"Oh, Charlotte," Amara says, kneeling next to me on my other side. "Your knee. It's all skinned up."

I look down and notice the displaced skin and the blood rising to the surface. "It's nothing." I try to stand up, but before I can even lift my butt off the floor, I find myself in the air, strong arms lifting and pulling me against a rock-hard chest. "Hey!" I cry out in surprise.

"It's not nothing," Henry says, following Amara as he whisks me toward the kitchen. "You fell down a fucking flight of stairs."

I don't know what to say. That's not true, I know what I want to say. "I'm fine." "Put me down, I can walk." "It's no big deal, this stuff happens to me all the time." I won't say any of those things. Not because I've been stunned silent, but because admitting I'm outrageously accident prone to this knight in shining armor will be the biggest embarrassment of my life.

Henry sets me on the counter of the kitchen island. "Do you have any antiseptic?" he asks Amara.

Amara nods and rolls her eyes because, of course, we have antiseptic. She spent the better part of my life bandaging me up. She pulls out a first aid kit from the pantry and brings it over.

Henry gets right to work, opening a package of gauze and squirting on the "stingy stuff." I hate the stingy stuff. Last month, I scraped my ear on the antique china cabinet in the dining room, I threw a fit when Amara tried to clean up my wound. Henry doesn't know it, but he is distracting me with the sinewy muscles bulging from beneath his T-shirt.

Henry and I lock eyes as he squirts antiseptic onto a square of gauze. He has little flecks of gold around the pupil which I hadn't noticed last time I saw him.

He shakes his head as if he's as entranced by me as I am him. "This might sting," he says before he dabs my knee with the gauze.

But I don't feel anything.

Until I do. *"Not the stingy stuff."* I shove his hand away and lift my knee up to my chin so I can blow the sting far, far away.

Henry takes a step back, his jaw slack with shock. Shock quickly morphs into amusement as a smile pulls at his lips. "The stingy stuff?" he asks, chuckling. "What are you? Seven?"

I hop off the counter, indignant and ashamed all at once. "No. I'm twenty-five." I step up to him so we're face-to-face. Except it is physically impossible for me to be face-to-face with him unless I have a ladder. He is insanely tall. I mean, I knew he was tall, but to someone who measures in at five-foot even, everyone is tall. But Henry? Henry is gigantic. Like six-five or something.

Instead, I speak into his chest, not willing to shed my pride by changing tactics and looking up to him. "And that stuff stings," I say, pointing toward the bottle of antiseptic. "I don't care how old someone is, it hurts. Every time."

His smile widens. "Okay, cupcake."

I let out a huff of frustration. Instead of acknowledging Henry's patronizing tone, I choose to stride past him and toward the staircase. "Come on, I'll show you where to put your things."

We climb the stairs to the third level, where my bedroom is, but I pass it and give it no acknowledgment. I'm not in the mood to tell Henry where I'll be sleeping. Instead, we walk to the bedroom next to mine. I thrust open the door and give a scooping wave inside. "This is where you'll be sleeping while you're here."

He pokes his head into the room and murmurs something about the size of his house. I don't catch all of it because he is so close to me, I can feel his heat radiating and bringing with it the faintest hint of cinnamon.

"Miss Sutton?" he asks.

It takes me a moment to realize he has walked past me and is now standing in the middle of the room, tossing his bag onto the king-sized bed.

"Yeah?" My voice is husky, and I hate the dreamy quality it has taken.

"I asked you where your room is?" His grin is broad as he checks me out from the top of my head to the tips of my toes.

"That's not important." The idea that he will know where I sleep can only lead to me conjuring fantasies of him climbing into my bed in the middle of the night. Not telling him brings about the images of him scouring the hallways to find me—determined to ravish me.

"Wrong."

"Huh?" Once again, I'm caught drifting off to La-La Land, where the occupants are myself and Henry.

"I said, you're wrong. I'm not going to be able to adequately protect you if I don't, at the very least, know where you sleep."

Good point. "Okay. I'm right next door." I point toward my room, and I can feel my cheeks flushing as fantasy number one plays out in my head.

"Great. Let's go have a look." He brushes past me in the

doorway, and I can feel the muscles of his abdomen rubbing against my breasts, my nipples instantly taking notice.

"We don't have to do that," I tell him, trailing behind. "There's nothing special about it."

He puts his hand on the knob. "It doesn't have to be special. I simply need to know the layout and look for potential security issues."

I try to come up with a reason, any reason, to keep him from going into my bedroom. One minute I'm having fantasies of this exact moment, but I will be mortified in reality if he sees my room. "No one is going to be able to get to me in my house," I tell him, rushing around him and blocking the door.

"If that were true, then you wouldn't need me to provide twenty-four-hour protection, now would you?" His gaze narrows with suspicion. "Why don't you want me to see your bedroom? What are you hiding?"

Henry reaches for the doorknob again, and I splay my arms and legs against the frame, convinced there is no way he's going to be able to get past me.

I am wrong.

He chuckles, then bends and places one hand on either side of my waist. He lifts me like I weigh ten pounds, turns, then sets me down. Just like that, I'm standing in the hallway behind him.

My words are stuck in my throat, and he opens the door and steps in. He turns to look at me, and I know he thinks my room is nothing special. He's only in the vestibule.

He takes three more steps. "Holy fucking shit."

Yup, completely and utterly mortified. If I thought falling down the stairs in front of this god-like man was embarrassing, I now have new standards. My bedroom is the exact same way it was when I was twelve. My walls are cluttered with posters of Fergie, Jonas Brothers, Hannah Montana, and horses galore. It's the dream bedroom of every tween, and I have it. Except now, I'm in my mid-twenties, and I'm still living in the bedroom from my childhood. I should have redecorated at some point in my adult life, but I didn't, and this is the end result of my procrastination.

"I know," I sigh as I walk past him, making myself comfortable on my Jonas Brothers comforter. "You don't have to say anything, I already know what you're thinking."

"That's impossible."

"You're thinking it's absurd that I still live at home, sleeping in a bedroom that's a flashback to the early two-thousands."

Henry walks over to the windows and begins inspecting the latches, then under the bed and inside the lampshades. "Actually, I thought it's funny that we have the same poster of Fergie."

"You do?" I can't believe a grown man would admit to something so juvenile.

"Yeah," he says as he walks out of the bathroom. "But not for the same reasons."

"I don't get it."

He pinches his lips and his eyebrows shoot to his hairline. "Seriously?"

I shake my head with a distinct awareness of my naiveté.

"I use it as a, uh, a spank bank."

"What's a spank bank?" From time to time, knowing I've been overly sheltered my entire life really frosts my cookies. It's left me at a disadvantage to mingle and identify with my peers.

"I'll tell you when you're older," he says, laughing.

What a jerk. Here he is being paid from my wallet, living in my home, standing in my bedroom, and he's treating me like a child. And I get it. I called the antiseptic "the stingy stuff," and I have Hannah Montana strewn across the walls. But a little respect can go a long way.

Fed up, I pull out the cotton candy pink chair which matches my makeup vanity, and stand on top of it.

Henry's forehead wrinkles in question. I wanted to be able to stand tall and look him directly in the eye.

"We have a meeting at four o'clock with my consigliere. I expect you to be dressed appropriately." I give him the same treatment he gave me when we were in the guest room. I start from his amazing pompadour and mentally undress him all the way down to his black leather boots. "Now, get out."

4

Henry

Charlotte is adorable, but I'm not sure if it's in a Julia Roberts as Tinkerbell kind of way, or a sort of endearing youthfulness. Her bedroom isn't at all what I had expected. Not that I had some image of a swarthy, sophisticated room with a seaside view. The exquisite Miss Sutton would be lying in the middle of the bed, her red hair fanned out on a pillow, wearing a silk nightgown, her hand traveling up her thigh.

The Jonas Brothers' posters that vandalized her walls were—I don't have the words. Besides the boyband and horse paraphernalia, I saw a young woman who has probably never experienced life on her own. The concrete walls that surround this mansion have kept her safe and unblemished from the filth outside. The reality of her lifestyle contradicts my first impression. She broke into a cop's house for Christ's sake. That takes guts. There aren't many twenty-five-year-olds with the balls to do that.

She's obviously naive, and by the shameful look on her

face when I mentioned my spank bank, she seems to know it. So then, what is it Charlotte does for the Scalise Family? What did her brother do? How can someone like Charlotte be of such importance and have enough clout that some degenerate would consider her a threat? It isn't adding up. When Charlotte kicked me out, I went back to my assigned room and took a few minutes to think things through.

The chauffeur who brought me here seemed more like a rental driver, and the used condom in the back of the limo certainly supported that theory. Charlotte told me she would have me picked up if I accepted, so I figured she had a personal driver or someone on the family's payroll. The driver's insistence for a tip was the clincher.

Then there was Amara. At first glance, she seemed like a bit of an old battle-ax, the kind of woman that even her boss would be afraid to approach. When Charlotte fell down the stairs, Amara immediately jumped into action and had everything we needed on hand and easily accessible. The look on Amara's face as she handed me the first aid kit was of pure motherly love. Even if Charlotte isn't her daughter, it's obvious she loves her as much as her own flesh and blood.

The driver, Amara, Charlotte. That's only three people. A place this massive must require an entourage for its maintenance, security, and day-to-day operations. So, where was everyone else?

The pipes in the bathroom rush with water. Charlotte and I share plumbing for the en-suite bathrooms. While she's in the shower, I take the opportunity to do a little snooping of my own.

The place is so massive the word mansion doesn't do it justice. "Compound" is more like it. Whatever way Charlotte is connected to the Scalise's, she's crucial and paid well for her talents. Considering the state of her room, I'd assume she's lived here her whole life. Either her immediate family was independently wealthy or had their hands deep within the Scalise organization long before Charlotte had a clue.

The home has four floors total, including a basement, which I've never seen in a Florida home. Ever. Seven bedrooms, nine baths. Forty-seven windows, not including the five doors which lead to the outside.

The windows are enough to cause me to have a stroke. Five doors? Really? Exits are great for getting out, like if there's a fire. However, every exit doubles as an entrance and a potential security breach. Factor in all the goddamn windows, and I know this place must require a small army.

Outside there is a twenty-foot concrete barrier that walls-in the residence. The sole access to the grounds is through the wrought iron main gate. There is a guard shack positioned right before the entrance. It looked like it was supposed to be manned by a guard and required clearance for entry. The shed was completely empty when I walked the grounds. I peeked through the gate, trying to get a good look into the windows. I saw a few CCTV monitors and a couple of clipboards, but not a single guard.

When I first arrived, I remembered the driver having to depress a button on the intercom—no guard then either. I walked the perimeter, rooting around for any potential holes in security. I was relieved to find the house was locked up nice and tight. Except for the lack of actual humans to provide protection.

Something's wrong here, and I have a feeling Charlotte has been a very busy girl. What she has up her sleeve is beyond me. I'm willing to bet the "consigliere" and myself are about to find out at the same time.

The only time I've ever heard the term "consigliere" was when I watched *The Godfather*. That person was the right hand of The Godfather. Maybe this family uses it in an informal, laid back sense.

In my room, I unpack my bag and assess my wardrobe of choice. Charlotte wanted me to "dress appropriately." I'm not sure what all that entails, but I have an entire duffle bag packed with outfits similar to what I'm wearing now, except with slight variations.

I change into a clean pair of dark-wash jeans and a burgundy T-shirt. The sunlight glints off the gun in my bag, and I consider whether or not it's appropriate to carry a weapon to the first meeting with the Scalise Family's consigliere. Deciding that it is, I opt for a Mexican carry and tuck the gun into the waistband of my jeans and cover it up with my T-shirt.

One of the first rules of gun safety is to never carry a weapon in an unsecured manner, such as what I'm doing. I know better. However, when I consider Charlotte hired me because she is scared for her life, I believe carrying in a holster might cause unwanted attention.

There's a gentle knock on my bedroom door, and I know it's Charlotte coming to collect me.

I open the door and peer down at the small woman.

Her gaze is cast downward as she twines her fingers with nervousness. "I'm sorry."

"For what?"

"You know, standing on the chair and barking orders at you."

I'm baffled she would find a need to apologize for standing her ground. I take a step forward and lift her chin to look at me. "Don't be. You didn't do anything wrong. I work for you, not the other way around."

She gives me a stiff smile and takes a step back. "Thank you," she says, "that's precisely what I needed to hear."

Charlotte guides me down a flight of stairs and through a long hallway until we come to a set of wooden French doors. It's an office that I had seen earlier when I had a look around.

"This was my father's office," she tells me as she pushes the heavy oak doors open. "So when I miss him, I come in here." She takes a deep breath, "Smell that?"

I nod. I can smell it, the faint odor of stale cigars.

"Cubans. He didn't have many vices, but Cuban cigars were his weakness." She waves to a set of chairs in front of a large desk. "Have a seat. Would you like a drink?" she asks as she uncorks a crystal decanter.

Like shoving a gun near my dick, drinking on the job is a truly terrible idea. "No, thanks."

She pours herself a glass of an amber liquid, and I walk around the office. There are large framed paintings, and the attention to detail is astounding. One is signed by Picasso. I'm no connoisseur of fine art, but even I can tell that, if these are reproductions, they're in a league of their own.

"You like that one," Charlotte says, pointing with her tumbler. "It was my father's favorite too. I, on the other hand, hate it. It used to give me nightmares."

The painting is a portrait with extremely distorted features. It's creepy alright, I can see why it would give a child nightmares.

"He used to say it reminded him that no matter how perfect someone seemed, there was something askew."

"Interesting interpretation. I thought it was more about the imperfections making their own kind of beauty."

"That's a lot less paranoid of a view than my father's. I like it."

The idea that she values my opinion enough to trump the memory of her father is surprisingly pleasing. I'm a selfish bastard. Our eyes meet, and I feel vulnerable like the first time I let a woman see me naked with the lights on. I'm dressed right now, but somehow, it feels like she can see right through me. In the capacity for which I've been hired, that is terrible news.

With a desperate need to look at anything besides Charlotte, my gaze lands on a family photo. It's of a man and two young children. "Is this you?" I ask, picking up the frame from the shelf.

"Yeah. Me, my brother, and my dad."

I can see all the changes from this picture of a preteen Charlotte hanging with her family in the backyard. A snapshot of happiness caught on camera. Her hair is longer, glossier, and a shade darker red than it was back then. Her body has transformed from a girl in her training bra to the soft curves of a woman. The man next to her is tall and familiar. The scar on his right eyebrow makes his identity clear.

"Is this . . . Are you—"

A man, dressed in a suit with shoulders as broad as the doorframe, storms into the office.

"*Charlotte,*" the man bellows. "What the hell do you think you're doing?"

5

Charlotte

Ray certainly knows how to make an entrance. His broad shoulders fill in the doorway, the sun glaring off his shaved head. A vein, dark and angry, bulges from his forehead. His cherubic cheeks do nothing to soften his features as his face brightens to an extraordinary shade of red. He's madder than a puffed toad.

He ducks as he crosses the threshold. "You've lost your goddamn mind," he says, his eyes narrowed and filled with murderous rage.

Henry's posture stiffens as Ray storms the office, and my new bodyguard takes three long strides before he's by my side. "You need—"

"It's fine," I tell Henry, pressing a hand on his chest. His impossibly defined chest. My fingers tingle as they graze the soft fabric of his cotton shirt, muscles flexing beneath my touch.

I have not one ounce of fear when it comes to Ray. He wouldn't harm a single hair on my head. Anyone else, he wouldn't hesitate to pull out his knife on the spot and scalp. Gruesome, but that's simply the way of the business.

Ray and I have dinner every Wednesday night. It's our ritual, a time to catch up with each other, to embrace the fleeting presence of a family unit. Flaking out on Ray is what has led us to this moment. Not once have I missed dinner. Chicken pox, the flu, not even when Joe Jonas got married, did I bail on Ray.

My brother, Charlie, and I lost our father when we were twelve. Ray picked up the pieces of our lives and worked tirelessly to give us a loving and stable home. Now that Charlie is gone, Amara and Ray are the only family I have left.

Family or not, it doesn't change the circumstances. I have a rat in my house, and I don't have a clue where it's hiding. I remind myself to keep the details to a minimum. Ray doesn't need to know what or how much I know because even though I love him with my whole heart, it doesn't change the fact that someone in this family had Charlie taken out.

"Let's have a seat, and we can talk," I tell Ray, trying to deescalate the situation.

"Fine," he harrumphs and makes his way toward my father's desk.

After my father left, Ray would use this office to work. When Charlie took over, Charlie refused to use this room. I think he considered it to be sacred or something.

This is my business and my office now, and I refuse to let him take the captain's seat. I make quick steps to beat Ray to the other side of the desk and swoop into the leather chair. Ray quirks an eyebrow and frowns but makes the correct choice, taking the seat across from me.

Henry walks around the desk and leans against the bureau, which lines the bank of windows directly behind me. He folds his arms and crosses his feet in a semi-relaxed pose. He may look calm, but vibrations of anger and suspicion thicken the air.

The proximity of my new bodyguard is distracting. I struggle to keep my head clear and my wits about me as I take a giant leap into the unforgiving waters of organized crime.

"Explain yourself, bug," Ray says, his demeanor shifting to his pseudo-father role.

"Where's Charlie?" It's a loaded question. Every fiber of my being tells me my brother is no longer of this earth. However, Ray doesn't know I know, and that's an advantage I will not relinquish.

"He had a meeting with," Ray's gaze flicks to Henry then back to me, "an associate in New York. You know that."

That's the story Ray has been feeding me. I'm sure he's trying to do what he thinks is best, it's probably more along the lines of paternal protection. I can respect that, but from where I'm sitting, the business is without a leader. As the next in line, it is my responsibility to make sure everything is on the right path.

"He left over two weeks ago," I tell Ray. "Nobody's seen or heard from him in days. I've called and texted him so many times I've lost count. And nothing. Not a peep."

Ray fiddles with his beard and looks up to the right corner of the room, it's his tell. He doesn't have many weaknesses, and the most stoic poker face I've ever come across—not that I've played poker, but I've seen it on TV. When he's suspicious or believes he needs to handle a situation with extreme caution, he tends to twist a knot in his beard while he calculates his next move. "That's strange. I talked to him two days ago, and he said everything was under control, and he should be home by next week."

I'm not sure what game Ray is playing, whether he's telling the truth or thinks he's telling the truth. But it doesn't matter.

"Good to know. Until Charlie shows up at the front door, I'm in charge," I tell him, my voice is sure, but my confidence wavers. Even though I'm sitting in my father's chair and behind his desk, I feel about two feet tall, unable to channel the ruthless power my father possessed.

"Do you want to tell me why you fired our entire security crew?" Ray asks, speaking to me the same way he did when I was a teenager and he caught me climbing out my window to put toads in Charlie's bed.

"It's time for a change."

"I see," Ray muses, knotting his beard again. "Did you consider the fact that we're now completely without protection until we get a new firm in here?"

"I did. And I don't think it's your personal safety which worries you," I tell Ray, nodding to the gun peeking out from under his jacket.

"Fair enough. But you and I both know the security was in place not only for the business but to keep you and your brother safe." Ray clears his throat. "Our business has its fair share of crazies, like everything else, but your father's top priority was to keep you and Charlie safe."

The mention of mine and Charlie's safety is laughable—it's a little late for that. Under normal circumstances, Ray's tactic of using my father's memory would whip me into shape and have me apologizing for my outlandish behavior. But not now. Not after losing Charlie.

"He did. And I agree that we need to take precautions. Which is why I've gone out and found someone I trust. Ray Thatch, this is Henry Cain," I say, jerking my thumb toward the man standing behind me.

The men don't say hello, shake hands, or utter any greeting at all. Instead, they remain planted in their spots and glare at each other. The tension between the two men is so heavy I could almost suffocate.

"And how did you two come to meet?" Ray asks, his attention turning back to me.

There's no way I can tell him the truth. Henry's brother owes us a lot of money, and Ray stays out of the nitty-gritty side of the business. He prefers to look at the bigger picture and let those beneath him focus on the details. It's because of this that seeking out Henry seemed like my safest option. I needed someone who wouldn't go blabbing about my situation and alert every other low-life that the Scalise Family was at its most vulnerable.

"At Pilates," Henry chimes in. "Miss Sutton here asked me for an opinion on a situation she was concerned about. We'd chatted a few times before that, and she knew about my previous experience with a private security firm in Iraq. I told her if she felt she needed further protection, I was available."

For Henry to so quickly volunteer that information floors me. Not that a single word of it is real. And how does he know I do Pilates?

"Okay, Charlotte. You've fired all of our security, brought in your own man," Ray says, pointing toward Henry. "So, what is it you're looking to gain?"

I don't think I'm gaining anything at the moment, not my footing, not a better life. Instead, I seem to be sinking further into the muck that was my father and brother's life. "Nothing. I just think since I can't get a hold of Charlie, maybe I need to step up. Keep things on track."

Ray opens his mouth to object, but I raise my hand to silence him. "I know you said you've spoken to Charlie, but I haven't. And the truth is that Charlie went to New York under some shady circumstances. This family is my responsibility. I owe it to Charlie, to you, to everyone else who works for us to keep this business up and running."

Ray purses his lips and nods as if he agrees with me. "And you think you're qualified to hold this position?"

What kind of qualifications does one need to run an illegal trade business anyway? "Absolutely. I know the ins and outs as well as anyone else. This lifestyle has inundated my entire existence."

"Fine," Ray concedes and gets up from his chair, buttoning his suit jacket. "Just one more thing."

"Sure," I tell him, ready to put this whole discussion to bed.

"You terminated an entire security firm from the property. Do you honestly think one man will be enough to keep you safe?"

My skin prickles at Ray's words. I'm not sure if it's a threat or a question. Knowing Ray the way I do, I know he would never hurt me, and his statement doesn't change that, it's just super unsettling. "I do," I answer, "and you can take that all the way to the spank bank."

6

Henry

I'm a fucking disgrace to the badge. I am obligated to march my ass down to the station and hand the captain my gun and shield. I am a failure as a cop.

I walked into this situation with my eyes wide open. Well, that's not accurate. I knew I was going to be somehow involved with the Scalise Family, and relatively close to the situation of their business. No matter how much I thought I prepared myself, I couldn't have conceived of this. I have entered the hive, and I'm not a simple worker bee, but bodyguard to the fucking queen.

After Ray Thatch leaves the office, I take the seat he had occupied and cross my ankle over my knee. "He's lying to you," I tell Charlotte with no regard to her feelings. There's no point in being gentle. Gentle isn't what she needs right now. I have a responsibility, to be honest.

"I know." Charlotte opens a drawer and removes a box of cigars and clips off the end. My dick twitches as she places the phallic object to her pouty pink lips and puffs on the end until it glows orange. What I would give to be that cigar.

"Charlie's your brother?" I ask, trying to focus on anything but her mouth.

She puffs out a ring of smoke. "Yeah."

"You said the other day that your brother's dead, but you told Ray he's missing. Which is it?"

"Charlie was my twin brother. He'd been in New York for almost two weeks. We talked every day while he was gone. It was our thing. Even when Charlie moved out, we still talked all the time. I hadn't lived a single day without my brother somehow being a part of it. Until four days ago."

I've never been close to Brian. We were on different paths. Mine law-abiding, his not, but I wish we could be closer. "What happened four days ago? What changed?"

Charlotte takes another puff of the cigar, then stubs it out in the ashtray. The smoke rises, and she whiffs it with her hand. "It's the smell I love," she says. "I've never been much of a smoker."

"You're avoiding the question." I can't hold back my irritation. This whole day has been a shit show. I've walked into the home of a fucking crime family, and I'm obligated to work for them.

She doesn't say anything, and I'm sure there's a better tactic I could use. Something gentler that encourages her trust, but I don't have the patience for it.

"Listen, you sought me out to protect you. From what? I don't know. Your answers have been cryptic and evasive, and it's starting to piss me off." I take a deep breath and count to ten, trying to calm myself. My anger will get us nowhere. I try again, this time softening my tone. "Whatever you think the problem is, you believe it enough to break into my house. You have the best security money can buy, but you've upended and fired everyone associated with it. The way I see it, you're worried that whatever the threat is, it's coming from inside. And that doesn't exclude Ray Thatch."

She blushes, and I can tell I've struck a nerve.

"I can't protect you if I don't have all the information."

Charlotte lets out a sigh and looks down at her hands as she twists her fingers, but she still doesn't answer.

"We're not playing games here, Charlotte. It's your life and my brother's future on the line."

She's stunned by my brash words, her head snapping up to look at me. "You think I don't know that?" she asks. "Why do you think I've gone to all this trouble to get you here?"

I run my fingers through my hair, annoyed at the whole situation, and pissed with myself for upsetting this adorable sprite of a woman. "I'm sorry. Let's start from the beginning." I need to dial back my emotions and look at the problem objectively. Like a cop. "How do you know your brother is dead?"

It hasn't escaped my notice that her references to her brother are past tense. This behavior can suggest a couple of things. One, her brother is dead, and she killed him, covering up the crime by taking extreme actions to appear blameless. Or two, she's seen the body. The proof is in the metaphorical pudding.

She shrugs her shoulders. "I don't know. I just . . . ," she trails off. "I know," she says, her voice confident. "I can feel it. It's like there's a light inside me I never knew was lit. Some kind of twin thing, I guess. Like in the movies. When he died, I suddenly didn't feel anything. It was . . . extinguished. I'm sure it sounds crazy," she says, looking back down at her hands, threading her fingers.

It does sound crazy, and it's a third possibility which I would never have considered. Then again, what do I know about twins? "Not at all."

At my words, her gaze flicks up to mine. The look in her eyes is enough to slay me. There's a brief glint of relief and something else I can't quite make out. Whatever it is, it strikes a chord in my heart, and my stomach flips.

"Let me see if I understand everything," I tell her, putting together the border pieces of an expert-level puzzle. "You and Charlie are twins."

"Yes."

"And your father was John Scalise?"

"Right again."

"Your brother took over the illegal family business and has now disappeared, but you know, in your heart of hearts, he's dead."

"Yeah," she sighs.

"And you need someone from the outside to protect you because you don't know who is friend or foe."

"Exactly," she says, leaning forward and perching her arms on the desk. "So?"

"So what?"

"Are you in?"

It takes every ounce of restraint not to break out laughing. "Are you serious? You're holding my brother's debt over my head. Even without that, I've associated with the inner circle of a crime family, and I'm a fucking cop. My choices are limited. Say no, and I'll be sleeping with the fishes."

She stands, her beautiful face marred with a frown. "Is that what you think of me?"

I swallow a lump in my throat. I don't know what I think of this woman. She's a contradiction of everything I've ever known about the fairer sex. Especially one with power. Take my mom, for example. Beverly Cain is a homicide cop. She's the reason I pursued a career in law enforcement. Despite her obsession with my love life, I don't think there is anything that can be misconstrued as soft and nurturing. She is all rough edges, and I don't think she possesses a maternal bone in her body.

In contrast, all the women I've dated have been almost the exact opposite. Soft and supple, warm and nurturing. I can't get a read on Charlotte Sutton.

My phone vibrates in my pocket, right on cue. I don't have to look to know it's my mom. She hasn't texted me since yesterday.

I ignore the message and look directly into Charlotte's beautiful shamrock eyes, searching for the slightest hint as to who she is. "I don't know."

It's the truth. I have no clue what this woman is capable of. One minute she's practically throwing a fit over a scraped knee. The next, she's firing her entire security team and putting the infamous Ray Thatch in his place.

"Well, that's not the way I operate," Charlotte insists. She stands and holds her chin high as she passes me, making her way toward the door.

With her hand on the knob, she stops and turns around to look at me. "At least, I don't think so," she muses, then waves her hand through the air as if she can swat away nefarious thoughts and strides out the door.

7

Charlotte

Henry Cain has a lot of nerve calling my character into question. Who does he think he is? Who does he think I am? If I were honest with myself—which isn't something I practice too much because I never like the answer—what do I really know about him? What makes him the man he is? Is he a good son, a faithful boyfriend, a gentle lover? Nope, not going down that road. What I do know includes the details of his bank account, his job history, and that his brother owes the Family money. Everything added together, puts Henry in a vulnerable situation.

And I exploited that.

But I didn't have a choice.

Okay, I did, but not any choices I liked. It was an opportunity I would have been a fool not to take.

The sun has set, and I've had a long day. There is no better cure for a bad case of the woes than a bubble bath. There are a plethora of options on how to prepare a proper soak. Lots of bubbles, or just enough to skim the surface. Scented or unscented. Candles or a hot washcloth over the eyes. Champagne. Champagne is non-negotiable. No bath worth its time would be complete without it.

As expected, the mini-fridge in my vestibule is stocked appropriately for such an occasion. I pour a glass of chilled Cristal and take long sips as the tub fills with a generous amount of honey and milk-infused bubbles. The combination will leave my skin soft as milk and smooth as honey. Huh, I guess that would make sense.

I tie my hair up in a loose bun and slip out of my silk robe, lowering myself into the steamy tub. I wring out a washcloth and cover my eyes, leaning back and letting the bubbles take me away to a world of unicorns and lollipops. Within minutes, the stress evaporates, and my brain decompresses from a seriously exhausting day.

Oh my stars, there is nothing that can compare to a good sudsy soak.

Time flies, and I don't realize how long I've been in the tub until my skin pebbles from the cooled water. I pull off the washcloth covering my eyes and notice my fingers might as well be prunes. All good things must come to an end. I slip back into my robe and head to my bedroom.

Pulling my hair out of the rubber band, I give my head a good shake, loosening the knots. My scalp prickles from the sweet release of freedom. In front of the vanity, near my bed, I apply creamy lotion up and down my legs. Something about the scent from the bath mixed with the lavender lotion makes me feel sensual. Images of Henry invade my thoughts. The way he looked so commanding and intimidating when he was sitting across from me. Sure, I hated the things he said, but jumpin' Jiminy was he hot when he said it.

My robe slips to the floor as I work the lotion onto my arms, neck, and across my breasts. A drawn-out wolf's whistle trills from behind me, and I shriek in surprise, jumping as I turn around.

What do I find? A shirtless man with muscles that go for days, sitting on my floor on top of a blanket.

It takes me a whole second too long to register what is going on. I'm disturbingly distracted by Henry's beautifully tanned skin and the dusting of hair leading to the waistband of his sweatpants. It takes another few seconds before it occurs to me that I'm completely naked.

My arms fly to my breasts, and I bend at the knees in a desperate attempt to cover myself. I snatch up my robe from the ground, turn around, and stab my arms through the sleeves.

"How long have you been here?" I demand. "Never mind, don't answer that. I don't want to know."

I march into my walk-in closet and slip on a pale pink, knee-length nightgown, and underwear. When I reemerge, my cheeks are still aflame from embarrassment, but I won't let that hold me back. I stand over the blankets Henry has arranged on the floor next to my bed. "What do you think you're doing?" This is a better, more concise question.

"Going to bed," Henry answers, his beautiful eyes laughing at my humiliation.

Not concise enough. "No. What are you doing here? Your room is next door."

"And it's a lovely room too. A huge bed, private bathroom. I bet the sheets are even one-hundred percent cotton."

"Egyptian cotton, actually."

"Fine, Egyptian. Trust me, I would much rather sleep in that bed next door than on this hard floor. But it seems someone couldn't contain her excitement and fired every last bit of security in this house. Leaving me," he says, waving a hand over his makeshift bedding, "to have to bunk next to my charge."

Henry cocks his head as he finishes his little speech, daring me to challenge him.

But I can't. He's right.

"Hmph." I round the bed to the opposite side and slip under

the covers. Nick, Joe, and Kevin stare up to the ceiling from my quilt. We lie in silence, and I can hear the frogs chirping outside my window. I roll onto my side, facing Henry's direction, but because he's on the floor, I can't see him. There's a perception of anonymity that comes with sleeping next to a person you can't see. It's as if nothing is real, and everything is sacred. It reminds me of sleep-away camp, or how I imagine it would have been if I had ever gone to one.

"Can I ask you a question?" I ask, finding the nerve to speak.

"Yeah, sure."

"Do you think I did the right thing?" The question won't stop festering in the back of my mind. All that hogwash about a light extinguishing, I don't know if it's even true. Maybe Charlie is fine, and I had an hour-long virus or something.

"Not sure about getting rid of all the security, but I can see why you did it. You don't know who you can trust. The best way to figure it out is to eliminate all the possibilities. So, yeah," he says, "maybe you did do the right thing."

It's therapeutic hearing someone validate my suspicions. It settles my self-doubt and helps dulls the fear that maybe I'm going nuts. In a lifestyle that demands controlled chaos for all its crazy inhabitants, it's nice to know.

We don't speak for a long time, and I think Henry has fallen asleep until he talks.

"Remember when you asked me what a spank bank was?"

I guess he's not the only one who considers the darkness to be a confessional.

"Yeah. You told me you would fill me in when I got older." I remember his statement like it was five seconds ago and not five hours. That insult stung.

"I don't think you can wait that long."

"Okay, then tell me now. What's a spank bank?"

He takes a deep breath. I'm not sure if it's because of annoyance or pity.

"A spank bank," he says, "is kind of like a, um, mental

collection of images that men, some women too, that uh, they find to be . . . erotically charged."

"Okay." I spend a few seconds mulling over the definition. "Why would someone need that?" I ask, and not because I'm ignorant. I'm not. I know people like to look at dirty magazines and websites; it just isn't something I've ever found appealing.

"You know for when a man, or some women too," he clarifies, "spanks it."

"Spanks what?" For the love of all that is good in this world, what are these people spanking?

"To be honest, I don't know how to put this any other way you might get it. Spanking is another term for masturbation."

May God have mercy on my soul. I told Ray to masturbate. My stomach churns, and I kind of want to throw up. I take a deep breath, swallow back the bile rising in my throat, and roll to my other side. I have no choice but to keep my mouth shut and go to sleep because, as it so happens, I am that ignorant.

8

Henry

After I defined the term "spank bank," Charlotte was mortified. The room became eerily silent. I didn't need to see her face to know she was redder than a strawberry—a deliciously sweet, freshly picked strawberry.

I think she was feigning sleep, too embarrassed to talk anymore. It wasn't until a couple of hours later that I heard her soft, adorable snores.

I barely got a wink myself, tortured by the images of her naked and applying lotion to her lean legs. I had to bunch the blankets around my crotch to hide the tent that made camp.

Normally, I can will the beast into submission, but he was having none of it. I was rock hard and stuck in the bedroom of the woman who had caused every problem I've encountered in the past few days. Even with that knowledge, it wasn't enough to tame my erection.

It took an astounding amount of determination to fall asleep, but still, the hard-on persisted. When I woke up this morning, it was just as hard as when Charlotte shed her robe.

Charlotte is still sleeping, and I peek up to look at her from where I lie on the floor. Her covers are pushed down to the bottom of the bed, her nightgown riding up her waist.

Fuck. I can't take my eyes off that pert ass. Silky white panties and creamy flesh are calling to me, begging me to grab it. My dick, if it's even possible, is harder now than it was two minutes ago. I have to make an executive decision.

I quietly tip-toe to the bedroom door and make sure it's locked because Charlotte's safety is my number one priority. My number two priority is practically drilling a hole through my sweatpants. I take one last glimpse at Charlotte before I head to the en-suite bathroom. As I do, she rolls over, her beautiful breasts shifting. My eyes are glued to the rose-colored buds winking at me from beneath her gown. I groan out loud, the torture, the temptation almost surpasses my ability to control myself.

I step into the bathroom and shuck my pants to the floor. "You're such a fucking prick," I tell my cock, staring down at it with disappointment. Hard-ons are a fact of life for men, and there are several ways to deal with them. Typically, I have more control over my body than I did when I was a teenager, a time when a light breeze was enough to make my dick rage. Being around Charlotte seems to have brought on some kind of sick time-warp back to adolescence. The most effective way to fix this is with the pathetic tricks of a teenage boy.

First, I try meditation. Clear my mind, think of something calming, soothing. I picture myself sitting in my recliner at home, looking out one of the large picture windows onto the beach. The waves are foaming as they crash onto the shore. The sun is shining down, not a cloud in the sky. A young family sets up for a picnic under an umbrella. A mom, a dad, and two kids with a beagle running in circles as they set up for a day sea-side. Off in the distance, four people are walking along the beach, the surf rushing up their ankles.

I take a deep breath, imagining the salty air filling my lungs, my dick is still hard, but the pressure seems to be letting up. The friends walking on the beach are getting closer. All women.

All naked.

Splashing each other.

Their heads are thrown back in laughter. The sun gleams down on them, so they appear to glow.

Oh, god. Now, the women's hands are roaming, caressing each other's bodies.

Shit.

I turn my mental image back to the sweet family on the other side, but they've disappeared. Only the beagle is left, and another dog is prancing along. A black lab. The lab circles the beagle and comes up from behind.

Damn it. I look away before the lab mounts the beagle.

Now the four women are lying on a blanket, a mass of limbs, tongues, and—

This isn't working. I need something else. I rewind my image to the women running along the beach. But this time, I try to think of something that will gross me out. Something unique from Miami. What do I hate the most? A familiar tune beats in my head, thanking me for being a friend.

Dorothy, Blanche, Rose, and Sophia. All four Golden Girls are running down the beach, splashing each other, having the time of their lives. Completely naked. Skin is sagging. Breasts are flailing. It's hideous, yet oddly erotic?

"Fuck." I'm completely out of control. Mental imagery was the worst idea ever.

Next option: Redirect blood flow. I start with my arms, flexing the muscles, then twist and turn, trying to work the muscles of my abs, clenching my calves—a real Mister Universe pose. After about five minutes of that, my muscles are exhausted, but the erection remains.

I try pinching myself, holding my breath, taking a piss—nothing is working. Out of frustration, I grab hold of my shaft and give a painful squeeze, hoping to strangle its life force.

All but giving up, I decide it's time to pull out the big guns. It's an oldie but a goody—a very, very cold shower. At this rate, I need the arctic waters of the South Pole to help. As I step into the stall, I let the water do its job, and bumps rise on my skin from the frigid temperature. I don't have any of my toiletries. I left it in the other room, the one I was supposed to be sleeping in until Charlotte changed the rules of the game.

I have no choice but to use her soap. It's feminine, lavender or lilac or something. It's purple, that's all I know. As I rub the soap across my chest, I get an image of Charlotte in this same shower, rubbing herself down.

I look down at my dick, and despite the cold water, it has done nothing to help. It's time to grab the bull by the horns. I have no choice.

I squirt some of the body wash into my right hand and grab onto my shaft, then stroke it from root to tip, giving an angry tug right at the head. My pace increases and my imagination kicks into hyper-drive. Flashes of Charlotte in the recliner at my house. What I wanted to do to her then, what I know I will never be able to do. Reality doesn't stop the onslaught of images of her legs spread wide, and my cock slamming into her silky wet pussy.

Spurts of hot cum spray onto the tile wall within minutes of the first stroke. My shoulders sag with relief and my cock deflates. Fuck, I needed that.

I rinse off and step out from the shower, and I feel like a new man. As I towel off, unwanted chub once again bulges. I look down and watch my cock grow before my very eyes.

"Shit," I mutter. "What the fuck am I going to do with you?" I ask my dick. Like the asshole that I know he is, he doesn't respond.

A light rapping at the bathroom door makes me jump. I'm not the kind of person who startles easily but come on, I just jerked off in the shower of the woman who happens to be the head of the Scalise Family.

"Is everything okay in there?" Charlotte asks from the other side.

I yank my pants up and open the door, holding the towel above my waist like I have some sort of intention for it. My intention for this piece of cloth is for it to cover up this impossible-to-hide erection.

My breath catches at the sight of Charlotte, donned in a silk robe that matches her nightgown and panties, and tangled sleepy hair. How is it possible that she's just as beautiful when she first wakes up as she is naked, running her delicate fingers along her smooth legs, up her belly, and—

"What's for breakfast?" I ask, holding the towel tighter against me. I'm going to have to figure out a way to harness this new obsession.

Charlotte takes a lingering look over my chest. I think she just deposited the first image into her spank bank. A small, greedy part of me revels in the idea of being at the center of her next fantasy.

9

Charlotte

Drips of water cascade down Henry's chest, captured by a small patch of hair between two magnificently sculpted pecs. Wait. One, no, two dewy drops have escaped and are making their way from his chest, down his stomach. They take different paths, yet still follow the sharp cuts of muscle which make up his abdomen. Now they merge in another patch of hair, except not on his chest, and not on his abs, but trailing farther down.

"My eyes are up here, cupcake."

I'm totally busted checking him out. I can feel the blush creeping from my neck up to my cheeks. "Yeah, I um," I clear my throat at a complete loss as to how I'll save myself. "Amara has a breakfast spread ready in the kitchen. I'm going to get a quick shower. I'll meet you down there."

Henry nods, but I can see the smile playing on his lips. "Sure thing."

Powering through my morning routine, Henry is at the

forefront of my mind. The way he teased me. The multiple ways I made a boob of myself. His heated look when I was naked and applying lotion. No, no, no. I can't go there right now. I need to focus.

Still, it doesn't mean I can't taunt Henry a little. I rummage through my closet and select an adorable, flowery—slightly too short—dress and a pair of strappy sandals, throw my hair into a ponytail, and head to the kitchen for breakfast.

"Good morning, Amara," I greet as I walk into the kitchen and snatch up a banana and a jar of peanut butter.

"Good morning," she replies. "How did you sleep?"

Henry sits on a barstool dressed casually in a pair of dark-wash jeans and a T-shirt. I wonder if he has a rotation of the same clothes but in different colors? The man wore the same outfit yesterday, even after he got changed for the meeting with Ray. Unlike the adorable shower-mussed hair from earlier, he has it combed into that pompadour I so love on him.

Henry smiles behind a cup of coffee as he takes a sip, and I know he's thinking back to me being naked. Or the spank bank conversation.

"I slept well, thank you," I answer Amara.

Amara smiles and hands me a mug of green tea.

"Thanks," I tell her, then take a sip.

"So, what's on the agenda for today?" Henry asks. "Yesterday was firing almost everyone who works for you. Today is what? Taking over the world?"

"Something like that. I have a lunch meeting with some business associates," I tell him. "Ray's supposed to meet us there."

"Sounds good. What are the plans until then?" Henry asks, looking at his watch.

My life has been in a total state of chaos since my brother left for New York. I've had a lot to consider and plans to make. Now that things seem to be settling down a bit, and for the first time since Charlie "disappeared" I feel safe in my own home, I'm going to take a few hours to myself. "We're going to the library."

Henry blinks a few times. "Alright then."

After we finish breakfast, I clean up the dishes. Some might think because I grew up in a house with servants, people who were paid to clean up after me, I wouldn't have had to lift a finger. Such is not the case.

I toss a towel at Henry. "You can dry."

He looks at the dishwasher and back to me, the question clear in his eyes.

"There's like seven dishes here. We're not running the dishwasher for that." I wash a coffee mug with a soapy rag, rinse it, and hand it to Henry.

He grunts out a small laugh and shakes his head as he takes the mug and dries it. "I figured you'd be too spoiled for doing dishes."

"Obviously, you have a low opinion of me," I say, and Henry opens his mouth to retort, but I don't let him speak. "And I know why. I didn't make the best first impression. Or second, or even a third. I'm not an idiot, I know what people think—that I'm some spoiled rich girl who's never known a day of hard work in her life."

"From a distance, I'm sure that is what people are thinking. I thought the same thing, and I'm sorry about that. But the more I get to know you, the more I realize you are anything but spoiled."

"Good. Just because I've grown up with a lot of advantages, it doesn't mean I don't have values and responsibilities. I've been doing chores my whole life, and I'm not too good to go out and mow the lawn," I tell him. "Except no one in this house would let me mow the lawn. And not because they, in any way, believe it's beneath me. But because the last time I did, I mowed over a rock."

He laughs. "Did you break a window or something?"

"Or something," I answer, not feeling up to telling the story of that particular trip to the emergency room.

When we finish the dishes, and the kitchen is cleaned up, I take Henry to the basement.

"I thought we were going to the library?" he asks, following me down the stairs.

"We are," I tell him as I shove open the door.

He takes a step in, then another. He spins in a half-circle, taking in the walls lined with books, and lets out a low whistle. "Man," he breathes out, "this is a lot of books."

"It is," I tell him. "It's my favorite spot in the whole house. As a kid, I used to spend hours down here. I could spend every waking second for the rest of my life in this room and still not be able to read all the books."

We walk down the aisles, and Henry runs his fingers along the spines of hardbacks. "You're probably the only house in the whole state to have a basement," he says, pulling a first edition copy of Tom Sawyer off the shelf and carefully turning the pages.

"Probably," I agree, shrugging my shoulder. "Something about the humidity and sea level or something. But when you have the money and the pull, you can have whatever you want, I guess." The library isn't the sole reason for this basement. A life of crime has other considerations which I'm not about to go into with Henry.

"This one," I say, plucking off a book from the shelf.

Henry takes a step closer to me, and I can smell my body wash on him. It's a heady mix of lavender and masculinity. The scent causes my brain to go haywire. I clear my throat and open the book, bringing it up to my nose, taking in a deep breath. "This one smells the best."

—

Henry

First impressions are entirely unavoidable. I try my damndest not to let that experience rule the truth of a person. Even though my first meeting with Charlotte was not on the best terms, I'm mature enough to know there is more to this woman than being privileged. She's also a goddamn tease. Her dress is indecently short and riding up her thigh as she drives. I can see the faintest hint of pink panties underneath and my dick twitches.

Down, boy. We have stuff to do.

Charlotte weaves through traffic on the highway like a getaway driver. She has a sleek Bentley Continental GT and the heaviest lead foot I've ever experienced. I want to tell her to slow down and obey the speed limit. Her car is as red as a candy apple and a magnet for being pulled over. The last thing we need right now is to be on the police radar for reckless driving. Charlotte is most likely on someone's hit list, and it could create serious problems if this mess runs deep enough. Not to mention, I'm a police officer. What if the cop who pulls us over is someone I know and realizes I'm consorting with a member of an infamous crime family? I can kiss any potential remnants of my career goodbye.

"What's this meeting about?" I ask Charlotte, distracting myself from fantasizing about finger fucking her as she drives, as well as envisioning the destruction of my career. She cuts off a late-model blue minivan who honks their horn at us. Where is that crappy limo driver when we need him? That's right, he was a rental because Charlotte gave her chauffeur the pink slip yesterday along with everyone else. It would seem she doesn't trust anyone in her network—no one except Ray, Amara, and myself.

I know she can trust me; I have a lot on the line. Amara seems like a nice person who genuinely cares for, and probably even loves, Charlotte. Ray Thatch? I wish I could say I'm on the fence about him, but my Five-O senses are telling me he is nothing but bad news. This entire situation is centered around a crime family, which could be throwing me completely off base. Regardless, I can't seem to shake the feeling.

We exit the highway, and Charlotte brings us to a quick stop at the light. My whole body flies forward, my nose almost touching the windshield. I've never been so grateful for a seatbelt as I am right now.

"You need to slow down. You're going to get us both killed before whoever it is that killed Charlie gets a chance to kill you," I tell her, my voice low, my teeth clenched.

She blanches. "Sorry. I don't get to drive often. I got this car for my birthday four months ago, and this is the third time I've gotten to drive it."

There is a tug of sorrow in my stomach. Charlotte's had all the amenities of an affluent lifestyle, but from what I can tell has never gotten to use them. "It's okay. Just slow down."

Charlotte gives me a meek nod, and the light turns green. To my relief, she listens and drives the speed limit. Two stop lights later, she takes a left and picks back up the conversation I had tried to start before I scolded her.

"To answer your question, Charlie had been working on some boundary issues. He was expected to be back by now. But since he's not," she says, and her natural glow turns ashen, "for reasons we've discussed, I'm going to step up and get it figured out."

"Why not let Ray take care of it?" I know the answer; she doesn't trust Ray. She hasn't come right out and said it, but if she did, she wouldn't have hired me.

She pulls into a parking lot and puts the gear shift in park. "Because this is a family business. And no matter how long someone has worked for us, become as close as any other member, in the end, they're still outsiders. The fate of the family is my responsibility."

"Understood," I tell her, taking a look around. We're in an old strip mall. The paint is chipping away from the facade. A large building that looks like it once housed a chain grocer is sealed up tight with vandalized plywood. A Blockbuster that never saw life after it shut down with its sign broken, so it reads *ock uster,* and the video return slot has become a faded blue. The only stores left in business are a head shop and an Italian restaurant.

Charlotte shuts off the engine and turns in her seat to look at me, her mouth a hard line of resolve. "There are a few things you need to understand. To start, I'm the one in control. You can fight with me about anything you want afterward, but not in front of these people. And not in front of Ray," she says, adding a little extra kick to the part about Ray. "These kinds of situations can get a bit tense, and I don't want you to go all cop on me. I need you to keep your cool. Sit back and watch for any potential threats of physical harm. That's your role."

In the small amount of time we've known each other, I don't think I've given her much grief—almost killing us on the highway excluded, of course—but man, is she putting me in my place. That I did not see coming. "Got it."

"All these men in the meeting, I've known my entire life. They have a backward band of brothers thing going on, an honor among thieves mentality. They all attend each other's kid's baptisms, weddings, bar mitzvahs, or whatever. One minute they're dancing with the bride, and the next minute they're whacking off the dad in the bathroom."

All I can do is blink. I'm struggling with what Charlotte said. "Whacking off?"

"Yeah," she says, her eyebrows furrowed. "You know, taking him out? Killing him?"

"We're going to need to work on your vocabulary, cupcake," I tell her, "Because you said . . . You know what? Never mind." Charlotte has a lot to focus on, the last thing she needs is for me to shake her confidence by telling her what she had actually said.

We walk toward the Italian restaurant. It figures we would be meeting in an Italian restaurant. Stereotypes tend to have a grain of truth.

To my surprise, we walk right past the restaurant and toward the head shop. Okay, this makes sense too. A tapestry of Jerry Bears hangs in the window as we stroll by. When we hit the end of the sidewalk, Charlotte turns down an alley between the Blockbuster and a self-storage lot. I keep two paces behind

Charlotte with my hand on my gun until we safely pass through to the other side. More storefronts line the walkway. We pass a massage parlor, and an old shoe repair shop before Charlotte stops in front of an art studio. Advertisements of friends painting masterpieces and sipping on wine cling to the door.

"The Painting Palate," Charlotte says, smiling as she hands me an apron. "It's therapeutic."

In the back of the store, we enter a room cordoned off by a curtain. What I see in front of me is beyond my wildest imagination. I can't help but stare. I'm looking at four men, with smocks hanging around their necks and canvases in front of them, sipping wine and chatting like women.

The first person to stick out to me is the Scotsman, Finlay McCabe, the ultimate authority of the Ambarsan Family. His hair is a flame of orange, and he sports the most impressive snaggletooth I've ever seen, almost vampiric. His clan is known for smuggling diamonds and other precious jewels from the Congo through the Port of Miami. How they get past customs undetected has been up for debate. No doubt they managed to pay off several customs agents. It's also theorized that some of the cruise lines are making a little extra dough on the side.

Next is the Brazilian, Francisco Diaz, head of the Santos crime family. With black hair, mocha skin, and a perfectly tailored suit, he has a sophisticated appeal that the women of Miami flock toward. The rumor is that he's slept with more women than Genghis Khan. The Santos Family has a reputation for bringing guns and other weapons into the city. Their biggest customer being TFO. The Faceless Ones are an up-and-coming street gang that received its name because no one is alive long enough to identify any of its members.

And of course, we can't forget the Sicilian, Carlo Messina. No crime organization meeting would be complete without the original Miami Mafia, the Catalano Family. But these Sicilians aren't known for leaving horse heads in beds. No, these guys have a reputation for gambling and drugs. Surprisingly, they will not break your knees if you fail to pay up. No. You will work for them until you have repaid your debt. However, most people don't live long enough to be in the clear.

I'm not certain how the Scalise Family fits into this well-organized world of crime. They all seem to have deep familial roots and connections to their mother countries except for the Scalise Family. There is nothing even remotely Italian about Charlotte—or her father or brother from what I've seen in that family photo in her father's office.

"Charlotte," Ray Thatch says, pulling my attention away from everyone else in the room. He looks like a damn idiot in his apron. Setting down his paintbrush and pulling out a stool, he says, "I saved you a spot."

I don't know what planet I'm on right now. I am a fucking cop standing in the middle of a fucking kindergarten art room with the most notorious crime families in the world. And there isn't a damn thing I can do about it.

10

Charlotte

My nerves are frayed, I've never done anything like this in my entire life. My father strove to keep me sheltered. No matter how hard he tried, he couldn't shield me from the lifestyle he created by being involved in illegal dealings. Charlie, on the other hand, was groomed to take over the business. Suffice it to say, I'm a bit out of my element. I don't know that I can do this, but I have to try. For Charlie.

Luckily for me, Charlie didn't feel as much of a need to protect me from reality. The moment he took over, Charlie kept me by his side, showing me every aspect of the business for this exact situation.

I've spent my whole life with the men in this room. I know more than I should about this dark world. The one thing which trumps money is pride.

The first time I realized my family was different from my friends, I was eight years old. I was at my Uncle Kevin's house for my cousin's birthday party. Celebrations among the families were enormous and ostentatious. A bouncy castle, petting zoo, clowns making balloon animals, the whole works. While my father was off talking with Uncle Kevin and a few other men, I snuck off to the pool house, in search of one of those high-powered squirt guns, like the kind in the commercials. I had no idea at the time, but that would become the moment that defined my life. My future.

Finlay McCabe and another man, whom I had never seen before, were in a heated discussion. The argument went from simmering to nuclear in the span of a blink. Finlay lifted the man up by the throat and pinned him against the wall.

To this day, I don't know what they were arguing about, but when I saw Finlay had pulled out a knife and proceeded to slice off that other man's ear, my understanding of the world had shifted.

I never told anyone, not even Charlie, what I witnessed at that party. It wasn't until a few years later that Charlie approached me when he found out what our father did for a living. Maybe it was because he was older when he discovered the truth, but he seemed to handle the whole idea much better than I did. I had nightmares well into my teens from that one birthday party.

And my dear old Uncle Kevin? I don't know what happened to him. That party, with my so-called cousins, whose names I can't even remember, is the last time I saw them.

As nervous as I am, knowing I have Henry to protect me—specifically me, not the Scalise Family's interests—makes me feel a heck of a lot better.

Henry stands at the curtains, looking suspiciously like a cop as he takes in three of the men on the FBI's Most Wanted list. I elbow him in the ribs and point to a chair, signaling for him to join the other henchmen.

Henry looks to the men huddled in the corner, playing cards, and frowns but does as he's told. I know he doesn't like it, but this is how it has to be. I have to show these men that I am the one in charge and not Ray. By the way Henry holds himself, I might have to convince them he's not a cop.

"Gentlemen," I greet. McCabe, Diaz, and Messina all stand, welcoming me, and dropping kisses on my cheek.

"Sorry to hear Charlie couldn't make it," Diaz says.

My heart hurts from his words, and I'm sure on some level he's sincere, but it seems Henry and I are the two people in this room who know Charlie is dead. "Yeah, me too," I reply, then take the seat next to Ray.

Ray gives me a reassuring squeeze on my shoulder. "You'll be fine, bug," he says.

His attempts to comfort me make me feel marginally better. I wasn't sure what kind of mood Ray would be in after our conversation yesterday. Would he support me or, as Henry had suggested, feed me to the fishes?

"Thanks. What's the theme this month?" I ask, picking up a paintbrush.

"Starry Night," Messina answers. "Seems fitting. Every day we start anew by ending what had come before it."

His statement rings true to me. I'm sure he doesn't have any idea of what I'm struggling with, but his wise words give me the confidence to do what needs to be done. I pick up a broad brush and dip it in the dark blue paint, working to cover the canvas. "Speaking of what happened before, what are the plans for the customs agents at the port?"

"McCabe has tried talking to a couple of officers, they're not budging," Messina tells me.

"What means are we using to convince them?" I ask, adding tones of gray to the bottom of the painting.

"So far, only money," Ray says, working on his own canvas, except he's not painting Starry Night, it's more like Dante's Inferno or something. It's kind of creepy.

"And that hasn't been enough to motivate them? That's interesting, money is almost fool-proof."

"Not this time around," McCabe pipes up. "U.S. customs have changed up every officer at the port."

I guess I'm not the only one who doesn't trust the people closest to me. "So, we find another way to motivate them," I suggest.

"Blackmail is too messy. You have to keep closer tabs on them, and they simply don't have as much invested as they do when we're talking money," Diaz says.

"Then maybe we need to make it a combo?" I say, sliding my paintbrush across the canvas. The lighter blue toward the top is starting to bring this piece together.

The men moan and groan at my suggestion, and I'll admit it's not the brightest idea. At the moment, I feel like the biggest dummy in the whole world, but I'm not willing to let this go. It could work. "It's not the best option, I know, but we don't have much choice. If we don't make this work, we're out of business. And that, gentlemen, is bad for all of us."

"She has a point," Ray says as he adds on a lake of fire. "We're going to have to up our game if we want to keep playing."

I'm thankful for Ray's backup. In a room full of men who are accustomed to working with other men, having the word of another man validates my suggestion. And it makes me feel a little less stupid.

The Scot, the Brazilian, and the Sicilian murmur amongst each other. Then the Sicilian asks, "When do you expect Charlie to return? I don't think we want to get too far ahead of ourselves without his thoughts on the situation."

I take a sip of my wine, needing the strength the alcohol provides. "I'm afraid Charlie has been unavoidably detained in New York. Things up there are going better than we had expected, and he's extended his trip by a few months," I tell them, hoping to buy myself some time to figure out what happened to Charlie. "I'll be the one who's running the operation down here until he returns."

I look to the corner and notice Henry playing cards with the other security guys. However, his focus is not on the game, but on me. He smiles, and butterflies flutter in my stomach. I think he might be proud of me.

I'm not sure the men from the other families are too impressed with me at the moment, but I've put myself out there and made my position clear.

11

Henry

During the ride back to Charlotte's house, I kept my thoughts to myself. There are so many things I have to consider, and I don't know if I can make sense of it right now.

Christ, what have I gotten myself into?

Once we're back in the house, I can't seem to stay in the same space as Charlotte. Seeing the way she commanded herself and the people around her? Hell, I don't know how to handle this. Yesterday, she told Ray to take his idea to the spank bank, today she's sitting in a room with professional killers and holding her own. I don't know if I'm impressed or scared.

"You haven't said a word since before the meeting," Charlotte says as she follows me upstairs. "Did I do something wrong?"

I squeeze my eyes shut and pinch the bridge of my nose, a migraine taking root. "I can't do this right now."

I take another shower and try to wash off the stench of betrayal. I've betrayed my profession in a way that was literally inconceivable to me last week. For all my doubts and anger, I know I can't leave Charlotte unattended for long. We might be in her home, but she has nothing between her and the very real threats from the outside. I've been gone too long as it is.

After searching the house for Charlotte, I find her in her favorite space, the library downstairs. She looks sweet. Like a fairy curled up on the couch, under a blanket, her nose in a book.

"What are you reading?"

"The Great Gatsby," she says. "It's my favorite."

I can't hold back my laugh. "Isn't that the one about the guy who gets involved in some illegal shit, so he can make lots of money for the woman he loves?"

"That's the one. But it's about so much more than that—"

"It doesn't matter," I say, cutting her off. I sit next to her and take the book from her hands. "We need to talk."

"About what?"

"Your plan."

She gives a deep frown and throws the blanket from her lap. "How much do you want to know? I mean, you're a cop."

That detail keeps coming back to bite me in the ass. Charlotte's right, I don't want to know too much, but . . . I let out a long breath. "I know, I know. But how can I protect you if I don't know all the threats."

"You're sure about this?"

"Not really." I signed up to do this to absolve my brother's debt, not worry about protecting the queen pin of the Scalise Family.

"Fine," she says. "Full disclosure."

"That would be great."

"A couple of months back, Charlie was working with the Petrovsky Family in New York, looking to expand our business and take it up the coast."

This is the one thing which no alphabet agency can figure out—precisely what pot the Scalise Family has their hands in. It's because of this that they can't seem to nail a single person in their organization. "Yeah, about that. Exactly what services does your family provide? Guns, drugs, gambling? What?"

"That's something you definitely don't want to be privy to," she says. "Anyway, Charlie went up north and made real headway with the Petrovsky Family and connections with a few other organizations as well. We don't typically deal with the Petrovsky's much, there's some, uh, bad blood from when my dad ran the family. The whole thing culminated when I was twelve. My father dragged Charlie and me from our beds and secured us in the panic room. I remember the look of defeat on his face when he hugged us. It would be the last time I'd see him. Anyway," she waves her hand dismissively, "from what Charlie said, the head of the Petrovsky's wants to let bygones be bygones. But then," she says, hopping up from the couch and grabbing her phone from her purse, "I got this message from Charlie."

She hands me the phone, and I read a text which says the Russians may be a problem. "Aren't the Russians always a problem in these kinds of situations?" I ask, thinking back to every movie with a Russian as the bad guy. And it's a lot.

"Usually," she agrees. "But then, Charlie texted me again two days later," she says, scrolling down the screen.

She leans so close to me I can smell her lavender-scented shampoo. Every cell in my body compels me to dip my nose into the crook of her neck and breathe deep. I tamp down the urge and read the message. Charlie tells her the Petrovsky Family was getting uneasy. "Uneasy about what?"

She shakes her head, and her tits sway slightly with the movement. "I don't know. That's the last time I heard from him."

"That's when the light went out?" I ask, referring to what she said when she told me she believed her twin brother was dead.

"Yeah. The next day."

"Do you know what the Russian's were after?"

"No. Charlie didn't want me too involved with the Petrovskys. He wasn't sure how much he could trust them. I guess he was trying to keep me safe."

I don't know how safe anyone can be when they're involved

with a crime family. "Maybe. Does anyone else know about this thing with the Petrovsky's?"

"I don't think so. A month or so before Charlie left, something changed. I don't know what, but he started to get all cagey and closed off. He told me to keep to what I know and let him deal with the Russians."

"So, Ray doesn't even know about this?" I don't like the guy, and I certainly don't trust him.

"Not as far as I know. But then again, I don't think Ray would tell me even if he did. He never liked my involvement."

"You got rid of everyone else in the house, why keep Ray?"

"That's not true. I kept Amara."

"Amara I get. But why Ray Thatch?"

She shrugs her shoulders. "He's like a father to me. After my real father died, Ray took care of Charlie and me like we were his own kids."

"What about your mom? Where was she at? Why didn't she take care of you?" From my experience as a cop, I know not all mothers are good mothers. For the life of me, I can't imagine any woman leaving her children to be raised into organized crime.

"She left when Charlie and I were little. From what I can remember, I look a lot like her. Charlie looked like our dad but with red hair. I guess the pressure of the lifestyle was too much for my mom. She left when I was five."

I don't know what to say to that. I have a fantastic family, they're not perfect, but they're mine. "So, you believe your life is in danger because Charlie died?"

"Yeah."

"From what you said, it sounds like the Russians may be at the root of the problem. What I don't understand is, if you trust Ray so much, why not fill him in and let him take care of it, and take care of you?"

She bites on her bottom lip, and my dick twitches.

"I do trust Ray, really I do," she says. "I honestly don't think he would do anything to put Charlie or me in any danger knowingly. People think this business has some kind of an honor code. But in reality, if one person believes you've crossed them," she drags her index finger across her neck, mimicking slitting her throat. "You don't even have to actually cross them, just the perception, the slightest hint you're out to get them or take something away, they'll whack you off."

I burst out laughing. Charlotte said it again. "Charlotte, I don't think you're using that term right."

"What term? Whacking off? Sure I am."

"No, you're not. Whacking someone off means that you're, um, giving a hand job."

"A hand with what kind of job?"

Jesus. "Have you been living under a rock your whole life? Didn't you go to school? You had to be exposed to some of this stuff. I know you said you were sheltered, but come on, there's no way you haven't heard these terms."

She blanches at my outburst. "If you must know, I was homeschooled after third grade. I didn't have a lot of friends. I spend more time reading," she says, waving her hand around the library, "than watching TV. Satisfied?"

I think I've walked into a minefield, and I'm not sure how to navigate this terrain. "I'm sorry. It's not my place to pry."

She stands from the couch. "You know what? Maybe this was a bad idea. You're right. I don't have any reason not to trust Ray. I should go and tell him everything, let him deal with this. I have no clue what the H-E-double-hockey-sticks I'm doing. So, go ahead and go. Consider your brother's debt paid in full." She storms out of the library and up the stairs.

I have no clue what the hell just happened. We went from talking about her past to her current problems, and the next thing I know, I'm fired. Fired? I'm not sure I was fired *per se*, but I don't know what else to call it.

I sit on the couch and pick up the book she was reading and start where she left off, deciding it's better to let her blow off some steam. I can't in good conscience let her fire me. She may not trust her instincts, but I trust mine, and I have no doubt this woman's life is in danger. She's just naive and reckless enough that she'll end up getting herself killed.

After twenty minutes, I decide it's time to go and talk with Charlotte, let her know what my thoughts are on the situation.

A barrage of metallic pops come from the first floor. I toss the book on the couch and run up the stairs.

Charlotte is under attack.

12

Charlotte

I escaped into the kitchen and assembled all the ingredients for chocolate chip cookies. Some days baking is the best way to soothe the soul. Maybe it's because I spent so many hours in the kitchen with Amara. We talked about anything and everything—current events, our hopes, and dreams, her family. I could really use her right now, but I sent her home an hour ago. I knew if I let her stick around, I would lay all my problems on her. No one knows what's going on except Henry and me, and that's how it needs to stay.

I feel so alone in this big empty house with only my indecision left to comfort me. I hate to admit it, but I might have overreacted to Henry's inquisition. Every question he asked was legitimate.

I do want to tell Ray, and maybe I should because right now it's raining bullets in my living room, and I'm hiding behind a couch. The couch, it seems, will not provide adequate protection and is being blown to smithereens with the onslaught.

"*Charlotte*," Henry is crouched low on the steps from the lower level. A bullet pulverizes a large floral vase on a table in the atrium. He ducks, covering his head, then calls out to me again. "Where are you? Are you okay?"

I crawl on my hands and knees toward a large wooden chest by the hallway. "I'm over here," I shout, waving my hand in the air.

"Are you hurt?"

I run my hands across my chest and over my face. "No. I'm fine. We need to get to the panic room," I yell. Just then a bullet whizzes by my head, it's so close I can hear the whine of the metal. "Now."

I scramble across the floor, and the edges of the tile scrape at my knees. I get to the doorway of the basement, and Henry reaches out and covers his body with mine.

"Where's the panic room?" he asks, his voice gruff and commanding.

"In the library."

Henry's arm is wrapped around my waist, tucking me into his side as we make our way downstairs. We wend our way through several rows of books until we are met with a steel door. I punch in the code, and the door makes a hissing sound right before it opens. Once inside, I yank the door closed, pull down the latch, and twist the lock, the room pressurizing again.

While Henry looks around at the equipment and provisions of our safe haven, I get down to business. There are eighteen twenty-seven-inch televisions that frame two ninety-eight-inch computer monitors. I flip the switches on a side panel to power the screens and wait for them to load.

"You've done this before?" Henry asks as I take a seat in front of the screens.

"We have a drill every six months. Ray insists on it." I key up some commands as the images in front of us come into focus.

"Were any of those drills not a drill?"

"A few," I tell him, focused on getting everything up and

running. A few more keystrokes and the entire compound comes into view. "There are cameras in every room of the house and all around the perimeter."

"Every room?"

"Every room," I repeat. "But the bedrooms, bathrooms, and my father's office kick on when the panic room is activated."

A breath of hot air blows on my neck, and I turn to look at Henry. "Everything okay?"

"Yeah, yeah. Except for, well," Henry points to the monitors.

"Right. Each screen shows nine cameras. Whatever's going on out there, we'll know about it."

As we stare at the screens, we don't see anything, not even bullets flying like they were when we got down here.

"That's strange," Henry says. "Everything looks how it's supposed to." The couch and the coffee table, the vase, all in perfect condition. "Who has access to this room?"

"Everyone who works here."

"That's Ray, Amara, and the entire security team that you fired. Anyone else?"

"There were a few other housekeeping staff, but I let them go too. The one person I kept on was Amara." The idea that Amara set this in motion carves a hole in my stomach. "There's no way she did this. Not Amara."

"I don't think so either," he says, "but Ray on the other hand—"

"It's not Ray. I know you don't like him; I get it. But it's not him. If he wanted to take me out, he would have done so right after Charlie died."

"So you do think Ray has something to do with Charlie's death?" he says.

"No. Of course, I don't. You're twisting my words." I crawl under the desk and fiddle with the wires. Once everything is in order, I scoot backward on my knees. As I stand, I knock my head on the underside of the desk. "*Peas and carrots,*" I holler as a stabbing pain spreads across my skull.

I try a second time to back out and keep scooting until I can see the lip of the desk with my own two eyes.

"Are you okay?" Henry asks, helping me off the ground.

I rub at the spot on my head. "Yeah."

He pulls the chair out. "Sit. I need to take a look."

"Really, I'm fine." I take the seat, but pout, my pride wounded from my klutziness. Again.

With gentle fingers, he parts my hair. "You're not fine, you're bleeding."

Of course I am. "There's a first aid kit in the cabinet," I tell him, pointing to the far corner of the room.

Henry tears open a box of gauze and squirts peroxide on a sponge, making quick work of cleaning me up. "This might sting a little. You're not going to freak out on me again, are you?"

"As long as it isn't the stingy stuff, I'll be fine," I retort, folding my arms across my chest, a little annoyed and a lot embarrassed.

He carefully dabs the gauze to the top of my head. It does sting, but nothing like the antiseptic.

"It's only a scratch. I don't think you need stitches," Henry tells me as he runs his fingers through my hair.

My scalp prickles at the contact.

"Would you look at that," Henry says, pointing to the computers.

I swivel in the chair to find the monitors have updated. Everything is how it's supposed to be, destroyed couch and all.

"How'd you do that?"

"There's a fail-safe. My father anticipated the live feed could potentially be compromised. There are only four people in this house who know how to access it. Well, three now. That's how I know it couldn't be Ray or Amara. They know as well as I do that we can override the system."

"There," Henry says, pointing to one of the monitors.

There are two men dressed entirely in black with matching ski masks in the backyard. They're just standing there, talking to each other, their semi-automatic guns lowered to their sides.

I pan over to the front door to find two more men dressed the same as the men before. The side door from the living room is kicked in. Within seconds the house is swarmed with men cloaked in black. The room goes dark, and the monitors fade.

"Shit," Henry says as he pulls out his phone, using the flashlight to illuminate the pitch-black room. "They cut the power."

"It's okay. The door is secure, and the backup generator will kick in after a couple of minutes."

We sit in silence as we wait for the lights to come back on. My outburst earlier replays in my mind. My sheltered life has its drawbacks, and my inexperience is foremost. Maybe I should apologize. "Listen, I'm—"

"Quit apologizing for standing up for yourself," he says, interrupting me. "I shouldn't have pushed so hard. I only want to keep you safe."

I release a grunt of frustration because now I feel like somehow, I've let him down. "But I do owe you an apology. I shouldn't have freaked out on you like that. My childhood is a bit of a touchy subject, I guess."

"That's an understatement."

The generator kicks in and the monitors come back to life. What I see steals my breath. "Holy cannoli."

The room is filled with men on a path of destruction. One rams the butt of his gun into the walls, punching holes. Another tears the upholstery with a knife on every piece of furniture. Glass is shattered, tables flipped. After they've destroyed everything they can, they turn toward another man who is standing in the middle of the room. He gives a lassoing gesture, telling them to wrap it up.

"Who are these guys?" I breathe, stunned by the vehement actions of total strangers.

"We know who it isn't."

"Maybe it's the Russians."

In the dim light of the safe room, Henry looks incredibly strong. He's the man who covered me with all his hard muscles to protect me as we rushed into the library for cover. I could feel the heat of his body through his shirt and straight to my core. He became hard when I needed him to, yet his embrace was soft and inviting. I didn't want him to let me go.

I've had to fight not to look too closely at him, a task which has proven near impossible. He is easily the most handsome man I have ever seen. His warm caramel eyes make my breath hitch with one look.

His jaw drops with shock. "Scratch that, it got uglier."

"What? How?" I look to the screen and see three men carrying in gas cans and spreading liquid across the living room, up the stairs. Men in the basement splash accelerant on the rows of bookcases.

The man in charge lifts his mask up to his nose, keeping his face concealed. The solitary defining feature is a giant mole above his lip. He pulls out a pack of cigarettes and a Zippo from his pocket. The man plucks out a cigarette and sticks it between his teeth. With a strike of the flint, he lights his cigarette, takes three long drags, and tosses the lighter to the floor.

—

Henry

"We need to get out of here." The camera in the living room goes black, then the kitchen. The fire spreads rapidly, climbing the curtains in the dining room.

Charlotte's hand flies to her mouth. "Oh, my stars."

"Tell me there's a secondary escape route from this death trap." I scan the room, hoping and praying for a way out.

Charlotte bites her bottom lip, the look on her face is all the confirmation I need.

"We have one option."

"Out there?" she squeaks. "With the fire? No way."

"If we don't try, we're going to die down here."

Charlotte goes pale, her eyes glazed with fright. She's in shock.

I swivel her around in the chair, so she's facing me. I put her cheeks in my palms and look directly into her beautiful green eyes. "We have to get out of here. We can do this. I need you to trust me."

She nods, and I let out a breath of relief, grateful she's able to focus. "Cover your nose with the neck of your dress." The dress that has been teasing me all day is totally useless. Unless . . .

I pull out a knife hidden in my boot and cut the dress up to her belly button. In one swift motion, I tear off the bottom half as she twirls with surprise. Her pearly panties shimmer in the dim light of the safe room. Fuck, she's gorgeous.

"Use this," I tell her, handing her the cloth of her skirt.

Once again, she nods, covering her nose like I'd instructed.

"Get down, I'm going to unbolt the door. Since the room is pressurized, there's going to be a strong pull of smoke. Keep your eyes closed. When I tell you, open them and follow me."

"Okay."

I twist the latch of the door, raise the arm, and brace myself for what comes next. I cover my nose with my shirt and squeeze my eyes tight as I pull open the door. A rush of heat and smoke funnels in, enveloping us.

I count to five and open my eyes, and they burn instantly. I take a look around. The furniture is on fire and spreading up the bookcases. Christ, it's an inferno. Even with the panic room being pressurized, we would have been cooked alive if we stayed.

I grab Charlotte's hand. "Open your eyes."

After a few hard blinks and a couple of hardy coughs, Charlotte regards our surroundings with her eyes squinted. Her mouth falls open as the horror of our situation blazes around us.

"Get down and stay as low to the ground as you can." I crouch as close as possible to the floor. "Follow me," I shout, the roar of the fire near deafening.

We crawl through the aisles of the burning bookcases,

glowing paper falling like rain toward the stairs. The stairs, that less than an hour ago were our salvation, have now become our only way out. We make it to the top step, but every room is ablaze, every exit blocked by fire.

"The only way out is up," I tell her. Five exits and not a single one of any use. Figures.

She sputters out a cough but gives me a thumbs-up, and we crawl higher, winding around the fire on the steps. When we get to the second floor, I realize it isn't a much better choice, it seems the men had made their way up here too, and every room, including John Scalise's office, is in flames. "We have to go up to the third floor."

Charlotte lets out a succession of deep hacks and is several paces behind me. The smoke is getting to her, weakening her. "Grab my hand," I tell her, pulling her next to me. "Don't let go."

"Okay," she mutters weakly.

We trudge another set of stairs and make it halfway up when Charlotte's hand falls from mine. I turn around to look for her; she's lying on the steps, her face flat on the floor.

I work my way back down and pull Charlotte's small, limp frame onto my back, and carry her up the stairs. When we ascend to the top, the air is clear, with no indications of fire. No exit signs either.

"Shit." I rest Charlotte on the ground and look for signs of life. She's breathing, they're shallow breaths, but she's still breathing.

I begin searching each room for a way out. I come across a guest room at the end of the hall. The important thing to note is that it's not on fire and has a large window. Beyond the window is the Olympic size pool. "This will have to be good enough."

I scramble back to the hall where I had left Charlotte and scoop her up in my arms. She groans as I shift her, and I pull her closer to my body. Standing at the window in the guest room, I ram my foot through the windowpane. The shock of force runs up my leg, pushing me backward. *"Motherfucker."*

I set Charlotte down on the bed and decide sheer bodily force will not be enough. A large, velvet-covered chair sits in the corner, and at the moment, seems to be my best option.

Heavier than I had expected, I lift the chair above my head with a guttural "humph" and walk toward the window.

"One, two," I count to myself, trying to collect all the strength in my muscles to make this work because if I don't, we're toast. "*Three.*" I heave the chair through the window. With a crash, the chair breaks through the thick glass pane and falls to the ground outside.

I rip off a curtain and wrap it around my hand and punch out the remaining glass, trying to make our new exit as large and safe as possible. Although I don't know that there's a safe way to jump from three stories.

With the opening as wide as I can make it, I gather Charlotte in my arms and walk her to the ledge. "I've got you, cupcake," I whisper, giving a small kiss to her forehead. Considering what I'm about to do, it may be the only time I will get to kiss her, and I won't die with that kind of regret.

The sound of crackling comes from behind me, and I turn to find that the fire has made it up to the third floor. There's no way out, except through this window. I take a deep breath and close my eyes because, well, I'm about to jump out a fucking window.

With Charlotte in my arms, I take the leap. The wind beneath my feet is the scariest thing I've ever experienced. Within seconds, we're making contact with the water. Pain lances through my body as we collide, lighting every nerve in my body on fire. My grip on Charlotte loosens, and I sink further to the bottom, while Charlotte floats to the top.

I kick my arms and legs, propelling myself upward. When I break the surface, I search for Charlotte and find her floating face-down in the water. I have no time to contemplate the meaning of life, only to react to the situation. I stab at the water with my arms until I capture her. Wrapping my arm around her chest, I pull her to the ledge and out of the pool.

I hop onto the concrete slab next to her and pull her from the edge of the pool. Her lithe frame is still, her complexion void of color. There is no rising or falling of her chest, she's not breathing.

"Fuck." With the palm of my hand, I start compressing her breastbone. "One, two, three, four, five," I count all the way to thirty. I seal my mouth to hers and plug her nose closed, blowing in two forceful breaths until I see her chest rise.

Nothing.

I start another round of CPR, trying not to think of all the things I regret having said to her. We only knew each other for a couple of days, but she was, no—is, the sweetest person I've met in my life.

I blow two more breaths into her mouth, and her body convulses beneath me, her arms flail while her chest heaves. I sit back on my haunches and watch as she coughs to expel the pool water from her lungs.

"Thank Christ," I breathe, running my hands over her cheeks.

The entire house is blazing, the heat of the flames already drying my clothes. We need to get out of here. I don't know if those guys are still here, but I won't wait around to find out.

Even though Charlotte is breathing again, she's still unconscious. I throw her over my shoulder and make my way to the garage. As far as I can tell, there aren't any men creeping around. If they're smart, they would have left as soon as the Zippo hit the ground.

The garage is not attached to the house, thank God, but as soon as I turn the knob, I realize it's locked. "Damnit."

I balance on one leg and kick the door open. Unlike the window, the door fractures and swings wide. Finally, a much-needed break.

The first car I see is a 1955 silver 550 Spyder Porsche. Its beauty beckons images of James Dean and one of the classiest times in history. I lower Charlotte into the passenger seat, her head lolls to the side, and she moans.

"I know, I'm sorry," I tell her, running a finger along her jaw.

With a jump, I slide into the driver's seat, ready to get out of here as quickly as possible, it's already taking too long.

"Keys, keys," I say to myself, searching through the center console and any nook and cranny which might be holding the damn keys.

"Fuck," I scream, banging the heel of my palms against the steering wheel. The goddamn keys are in the house. I throw my head back on the headrest, taking a breath, trying not to give up. I glance toward Charlotte, she's pale with her eyes closed. I need to get her out of here.

As if some higher power could hear my plea, a twinkle of light catches my attention from the ignition.

"Thank fuck." I turn the key and check behind me.

The power is out, and so is the garage door opener. I have no choice. I throw the gearshift into reverse and slam on the accelerator, busting through the garage door and the gate. The grown man part of me hurts to think of doing something so reckless to such a beautiful vehicle.

I swing out wide onto the street where sirens are blaring. Fire and police are on their way. I slam the gear into drive and speed through the neighborhood.

After an incident like this, there are so many things to consider. Where do we go? Who can we trust? My options are limited, so I pull out my phone and call the best person I believe can help.

"Mom, I need a favor."

13

Charlotte

My throat is so sore it reminds me of when I had a terrible case of tonsillitis and I had to have my tonsils removed. Sure the ice cream was great, but back then, they believed eating rougher foods like potato chips would help speed up the healing process. That's how I feel—like I've been eating potato chips after a tonsillectomy.

I open my eyes, and they burn like I've spent the past six hours swimming with my eyes open. Except I haven't. A chill skitters across my skin, and I realize my clothes are damp.

Did I go swimming?

I stare at the popcorn ceiling and try to recall my last memory. Images of bullets, the panic room, and Henry's face contorted with fright.

Wait. I don't have popcorn ceilings.

"She's waking up."

A grizzly-looking woman is standing over me, her hair cropped short and flitted with silver. Who is this woman, and where am I?

What is this thing on my face? I rip off the mask covering my nose and mouth and bolt upright, my head spinning with the quick movement.

"Man alive, my head hurts." My hands fly to my temples in an effort to dull the pounding.

"How are you feeling?" the strange woman asks.

"I'd feel a lot better if I knew who you were." I toss my feet over the edge of the couch.

"Sorry. I'm Bev, Henry's mother," she says with a warm, nurturing smile. "You've had quite an evening from what I've heard."

"Really? Would you mind filling me in?"

"She's awake," says another woman, this one younger, and she's dressed in an EMT uniform. "How are you feeling?"

With dark hair and soulful eyes, I know she must be Henry's sister. I'm sitting in the home of Henry's family and meeting them for the first time since blackmailing him into working for me. I don't know if this could get any worse.

"I'm okay, I think. A little thirsty, I guess."

The woman I assume is Henry's sister, sits next to me on the couch, grabs my wrist, and looks at her watch. When she's done, she pulls out a little contraption from her bag and sticks it on my finger. Then she plucks out a penlight and looks into my eyes.

"Open your mouth," she demands, and I do as I'm told. "Her oxygen saturation is good. Her throat looks pretty red, but she seems to be breathing okay. Any nausea? Dizziness?"

I swallow hard. "Um, dizzy, I guess. Maybe a little nauseous."

She clicks the penlight off and tosses it back in her bag, then pulls the thing off my finger. "Possibly a slight concussion. You're lucky."

"Great, you're awake," Henry says as he walks into the family room, tearing a bite from a sandwich. He looks gritty, weary, and only the slightest bit concerned for my welfare.

His sister stands up. "I think she's going to be okay, Henry, but you should still take her to the hospital. She might have a concussion. And smoke inhalation is a serious problem. She's fine for now, but the swelling can creep up and obstruct her airway. She needs to be under observation."

Henry glances toward me and then to the ground, his jaw ticking with consideration. "I understand. Tell me what to look for and what to do if it happens."

His sister shakes her head with a laugh. "There's nothing you can do. She would have to be emergently intubated. I know you're CPR certified, but you're not trained in placing an artificial airway."

All this talk about me, but not to me, is making my head pound harder as I try to put the pieces together. "Okay, stop it. I'm tired, I'm cranky, and I don't have a clue what happened or how I ended up here with a bunch of strangers."

"She's awake," another man says as he enters the room. Everyone turns to glare at him.

It's Brian Cain. It would appear the entire family has a low opinion of the man. I imagine his trouble with the Scalise's isn't an isolated incident.

"I can take a hint," Brian says, then walks down the hall and out of sight.

"I get it, Bea," Henry says to his sister, getting back to the conversation from before Brian interrupted. "I'll keep it in mind. Thanks for your help."

Bea huffs with exasperation as she swipes up her bag and slings it over her shoulder. "Yeah, any time," she says, her tone harsh. I'm confident she's sincere in the offer, but she probably hates that her brother is ignoring her advice.

"I have to get back to the rig, Mom," she says, dropping a kiss on Bev's cheek. She turns to me. "Glad you're doing okay. Drink plenty of cold fluids and take some ibuprofen to try to prevent inflammation. If you start feeling short of breath, go to the hospital immediately. Good luck."

I nod. "I will. Thank you."

After Bea leaves, Bev claps her hands. "Let's get you some ice water. Sound good?"

"That'd be great." To say I'm parched would be a massive understatement.

Henry takes the last bite of his sandwich, then sits on the couch next to me. "You doing okay?"

Everyone keeps asking the same question, but no one is telling me what happened. "Yeah. I think so. It's just," I halt my thought for a second because I'm kind of embarrassed that I don't remember. Everyone else seems to be in the know, except me.

"What's the last thing you remember?" Henry asks as if he's reading my mind.

"The panic room. Fixing the live feed." I leave out the part about his eyes, it might scare him off, and I kind of need him right now.

Bev hands me a glass of ice water and then sits on the loveseat across from Henry and me.

As I drink my water, Henry fills me in on the details. The fire, jumping into the pool from the third floor, and me stopping breathing and needing CPR. Tears well in my eyes. I haven't cried since my father died. Not even when I lost Charlie—maybe because that isn't confirmed, and it's simply a gut feeling.

Without any warning, the tears turn into a waterfall. "I died?" I cry. "And my house. Everything is gone. Every memory of my dad, my brother, my entire childhood, is gone. Is there anything left? Maybe the fire wasn't as bad as you thought," I suggest, desperate for the tiniest sliver of hope.

Henry shakes his head. "I don't think so. I made a few calls. It's a Five Alarm fire. Over a hundred firefighters and twenty trucks, some from other counties. They're still working to put it out. I'm so sorry."

Bev hands me a tissue because it's obvious I'm about to lose my cool again. And I do, but this time, I manage to collect myself a little quicker. My mind is fuzzy, and everything feels surreal.

All I can do is think about one task at a time. "I need a shower," I say, rubbing at the gunk caked between my fingers. "But I don't have any clothes."

"It's okay," Henry says. "We'll figure something out."

He stands and offers me his hand. I accept, and the feeling of his palm against mine warms my cold, shocky heart. He gives me a pained smile and guides me to a bathroom down the hall. "There's a robe on the back of the door and towels in the closet. Help yourself to whatever you need. I'm going to find you something to wear."

I don't know what to say, and I stand there like a dumb dumb staring at him. He must have some idea of what's going through my mind, which is nothing at the moment. He walks to the tub and turns on the faucet, puts his hand under the water. When it's warm enough for his liking, he turns on the shower.

Steam fills the bathroom, and Henry helps me out of my clothes, lifting what's left of my dress above my head. There's no skirt anymore, and I have no idea how it happened. Not even walking from the living room to the bathroom did I notice I was only in my underwear.

Wrapping his arms around my waist, Henry places me under the showerhead. The curtain is open, and water sprays everywhere. The tub floor turns gray from soot sluicing off my body.

Henry frowns at me, strips naked, and steps into the shower. "It's okay. I'll take care of you." He picks up a bottle of shampoo and squeezes the liquid into his hands. With a delicate touch, he rubs my scalp as he works the shampoo into my hair, cautiously cleansing the spot I had bumped earlier in the panic room.

I'm naked. Henry is naked. And we're in the shower. Together. Even with all these facts, it does nothing for me. My first shower with a man, and there is nothing erotic or pleasurable, only comforting.

After rinsing my hair, Henry grabs a washcloth and lathers it with soap, and with the most tender touch, washes away the trauma left behind from the events of the night.

To my amazement, he's a complete gentleman about the whole situation, not taking advantage of my mental or physical state. With each stroke of the washcloth, he keeps his eyes trained on mine.

For the first time in I don't know how long, I feel genuinely cared for. Amara was like a mother to me, but there's a difference between a mother and like a mother. There was always something missing. Same thing with Ray. He never treated me poorly, provided me with all the things a good father would, but he still wasn't my father.

At this moment, in the shower with this man, there's an air of unconditional acceptance. It has been gone so long, I hadn't realized I missed it. However, even in the chaotic mental state I'm experiencing, I know better than to rely on this feeling because it's hyper incensed from the situation. Still, that doesn't mean I can't enjoy it while it lasts.

Henry quickly washes his hair and body, steps out of the tub, and grabs a towel from the closet. He takes special care as he dries me from head to toes, wrapping me in a fluffy pink robe.

He towels off himself and wraps it around his waist. "Feel better?"

I nod, incapable of higher-level thinking.

"Good. Come on." Grabbing my hand, we walk to a bedroom down the hall.

The room is decorated with striped navy blue and white wallpapered walls and sports trophies on the dresser. "Is this your bedroom?"

"Yeah. Well, it used to be," Henry rifles through a bag he pulled out of the closet. "I keep an emergency bag in the closet, just in case. Here," he says, handing me a wad of fabric. With his back to me, he drops the towel, and I try to look away but fail miserably. His ass is toned with two adorable dimples nestled above each cheek. I was literally naked with him in the shower, and not once did it occur to me that I should take a peek at the goods. I guess my wits are returning.

He slides on a pair of boxer briefs. He looks just as amazing wearing them as he did naked. How is that even possible?

"I'll give you some privacy and grab another glass of water and some ibuprofen," he says, his shoulders tensing as he stares at the wall.

"That would be great. Thanks."

When he returns, I've changed into the clothes which he handed me—a pair of dark gray boxer briefs and a white T-shirt. They're three sizes too big but smell like Henry, and I think they're my new favorite pair of pajamas.

Henry stands still at the doorway, staring, then swallows hard. He looks away as he hands me a glass of water, sets down a second glass, and then hands me some pills. "You need to take these and drink both glasses before you go to sleep."

I toss the pills in my mouth and follow it up with an entire glass of water. "One down," I say, giving Henry a smile.

"Good."

I'm not sure what has happened since he left the room and returned, but there's a definite shift. He seems cold, indifferent.

"I'm going to go lock up," he says. "I'll be sleeping down the hall if you need anything." He turns and walks toward the door.

As he makes to leave, my heart pounds with dread at the idea of being alone. Not simply alone, but without him. "Wait."

He turns around, his eyebrows arching up in surprise at my sudden plea.

"Please don't go. I . . . ," I fiddle with the hem of my shirt. "I don't want to be alone tonight. Would it be too much to ask if you slept in here with me?"

"Uh," he looks around the room as if it will offer the right answer. "Sure. No problem. I'll grab some extra blankets and pillows."

"No. Not on the floor. In the bed. With me."

Henry blinks hard then takes a deep breath. "Are you sure?"

I sound desperate right now, and it's kind of hard not to hate myself. I've never asked a man to share a bed with me, except when Charlie and I were little, so that doesn't count.

Henry throws back the blanket, gestures for me to take my place, then slides in next to me. We lay on our backs, staring at the ceiling fan above, me wearing his underwear, him wearing his underwear. Heat radiates beneath the covers from Henry's bare chest. It's a needed distraction as my mind whirls with memories and emotions. Emotions with the strength of a hurricane. "Did I really die?"

"You stopped breathing," he breathes out. "I had to give you CPR."

My bottom lip quivers. I think Henry could tell me a hundred times, and it wouldn't affect me any less. Tears fall from my eyes, and my nose becomes stuffy. I try to stifle the onslaught of feelings with a couple of sniffles.

"Hey, hey," he says, rolling over and pulling me into his arms. "It's okay. Everything is okay."

I nod my head vigorously, needing to believe what he's telling me. I don't know if I can keep going if I lose hope in our mission. After everything that's happened, my faith is faltering.

With his index finger, he lifts my chin from his chest to look at me. "It will be okay, I promise. I won't let anything happen to you."

His lips are so red, sexy, and—

Without a second thought as to the consequences, I rub my finger across the smooth skin of his mouth. I peer up to check his reaction.

His eyes are dark and intense, but they aren't telling me no. I take the next step and press my lips to his. They're warm and delicate and taste like mint. It takes a couple of seconds before I realize he isn't kissing me back.

"I'm sorry. I didn't . . . I'm sorry."

"No. Don't be. It's not uncommon to seek affection after a trauma. It's completely normal."

Why is he so clinical? I feel like I'm talking to a therapist, not a bodyguard. "What about what you experienced?"

"What do you mean?"

"Sure, you're a police officer, and you see a lot of stuff. But you were in a house fire, jumped from a building, and did CPR. It seems to me your experience was just as terrifying as mine."

He takes a breath. "It was. It was hard seeing you there, floating lifeless in the pool. I didn't," he stutters, "I didn't know if you were going to make it."

He squeezes his eyes tight like he's trying to hold back. He doesn't need to, I know he feels the same vulnerability and insecurity as I do.

Just as I consider trying to kiss him again, his lips are coming to mine. This time when they meet, there's a spark that ignites between us. The kiss is soft and gentle.

When he pulls away, we're both panting, the experience intense and breathtaking.

"Shit," Henry says, rolling onto his back. "I'm sorry. I shouldn't have done that. I don't want to take advantage of you."

I shift onto an elbow and place a palm on his chest, fingers playing at the hair there. "You aren't taking advantage of me. I kissed you first, remember?"

"It doesn't matter. I promised to protect you. Kissing you after everything that happened isn't a good way of doing that."

I'm not sure what he's more stuck on, the idea that he took advantage of me, which is ridiculous, or the fact that he wasn't able to protect me. "None of this is your fault. You know that, right?"

He doesn't say anything.

"I'm serious. I hired you because I was scared for my life. It turns out my worries were completely valid. And you know what? If it weren't for you, I wouldn't be here tonight, wearing your underwear, in your childhood bed, having this discussion. And I'm so sorry I didn't say this before but thank you."

I climb on top of him, his eyes wide and startled. My fingers thread through his, and I place his arms over his head, leaning in to kiss him.

He doesn't return the kiss immediately, so I nibble at his lip, coaxing him. After a few rough tugs, he caves and captures my mouth with his.

Releasing my hold, I caress his face, the stubble on his jaw pricking my fingers. He pulls my body flush against him, and he rolls me over so I'm on the bottom with my arms pinned above my head. His free hand roams down my leg while he grinds his hard cock into my center.

As I thrust my hips toward his, he stops. "We can't do this."

"What? Why not? You're not attracted—"

He puts two fingers over my mouth. "You are a stunning woman, Charlotte Sutton. But if we do this, no, when we do this, I want it to be someplace nicer than my parent's house. You deserve better, cupcake."

As much as I want to, I can't argue with that kind of gallantry.

14

Henry

Charlotte and I spent the entire night in each other's arms. It felt good. Surprisingly good. A part of me wanted to kick my own ass for not taking what she offered, but I couldn't do it. Charlotte is an exceptional woman. She may have been raised in a less than ordinary lifestyle, but the Family's decisions are not what defines her. She's kind, spirited, and giving. I have no doubt when she's ready, she'll find the perfect man. Someone who will love her and support her, give her the life she's dreamed of.

However, that person can't be me. She reigns queen over an illegal business. The benefits of her position provide her with a higher quality of life than I could afford—not on a policeman's wages. I sneak out of bed as the sun rises and make my way to the kitchen to start a pot of coffee.

"Good morning," Dad says. He's dressed in a striped terry cloth robe and moccasins. "How'd you sleep?"

I scratch my head, then my chest. "Okay, I guess. You?"

He pulls out a coffee mug and pours from the carafe. "Fine."

My father isn't a great conversationalist, but I don't mind. It's often therapeutic to simply sit in a room with another person and not be burdened with tête-à-tête.

"Would you like an omelet?" he offers, pulling out mixing bowls.

"Sure. Better make it two."

He raises an eyebrow. "Two?"

"Yeah. I brought someone home with me." Dad wasn't home until late last night and missed all the excitement.

He laughs as he cracks eggs into a bowl. "I bet your mom loved that."

"She did," I say, smiling behind my cup. When I had gone downstairs last night to grab Charlotte's water and pain medicine, Mom was all too happy to talk about the woman in the guest room.

"She's the one," Mom said. "Don't do anything to scare her off. I need grandbabies." After the fire yesterday, I called Mom for help. I had to give her some details but kept it to a minimum. However, those tidbits of information didn't deter her from instantly loving Charlotte. What Mom's fascination is with my love life, I'll never know, but she's hellbent on the idea of me settling down and popping out a few grandkids.

"Good morning," Charlotte says as she traipses into the kitchen. She's donned in the pink robe I put her in last night, her hair adorably mussed.

"Coffee?" I ask, holding up the half-empty pot.

"No, thanks. Orange juice would be great."

"You got it."

"This must be the young lady you were talking about," Dad says as he steps out of the pantry.

"It is," I confirm. "Charlotte, this is my dad, Benny. Dad, this is Charlotte Sutton."

Charlotte stands from the table to shake Dad's hand. Dad kisses the back of her palm. "You sure are a beautiful young lady."

Charlotte blushes. "Thank you."

Mom charges in from the lanai. "Good morning, everybody. How are we feeling today? Charlotte, you look better. Are you feeling better too?"

"My throat's still sore, but definitely better," Charlotte replies, flicking her gaze to me and smiling.

"Good. Now, why don't you and Henry set the table? Benny and I will carry the breakfast out."

Charlotte and I set up the dining table for a family breakfast—excluding Brian, who went to bed an hour ago after burning the midnight oil to play Call of Duty.

Mom is probably stalling in the kitchen so she can update Dad on the events of last night. With Mom being a retired homicide cop, I knew she wouldn't be able to leave this alone. She doesn't know who Charlotte is, but she's an intuitive person—a requirement of the job. I wouldn't be surprised if she hasn't done some checking around, interrogated Brian, and watched the news all before 6 a.m. If she hasn't had confirmation yet, I have no doubt she's close.

"What you need, Miss Sutton," Mom announces, bringing in a platter of bacon and sausage, "is a good meal."

The fact that Mom referred to Charlotte as "Miss Sutton" does not bode well for the direction of the impending conversation.

My father enters the dining room carrying another platter, this time with omelets. "I hope everyone likes feta," he says, setting the plate in the center of the table.

"I love feta," Charlotte says excitedly.

I lean in and whisper in Charlotte's ear. "Dad's an executive chef at La Jolliesse."

"Very nice."

We pass around the platters and fork food onto our plates.

"What do you do, Mrs. Cain?" Charlotte asks.

"Bev, please," Mom says. "I'm retired."

"Really? What did you do before you retired?"

"I worked homicide for the Miami Police Department."

Orange juice splutters from Charlotte's mouth. "A homicide detective?"

"Yes," Mom confirms. "And I think we all need to talk about what your plan is now."

"My plan?" Charlotte squeaks, looking like a deer in the headlights.

"Mom," I interject, "Cut her some slack. Someone just tried to kill her and then set fire to her house. Take it down a peg."

Mom frowns at my reprimand. "Old habits die hard. I guess what I'm trying to say is, what do you plan to do next, Charlotte?"

"I don't know. Go back to see if I can salvage anything? Call Ray. Oh my gosh," Charlotte gasps, her hands flying to her cheeks. "I never called Ray. He must be worried sick. Where's my phone?" She stands from the table, knocking over her orange juice, the glass shattering to pieces. "Geez oh Pete, I'm so sorry," she cries, fretting about cleaning the broken shards.

"Sit down, cupcake, we'll get it taken care of. Eat your breakfast first," I croon, trying to help Charlotte calm down.

The mess is cleaned up in no time with Mom's help. Charlotte picks at her food nervously. I grasp her hand, giving it a reassuring squeeze, and she gives me a small smile.

"You know," Dad chimes in, "it seems to me, from what little Bev has told me, is that if whoever tried to kill you thinks you're dead, why not let them keep thinking that?"

Me, my mom, and Charlotte all stare at Dad.

"And," Dad adds, "I don't know who this Ray guy is, or how he's related to all this, but I would let him think you're dead too."

I toss my napkin on the table. "Wow. That's . . . an excellent idea."

"And to think, we're the cops." Mom shakes her head with disbelief as she shrewdly assesses her husband.

"Don't sound so shocked," Dad says, sounding offended. "Just because I'm a chef doesn't mean I'm dumb."

Charlotte has remained suspiciously mute through the whole exchange. It doesn't seem in her nature to stay quiet. But I get it, she's had a lot thrown at her, and I can only imagine what it's like to try to figure it all out.

A minute later, she speaks up. "I have to tell Ray. He must be worried sick. It would be, I don't know," she blows out an exasperated breath, "cruel."

"I understand why you feel that way. But if we let everyone believe you're . . . ," I wave my hand in the air, searching for a more delicate way of saying it.

Charlotte beats me to the punch. "Dead?"

"It gives us the advantage. We can find out who tried to kill you. And," I tack on for an added bonus, one I know will allay many of Charlotte's doubts, "Find out what happened to Charlie."

Charlotte sits silently, chewing on a slice of bacon.

"He has a point," Mom says. She doesn't know anything about Charlie, I didn't go into detail about who Charlotte is, and for the moment, it doesn't seem like she's looked too far into it. However, she would know a good idea when she hears it.

"I hate it," Charlotte says, "but I don't see any better alternatives at the moment."

I bolt up from the chair, the legs scratching against the floor. "Great. Let's get dressed and head out."

"Wait a minute," Charlotte says, grabbing my arm before I can leave the table. "Where are we going?"

"New York City."

15

Charlotte

Bea stopped by this morning after her shift and brought me some clothes to wear. The jeans are a bit long and have to be rolled up and the kitten T-shirt is a little frumpy. However, I'm grateful for the help, otherwise, I would be wearing Henry's emergency sweats, and I'm sure I would look downright ridiculous.

"You look adorable," Henry says as I come out of the bedroom.

"You're a liar."

"No, seriously, you do." He looks me up and down, a lazy smile curling at the edges of his mouth. "We'll get you something better after we get on the road."

"Great," I mutter as I follow him down the stairs. I've never considered myself spoiled, but I always had beautiful clothes from chic Miami boutiques. I am not looking forward to a new wardrobe from Wal-Mart.

When we get to the kitchen, we find his mom, dad, brother, and sister. The whole family is here to see us off.

Bev embraces me in a hug, and it's warm and safe, and I kind of want to stay here for the rest of my life. "Now, you two be careful. And if you get into any trouble, you know where I am."

"Thanks, Mom," Henry says. "We'll be fine, I promise."

The entire family takes their time, giving us hugs, watching as we exit into the attached garage, waving goodbye.

That's when I see it. "The *Porsche*," I cry in horror. I cover my entire face with my hands, not wanting to see the hideous sight any longer than necessary.

"I know," Henry murmurs, sounding as disappointed as I am sickened. "Sorry about the damage. We were trapped in the garage, and, well, I didn't have much choice."

"Fiddle dee dang, that's a good reason. Okay, so how are we supposed to get to New York? We can't risk flying or taking a train."

Henry dangles a set of keys from his fingers, waggles his eyebrows, then presses a button to open the garage.

As the door opens, Henry says, "Normally, my dad keeps his baby in the garage. But after the damage to your car, my mom didn't want a suspiciously wrecked vehicle in the driveway."

When the door lifts up, I find a steely blue Ford Thunderbird in the driveway. Like Thelma and Louise, we're making this trip in style—hopefully with a better ending.

"My dad's pride and joy." He tosses the keys to me. "Wanna drive?"

"Really?" I ask, stoked by the offer.

"Only seems fair."

I rush around to the driver's side and hop in. Henry gets in on the passenger side.

"Okay, set the GPS for NYC," I order, the promise of a road trip renewing my purpose.

"Yeah, about that." Henry tosses a large book in my lap and gives me an incredulous look. "We're gonna need to stay off the grid. Atlas only."

I groan with disappointment. "You can't be serious. No

phone?" Reality strikes me with impeccable aim. When we left the house, it was on fire, so it's not like we had time to grab the important things—like my pocketbook. I've been so distracted by all the life-altering information that it didn't occur to me that I don't have my purse. Or my phone. Or any money.

"What are we going to do for money?"

"I have a little bit of cash tucked away for a rainy day. If we're careful, we can make it work."

I shake my head. "Not in New York." I put the car in reverse and back out of the driveway.

When we hit the highway, Henry speaks up. "You're going in the wrong direction."

"I know it's out of the way, but I have some money stashed for situations like this," I tell him as I change lanes.

"Like this?"

"Think about it. I'm the daughter of a crime lord. I've had some close calls in my life, nothing like this, but there is always a need for a contingency plan."

"Charlotte, we can't go back to the house. Whatever you had, is long gone. Toast. Toasted."

"We're not headed back to the house," I tell him, making my way onto an exit ramp for Gertrude's Gator Farm.

I pull into a deserted parking lot. "They don't open for another hour, so I think we're going to have to break in. Unless you want to wait."

Henry lets out a small growl of frustration. "No. Let's get this over with so we can move along."

Henry and I walk toward the back door, and he works to try to pick the lock.

"Where'd you get the lock picking kit from?" I ask.

"Stole it from my mom. I thought it might come in handy."

Through a string of curses, Henry works to pick the lock. A few feet above us is a window that is slightly cracked. "There's a window we could try," I suggest.

Henry must not hear me because he continues to pick at

the door. "How does a piece of shit building like this have such stingy locks?" Henry mutters to himself.

I look around and spy a few empty crates. Obviously, Henry's way is not working, and he's too focused on that to hear my two cents. I grab a couple of containers and stack them on top of each other. The poorly constructed ladder wobbles slightly as I step up. Putting one hand against the brick wall of the building, I steady myself as I pull the other leg up.

The window is just in reach, and I lift the pane up, moving the window another inch, maybe two. The crates beneath my feet waver. "Uh, oh," I say, using my legs to regain my balance.

It doesn't work, and the top box which I'm standing on slides off the bottom one. I grasp for the ledge of the window as the crates fall away, leaving me dangling. "Hey, Henry?"

"Yeah?" he says, half paying attention as he pulls hard against the door in frustration.

"Can I get a little help here?"

"What?" Henry asks, then looks up. "Oh, shit." He drops the kit from his hands and runs the few feet between us, grabbing onto my feet and pushes me upward.

I am so thankful for the break on my muscles, I was kind of worried my arms were going to fall right off.

"What the hell are you doing?"

With my feet planted on Henry's shoulders, I work to shove the window up further. "The window was open."

"So you thought you would climb in since the lock picking thing wasn't working?"

The window wiggles just enough that I can squeeze through. "Right. Now, give me a lift."

He pushes me up high enough that I'm able to leverage my weight against the windowsill. I snake my body into the opening and crawl in headfirst. Except, now that I'm halfway through it, I realize it's closer to ten feet to the ground from the inside.

The giant vat of alligator feed—a concoction of snakes, turtles, fish, and other things I don't want to think about—

beneath me doesn't make the situation more appealing. "Never mind, not going to work," I holler behind me. As I try to shimmy myself back outside, my hand slips on something gooey, and I lose my balance, propelling me inward and closer to the grub. I'm balancing like a seal on an imaginary ball. "I could use a little help here."

Henry mutters something I can't understand, but he definitely sounds angry. His thoughts don't matter right now because my balance is precarious and also my main focus as I spin my arms in a pathetic attempt to fly. I fail miserably and am helpless as the chum rushes toward my face.

I stand, soaked in fish guts, spoiled chicken carcasses, and whatever else constitutes a nutritious meal for alligators.

"Are you okay?" Henry calls up, and that, I hear.

I pull a frog leg from my hair and throw it back into the cask. "Yeah," I holler, flinging my hands to get the bits and pieces of flesh off me. Then the smell hits. It's like a mixture of iron and the rotting entrails of Moby Dick.

I cough and heave as I climb out of the bin, making my way to the door to let Henry inside.

"Jesus Christ," Henry gasps, swatting the flies swarming around me. "What the hell happened to you?"

Another heave rolls from my belly, and I bend at the waist, tamping down the vomit. The one thing that can make this whole experience worse is if I throw up. I point toward the tub of gross. Henry lets out a laugh. Not a "you're so adorable" laugh, but a full-bodied guffaw that keeps going.

After what feels like an eternity, Henry manages to collect himself. "Okay, where's this money you were talking about?"

Still unable to use my words, I point toward a row of lockers.

Henry nods and ambles toward the employee area. "Why in the hell did you pick a gator farm to stash extra cash?"

Telling him the truth is precisely what I need to make this whole thing worse. As a child, Ray used to take Charlie and me here. Ray always had some other person with us. As an adult,

I can see it for what it was, but back then, I simply thought Ray was entertaining a new friend. At some point during the middle of the show, Ray and the mystery friend would walk off. By the end of the performance, Ray would return with a bag of popcorn, and his so-called friend left for an emergency. Every. Single. Time.

I smile at Henry, and the blood drying on my face resists my strained grin. "Childhood memories, I guess. It's a place I would never forget. Locker two-forty-two."

Henry scours the lockers and dials in the numbers of the combination I gave him. "You weren't kidding," he says as he stares at the stacks of one-hundred-dollar bills.

"Nope." I stretch across him and gather the stacks in my arms.

Henry snatches the money from my hands. "Don't touch it," he hisses.

He has a lot of nerve. I prop my hands on my hips and give him a fierce glare. "Why not? It's my money."

"Because you're getting blood and shit all over it," he says, pointing to my chum-painted body.

I drop the cash onto the floor and fold my arms like a petulant child. "Fine."

My attitude doesn't distract Henry in the least. He kicks the money into a pile. "I can't carry all of this in my arms. There's a bunch of grocery bags in the trunk. Go out and grab a few."

He tosses the keys at me, and instead of reaching to catch them, I duck out of the way.

Henry snorts back a laugh and picks up the keys, this time handing them to me. "Hurry up. I don't want to be here when they open."

I rush to the car, skittering across the gravel, and unlock the trunk. As I pull out the plastic bag stuffed with more plastic bags, the crunch of gravel and the roar of an engine catch my attention. I slam the trunk shut and go low to the ground, trying to hide.

The unexpected visitor's car pulls beside the Thunderbird, and the door creaks as someone steps out. I peak around the taillight and immediately recognize the vehicle as Ray's.

"Get out," Ray says. I don't have to see to know it's him. I can identify that man's voice anywhere.

"It wasn't me, I swear. It was Simon," says another man.

The men walk around the car, and Ray turns, eying the Thunderbird suspiciously. Nobody's supposed to be here right now, and Ray knows that.

"I don't care," Ray tells the whiny man. "Keep walking."

Ray takes his new friend in the opposite direction of the building, where Henry is waiting for me to return. I don't know who that guy or Simon is, and it doesn't matter right now. What does matter is that Ray has business to conduct, and mine and Henry's window is closing. Once Ray is finished, he will be back to figure out who the heck the Thunderbird belongs to.

Once Ray is out of sight, I dash into the building. "Here," I say, throwing Henry the bags. "We need to hurry."

Henry starts tossing the money into the sacks. "What's going on?"

He's taking too long, so I stretch across him and start shoving the money in as quickly as I can, emptying the locker completely. "I'll tell you when we're on the road."

We make our way out of the building and hop in the car. Henry takes the driver's seat.

"Where are the keys?"

"Fuddy. Hold on," I jump out of the car and run to the trunk where the keys are dangling. As I pull them out of the lock, a loud bang pierces my ears.

Henry turns in his seat, looking at me, his eyes wide.

"*Come on.*" I run to the passenger side, hop in, slam the door shut, and toss him the keys. "Go, go, go!"

Within minutes we're back on the highway. My heart is pounding in my chest. "Oh my stars, oh my stars, oh my stars," I repeat, trying to grab hold of reality. I'm covered in fish guts and blood, and I witnessed Ray carry out a hit. Of course, we can't forget everything else that's occurred in the last twenty-four hours.

"You want to fill me in on what happened?" Henry asks, his hands gripping the wheel so tight his knuckles turn white.

Not really. "You know, your whole family has 'B' names. Benny, Bev, Bea, Brian. How come you're not a Bobby or Buddy or something?"

"I'm named after my grandfather. Now quit deflecting and tell me who that was back there."

"It was Ray." I fill him in on the childhood experience of the gator farm and the man who was accompanying him.

"Who do you think it was?" he asks. "Did you recognize the voice?"

"No. I don't think I've ever met him. I didn't get a good look. I was too busy trying to hide."

"What did they say?" he asks as he passes a minivan.

"He said it wasn't him."

"What wasn't?"

"I don't know for sure. Do you think it had anything to do with the fire?"

Henry shrugs his shoulder. "Maybe. But if Ray is rounding people up, it means he's looking into everything. If they haven't found out already, it won't be long until they realize there aren't any bodies burned in the fire."

"Now what?"

"Stay the course. Get to New York and see if we can't follow your brother's tracks."

"And how do you suggest we do that if I'm supposed to be dead?"

"We'll figure it out along the way. But first, we have more important things to do."

"What can be more important than that?"

"Getting you in a shower. You fucking reek."

16

Henry

The stench filling the car is practically unbearable. If I think it's terrible, it must be worse for Charlotte—she's wearing it. After a few hours on the road, we stopped at Target for supplies. Charlotte was remanded to the car since she looked like *Carrie* at Prom.

I pull into a parking lot of a little roadside motel. The rooms still use regular keys, and the front desk offered to let us pay by the hour. As we climb the stairs to our room on the second floor, a bum sits in a corner, throws up, and takes a swig of a bottle disguised by a brown paper bag. At least Charlotte won't stick out. There are probably a few serial killers holed up in this joint.

When we get to the room, the stench of mold is pervading. The lights flicker, and the walls are yellowed with smoke. There is no doubt in my mind that the bedspread is covered in semen.

"Body wash, shampoo, conditioner, vinegar," I say as I pull the items out of the bag.

"Vinegar?" Charlotte asks with a raised eyebrow.

"To help neutralize the, uh, the odor."

She wrinkles her nose at the mention of her smelling like decaying fish.

"Fill the tub with water, add the vinegar, and soak. Then take a shower."

She folds her arms in front of her, speculation written on her face. "How do you know so much about getting rid of the smell of fish guts?"

"When I was a kid, my family and I visited some relatives in Indiana. There was a surfeit of skunks in my aunt's barn. Brian was too stupid to listen to me when I told him not to play with them. He got sprayed. Like ten times over. My mom and aunt tried everything. Tomato juice bath, smothering him with lemon juice. The one thing that worked was the vinegar. I figured it should work for you too."

She grunts her frustration and puts the supplies back into the bag.

It seems my little story wasn't enough to earn her forgiveness. Why she's mad, I don't have the faintest clue. She makes her way to the bathroom and mutters something about adding olive oil to toss her salad as she slams the door shut. I choke on a laugh, she has no clue what she's saying, and my amusement will piss her off more.

Charlotte brines in the tub for over an hour. As I wait, I pull back the bedspread, and rest against the headboard, kicking my feet up on the springy mattress. I flip through the channels to kill time. Police procedural—no thanks, I live it. Hospital drama—I've got enough drama in my life right now. One more click and the background music catches my attention.

"My, it's sweltering in here." A gorgeous woman with hair the same shade as Charlotte removes her shirt.

I can't agree more. I scoot to the end of the bed, my interests piqued.

"Well, I wouldn't want you to get over-heated, yet," the man says as he too takes off his shirt.

The pipes in the wall groan as Charlotte drains the tub and starts the water for the shower. My dick is rock hard from last night, and there is a porno with a woman giving a man a blow job on TV. By my calculations, I can rub one out in five minutes. After everything that went on in my bed with Charlotte, it might not even take that long.

The lotion I bought for Charlotte at the store earlier is going to pull double duty. I grab the cream and hop back in the bed, practically tripping over my own feet as I pull my pants down at the same time. A squirt of lotion in my palm, and I'm ready to go. I stroke from root to tip, watching as the man spreads the woman's legs apart. One of my favorite parts of a woman is the delicate, pink tissue that feels like silk on my cock.

I give another stroke, with a slight squeeze at the head of my dick, and my balls draw up close.

The man runs his tongue up the woman's pussy, and she lets out a gasp of pleasure. Fuck, I love it when a woman makes noise, it is the ultimate ego stroke, confirming I am the master of a woman's pleasure.

"Oh, please," the woman begs the man.

"Oh, please what?" a shockingly familiar voice asks.

Charlotte is standing in the doorway, her strawberry hair damp and gorgeous against her creamy skin.

My cock is in my hand, and the man on TV is pounding into the woman from behind.

"Yes, yes!" the woman screams. "Fuck me, fuck me!"

My eyes bug out of my head as I realize what is going on. I let go of my dick and scramble for the remote sitting next to the lotion on the nightstand. I snatch it up and click off the TV.

Charlotte blinks a couple of times and then glances down at the bed where I'm sitting.

I look too, and my dick is sticking straight up for all to see. I quickly cover myself with a sheet, and my cheeks burn with embarrassment.

"Whatcha doin'?" Charlotte asks, a smile tugging at the

corner of her mouth.

"Um, I was, uh, it was just, and the TV . . . shit."

Charlotte walks toward me. "It's okay, it's completely natural." She sits on the edge of the bed.

I'm not sure how I feel about sitting this close to her when I was jerking off five seconds ago.

"I think the vinegar worked," she says, lifting a handful of hair and sniffing.

Unable to resist, I lower my nose to that spot between her neck and shoulder and take a deep breath. She smells of ivory soap and a uniquely feminine scent that's all her. Not the slightest hint of chum or vinegar.

The temptation is immense, and I squeeze my eyes tight, trying to halter the urge to do more than inhale. However, I'm a weak man. The weakest of the weak. I rub my nose along her shoulder, dropping small kisses along the way.

She lets out a moan, and I know she's as sunk as I am. It would require a disaster of epic proportions to keep me from sleeping with her.

Charlotte lolls her head to the side, extending her neck, gifting it to me. I seize the offer, running my lips along the slim column of her throat.

She sinks into my kisses and presses her body against mine. Her softness is almost my undoing. I haul her across my lap and pin her to me. Charlotte is easily the most beautiful woman I have ever seen.

She's also experienced more in two days than most people do in a lifetime. Only an asshole would take advantage of a woman after everything Charlotte's been through. I can't be sure I'm not that asshole.

"Are you sure?" I ask, hoping for the green light to absolve me of my shame. Last night, I refused to have sex with her, telling her she deserved better. Now, here we are in a shitty motel, and all my morals are tossed out the window. It turns out I am, in fact, that asshole.

She wraps her arms around my neck and pulls me to her. "More than ever."

Every ounce of frustration and frenzied sexual tension since we've met has culminated to this moment.

I unwrap the towel from around her and sit back on my heels, gazing at her creamy, supple breasts. No longer able to restrain myself, I lower my head and suck one into my mouth. My fingers tweak and manipulate the other breast.

She arches her back, feeding her breast to my mouth, and it's so damn hot. She lets out a moan and wraps her legs around my waist, pulling me to her. My cock twitches as it rubs against the slick warmth of her sex.

"Fuck. You feel amazing." I'm about to lose my damn mind, and I'm not even inside her yet.

I scoot down the bed, spreading her legs wide for me. My breath hitches. She's as amazing as I imagined. The other night, when I saw her naked after her shower, I knew the carpet matched the drapes. But I had no idea she would smell so incredible.

I run my nose between her folds. "Your pussy smells like heaven."

"Really?"

"Yes. And I bet it tastes even better." I run my tongue along the same path, and I was right—she's delicious. I delve into her folds and lave at the sensitive tissue, savoring every single flavor as it dances on my tongue.

"Wow." Charlotte breathes, her fingers running through my hair, tugging at the roots.

Her clit is red and swollen, begging for attention. I suck it into my mouth as one finger circles her entrance. My finger slides inside her, and immediately, her pussy grips my finger. She's so damn tight.

"Oh," she cries out, but I think it was more from shock than pain.

I continue to suck and finger fuck her. When I add a second finger, she goes still.

There has been a definite shift in tenor. "Is everything okay?" Thirty seconds ago, she had been loose-limbed and rubbing her pussy against my face. Now, she's wound so tight she could snap like a twig.

"Um, do you think you can come up to the top of the bed?"

"Sure." I lay on my side, my head propped on my elbow. "What's going on? Did you change your mind? I understand if this is too much. I don't want to pressure you."

Charlotte gets out of bed and pulls the sheet with her. She wraps it around her body and starts pacing the room. "No, it's not that, it's just . . ." She starts nibbling on her fingernails.

I haven't seen her do that before. Not even after I told her I had to give her CPR. If ever there was a stress-inducing incident, that should be it. "It's what? I have protection in my wallet if that's what you're worried about."

"No, it's not that. I mean, I'm glad you have protection, but that's not it. It's well," Charlotte takes a deep breath. "You know, I've had a privileged life." She rips the top part of the nail off the index finger and spits it onto the floor.

"I see," I mutter, stunned by the direction of the conversation. I hop out of bed, my hard-on flinging around.

I fumble for my pants. "I'm not good enough for you. You were raised in the lap of luxury. You wouldn't want to sully yourself with a lowly cop."

Charlotte's eyes go wide, and she removes her finger from her mouth. "No. No. That's not at all what I'm saying." She sits on the corner of the bed and drops her head in her hands. "This is so embarrassing."

Whatever her issue is, it's freaking her out. What she needs is support, not the flare of my bruised ego. I toss my pants on the chair and sit next to her. "What? What is it? Whatever it is, we can figure it out. Together."

"Really?"

"Yes, really."

Charlotte nods her head a few times as if this will somehow

give her the strength to divulge her secret. "Okay, but don't freak out."

"Cross my heart," I promise, marking an "X" over my heart with my finger.

"Fine. Like I said, I grew up with a lot of privilege. But with the business, I didn't have a lot of socialization with people my own age. So, I missed out on some of the normal, um, teenage-type things one might do. Like when they're sixteen."

I nod as if I'm following, but I have no clue where she's going with this.

"Or eighteen, or twenty-one. And here I am at twenty-five, and I've never," Charlotte clears her throat, "slept with a man."

My mind goes blank. Nothing is rattling around in my head except a Roadrunner cartoon. At last, the problem before me comes back in full force. "Are you saying . . ." Now I'm pacing the room and biting my nail. "Are you saying . . ." I can't even speak the word.

"I'm a virgin."

And the anvil has fallen on my head. "You're . . . You—" I point toward Charlotte. "You, you, you're a . . . virgin?" I wince the moment the word comes out of my mouth. I made it sound like it was dirty or wrong or something. It's not, it's just unbelievable.

"You don't have to say it like that. There's nothing wrong with being a virgin. It's not something I should be ashamed of."

Even as she speaks—and I know she's right—it sounds as if she's trying to convince herself, not me.

I climb out from under the proverbial anvil and gather Charlotte in my arms. "Cupcake, you are the most beautiful woman I have ever met." I kiss the shell of her ear and down her neck. "And I'm honored to be your first lover." I pull back a little, searching her face for understanding, acceptance of my fuck up.

"But?"

"But, not like this."

She sags against me, and I know it had to be a monumental blow to her pride.

"Not because I don't want to. God, do I want to. But not here. Not in a shitty motel. You deserve better for your first time."

Her eyes fill with tears, and I know I've hurt her, and I hate that I'm the reason for her pain. At the very least, I can offer a temporary fix.

I lay her on the bed and unwrap her from the sheet. "I don't know how far you've gone with anyone before, and forgive me if I sound crass, but have you ever had an orgasm?"

Her face scrunches with embarrassment, and she shakes her head.

"It'll be my pleasure to give you your first."

17

Charlotte

"I had no idea it would feel like that. If I'd known, I would have . . . I don't know, but that was great," I tell Henry as I roll over and place a hand on his chest.

"I think it's a good thing you waited." He rubs his hand along my arm. "From what I've heard, most girls have their first with an inexperienced high school guy. I doubt they figure out it's supposed to be good until a few years later."

I chew on Henry's thought for a few seconds. From what I've seen on TV, he might be right. I didn't have a lot of girlfriends as a teenager, so those moments when friends gossip after their first time didn't happen for me. Yet another thing I've missed out on because of the family business.

"Yeah, maybe you're right," I say, settling into his arms.

He holds me a little tighter. "This is nice."

"It is." Warmth floods me, and I'm powerless to stop it. This is the most extraordinary feeling in the world.

Henry falls asleep as the newscasters on the eleven o'clock

news sign off. I lay in his arms in a questionable motel, a little bit less of a virgin, and my life changing in ways I never imagined. As the glow of the TV dims, so do my thoughts, and I fall languidly into a restful sleep.

Morning arrives before the sun even rises. I'm in desperate need of caffeine, which I never require to function. However, after the events of yesterday, I'm exhausted, and every muscle in my body aches. Luckily, the faint odor of alligator food has dissipated. I thought I got it all, but the scent kept waking me up. Maybe it was in my sinuses or something.

Henry said we could stop one time before lunch. So if I needed a bathroom break, I better make it count. He seems to be quite hard-nosed when it comes to travel. I grab a cola from a vending machine at the motel and count that as my caffeine. It works, and as the sun crests the horizon, I finally feel human.

The hours spent in the car this morning have been quiet. Henry doesn't even want the radio on and doesn't seem particularly chatty. I've only had my thoughts to keep me company. My mind whirls with the high ideals and fantasies I had when I was younger about how I would lose my virginity. All the typical scenarios: Prom, the back of a pickup truck on the beach. A young man who couldn't wait to be with me in the most intimate ways two people can be. I may not live a traditional life, but every girl has some classic dreams, and Henry and I are anything but conventional. Nothing about the way we met, or have ended up in this car, can be spun into a far-fetched scenario of traditional norms.

This isn't the most romantic situation. I'm realistic enough to know that losing my virginity is not going to be all roses and fireworks. But, at the very least, I want to know something personal about him. Something lovers would share.

"You know a lot about me, but I don't know much about you," I tell him as I finish off the last of my cola.

He gives me an incredulous look.

He knows I've looked into him, he wouldn't be here if I

didn't. "Besides that stuff."

"Okay, what do you want to know?"

"How about," I take a moment to pretend to think about it. "How old were you when you had your first kiss?"

"Six, the neighbor girl and I during a game of 'I'll show you mine if you show me yours.' You?"

"Sixteen. Jamie Hopkins during a homeschooling event at an aquarium."

He smiles. "You were a late bloomer, huh?"

"Yeah. How old were you when you lost your virginity?"

"Fourteen. Same neighbor girl."

"Wow, you were so young. Did you even know what to do with it?"

"Not really," he laughs.

"Your first kiss and your first time were with the same girl, was she your first love?" I don't know that I want the answer. What if he says, "yes?" I'm not in love with the guy, but I definitely don't want to hear he was in love with someone else.

"I don't think so," he answers. "She was just convenient."

His response grates against my ego. What if I'm just a convenience? Will he use me the same way he used his neighbor? Is he the man I want to give my most precious gift to? Or is my virginity a monumental inconvenience that I'm practically begging him to take?

"Is that what I'll be? I mean, if we ever, you know?" My cheeks are practically on fire with embarrassment.

He glances at me, his lips pressed into a hard line. "Have sex?"

"Yeah."

"Cupcake, from the first time I met you, you have been anything but convenient. Why start now?" Henry's forehead bunches with confusion as he glances into the rearview mirror. "Shit."

"What?" I turn around to find flashing red and blue lights. "Holy smokes. What are we going to do?"

Henry runs his fingers through his hair as he thinks. "You don't have any identification on you either. Shit."

I force my entire body to go limp, and I fall against the door, my ankles crossed awkwardly.

"What the fuck are you doing?"

"Trust me."

A stout state trooper knocks on Henry's window. "Driver's license and registration, please."

Henry digs into the back pocket of his jeans, digs around in the glove compartment, and hands the policeman the requested information. "Did I do something wrong, Officer?"

"You were speeding," the state trooper replies, his tone cold and indifferent. "I'll need your ID, too, Miss."

I moan and spew gibberish, pulling on my hair, and follow it up with an ear-splitting cry.

"Is she okay?" the trooper asks Henry, his demeanor doing a complete one-eighty.

Drool trickles from my mouth for good measure, and I pound on my forehead with my palm, shrieking.

"Jesus," Henry mutters under his breath as he stares at the spectacle I'm making. "She's fine," he tells the cop. "We're on our way to New York. My sister needs special care. My parents don't have the energy to provide the twenty-four-hour assistance she requires."

The story is sad and unfortunate for those who live this reality. I can't imagine how that must feel.

"Well, I, uh . . ." The state trooper trips over his words. "I'll let you off with a warning. Watch your speed."

"Thank you, Officer. I'll do that." Henry replies.

I let out one last over-the-top cry as Henry rolls up his window.

He turns in his seat to look at me, and I detect the faintest hint of admiration in his smile. "What the hell was that?"

I shrug my shoulders. "Does it matter? It worked."

Henry leans toward me and pushes my hair behind one

ear. He's so close, I can detect the scent of coffee on his breath. My, my, does he smell good. Visions of last night flit through my mind, and a pang of regret settles in my belly. He did the honorable thing. He wants to make it special for me. However, at the moment, my libido could care less about his good intentions.

"You're bleeding," Henry says as he rubs his thumb across my temple. "You must've cut yourself at the gator farm. Pounding your head probably reopened the wound. There's a truck stop a few exits away. We'll stop and get you cleaned up."

Just like that, my libido has been checked. I wonder if Henry even sees a woman in front of him, or if I'm the same girl he met who hated the stingy stuff.

My hand flies to my mouth at the thought. "No stingy stuff."

Henry laughs as he shifts the car into drive. "Okay, no stingy stuff."

18

Henry

The blood dribbling down Charlotte's face has me doubting my ability to be objective. If I hadn't been so enamored with the idea of sleeping with her last night, I might have noticed she had a gash in her hairline.

We pull into a truck stop, and I fill up the tank while Charlotte heads into the shop. I meet her by a bank of payphones. This place is severely outdated, with wood-paneled walls and no women's restroom.

"I have to pee," Charlotte whispers as she knocks her knees together.

"Hold on a second. Let me grab a few things, then I'll stand guard."

I tread up and down the aisles. Past the wiper fluid, cassette tapes of John Denver, and the condoms, I find what I'm searching for. I gather the supplies in my arms and pay at the register. The woman cashing me out glares suspiciously while a cigarette hangs from her lips.

When I return, Charlotte is pressing the buttons on one of the payphones. "It feels so weird to hit buttons like this. It's been so long."

"Yeah, okay. We need to get a look at that cut on your head. Is anyone in the men's room?"

She rolls her eyes. "As opposed to the women's room? No."

"Good." I grab her hand and push open the door.

She digs her heels in and stops moving. "I said I have to pee."

"That's fine. You can pee while I go through the bag to fix you up."

"No, I'm not peeing in front of you."

Seriously? "It's not like I haven't seen you naked. It's fine."

She puts her hands on her hips. "It's not fine. You've seen me naked, but you've never watched me empty my bladder."

"Whatever." I shove the door open and wave her in and stand guard while she does her business.

A few minutes later, I hear the flush of the toilet, the water from the faucet, and the door opens.

"Sit on the pot, so I can get a good look at you," I tell her, pointing to the toilet. For once, she doesn't argue.

I set the bag in the sink and turn to Charlotte. She looks worn out with circles under her eyes. It doesn't take a genius to figure out how much of a toll this whole ordeal is taking on this sweet, gorgeous woman. A small part of me hates that I have not been able to protect her the way I promised. True, she is still alive, but at what cost? She has lost so much in her life, and here she sits in a grungy truck stop men's room, strong as ever. Maybe at her strongest.

The shadow of a bruise settles above her temple, and her left eye looks a bit swollen. I tilt her chin up so I can get a better look. "I think you may have overdone it when we got pulled over. You're going to end up with a black eye."

"Sacrifices must be made for success," she says with the shrug of her shoulder.

Upon further inspection, the wound is worse than I thought,

and I'm glad I prepared for it when I was assembling my makeshift first aid kit. "It's pretty deep," I tell her as I brush my thumb across her forehead. "I'm surprised it stopped bleeding at all."

"So, what then? Go to the hospital? Get stitches?"

"No, a hospital would require ID, and we can't afford to raise any suspicion." I wet a paper towel under the faucet and work to clean the wound, then pull out a bottle of antiseptic.

Charlotte stiffens at the sight of the red, white, and green bottle in my hand. "You promised there wouldn't be any stingy stuff."

Not this again. "I know, I'm sorry. But you were swimming around in a vat of bacteria. At the very least, we have to clean the wound before I close it up."

Her face goes pale at the mention of closing the wound. "You're not stitching me up!"

I spray on the antiseptic while she berates me, and she doesn't even notice. I let her continue her tirade and lean back against the sink, amused. She's adorable when she's angry.

"Don't look at me like that!"

My smile widens. "Like what?"

"Like I'm a joke. I'm not a joke."

"Of course not. Now that the wound is clean, are you ready for me to finish? I'm hungry, and the buffet in the restaurant is closing soon."

She runs her fingers along the skin near the gash on her forehead, and I know she realizes I sprayed it clean. The glare she gives me suggests she's none too pleased. "Fine."

The last item in the bag is a bit unconventional but perfect in a bind.

"What's that?" Charlotte asks.

"Superglue."

She nods. "Smart."

Once Charlotte is all cleaned up, we head over to the restaurant and order the breakfast buffet. I load my plate with bacon, sausage, pancakes, and home fries.

"How can you eat all that?" Charlotte asks as she stirs Splenda into her bowl of oatmeal topped with blueberries.

I plop a bite of pancake drenched in syrup in my mouth and chew. "How can you eat that? It looks like snot."

"But it doesn't taste like it. I love oatmeal. It's hardy and nutritious, and it can be dressed up in so many different ways."

"Whatever you say, cupcake."

"So what's the plan once we get to New York? Where do we start?" Charlotte asks after taking a sip of apple juice.

"I'm not sure. Do you know who Charlie was in contact with when he was up there? Who was he working with? Charlie's last text said the Russian's were getting uneasy. What do you know about the Petrovsky Family?"

"Not much. Other than the bad blood between our family and theirs, there isn't a lot of history."

She's lying to me. She knows a lot more than she's willing to let on. "Cut the bullshit, cupcake. You're not as innocent as you look. What's the bad blood between the two families?"

Charlotte let out a resigned sigh. "A million years ago, there was an attempt to merge the two families. But greed is such a force that it was impossible. Now Vlad, the head of the Petrovsky Family seems to be trying to make amends."

I take a sip of my coffee. "If that was true, your brother would still be alive."

"Yeah. He would be," she admits, twiddling her fingers in her lap.

"What are the Petrovsky's into?" I ask, tired of skirting around Charlotte's feelings. This trip has taken a toll on both of us, and I need to know all the parts to this puzzle.

Charlotte shrugs her shoulder and frowns. "Last I knew it wasn't anything too crazy. Weapons and money laundering. But that was forever ago, who knows what they deal in now."

It blows me away that Charlotte believes weapons and money laundering are the same as robbing a liquor store. "Charlie didn't say what his business was in New York?" I ask. I have a hard time believing her brother didn't fill her in to some extent. Charlotte's hands are all over the Scalise Family business. Why would he leave her on the outside now?

"If I was to guess, it's something pretty ugly if Charlie was trying to shield me from it," she says before filling her mouth with oatmeal. She gazes out the window and her demeanor turns cold as she eats silently.

I've hit my limit on questions for the time being, so I change the subject. "I was thinking when we get to New York, we'll hit different neighborhoods until we get the feel of things. Maybe we'll get lucky."

She nods and smiles, the glow of her innocence and youthfulness returning in full force. God, she's beautiful. "Let's say, for argument's sake, we find who we need. What then, we just walk in guns blazing?" She clasps her hands together, miming a gun. "Pew, pew-pew."

She's too damn cute. "Doubtful," I laugh. "We'll have to do a little research, figure out the best angle to go at it. We can't rush in like a bull in a china shop."

She slams her hands on the table, the silverware clanging. "I hate that saying. What does it even mean? I've never understood why a bowl in a china shop is a bad thing."

At a total loss for words, I stare at her, blinking. "Well," I pause a beat, trying to figure out how to explain the common saying. "I guess bulls would cause a lot of destruction."

She folds her arms and leans back in the booth. "How? It's a bowl. And why wouldn't there be a bowl in a china shop? They have plates, saucers, cups. Why not bowls?"

"Wait. Are you saying 'bull' like the male cow or 'bowl' like the dish?"

Her cheeks flush crimson. "Like the dish," she murmurs, staring at her fingers.

Humor bubbles through every cell in my body until it releases in raucous laughter.

"It's not funny," she hisses. "Anyone could make that mistake."

"No, cupcake, only you could come up with that."

19

Charlotte

The traffic in New York City is a disaster 24/7. How is it that no one who lives here wants to own a car, but the vehicles are bumper to bumper?

Henry slams on the brakes, narrowly missing a pedestrian who is too focused on her phone to look both ways. "This is fucking ridiculous," Henry gruffs, gripping the steering wheel. "Maybe we should find a hotel in New Jersey and take the train into the city."

Times Square is as bright at midnight as it is at high noon. The jumbotron catches my attention, advertising a new vodka that recently hit the market. "Maybe you shouldn't have opted to drive through the busiest intersections in the world," I say flippantly. "Besides, no one wants to stay in New Jersey. Not even the people who live in New Jersey want to be there. New York is the greatest city in the world. Take a left at this light, we'll try The Kaplan."

Henry follows my direction, and we make our way toward

Central Park. The Kaplan is a beautiful 1920's historic hotel, built by a wealthy Texas oil tycoon after his entire family fell victim to the Spanish Flu in 1918. Only the uber-rich and famous deign to pay the exorbitant cost.

"Without a reservation? You've lost your mind," Henry says, passing the valet stand.

"You're being ridiculous. The Kaplan is beautiful, luxurious, and has the hottest restaurant in the city. Not to mention a lot of Goodfellas come here to cheat on their wives, pamper themselves at the spa, and plan to take over the world with their cronies in the cigar room. This is an opportunity."

Henry turns the corner, and we circle the block. "You know what? You're right." He pulls the car in front of the valet. "Besides, I'd love to see you try to get us a room."

We walk to the front desk, where a snobby concierge talks down to some girl next to him. "Sasha," he screeches. "The Landrigan's specifically requested no Calla Lilies in their room. How many times do I have to remind you that Mrs. Landrigan's cat is allergic? Your incompetence is astounding. Take your break, I'll clean up this disaster."

Poor Sasha. Her eyes brim with tears as she nods and walks away, her shoulders slumped.

"And Sasha?" The concierge calls after her. "Feel free to never come back."

What a turd. I mull over a few ideas, trying to figure out the best strategy. The front desk guy will be a tough nut to crack, and I'm going to have to play it big if I have any hope of succeeding.

"Are you picking your nose," Henry whispers into my ear, seemingly embarrassed.

"No." I pluck what feels like a hundred hairs out of my nostril, my eyes stinging. "Stay back here. I've got this."

Both Henry and I are travel weary. Our clothes are wrinkled, I have a ketchup stain on my shirt, Henry's armpits are stained with sweat. My hair is knotted on top of my head, Henry looks like he's never seen a comb. The clincher is the odor—the recycled air of being trapped in a car for hours on end. I can only hope these tiny details will add up to work in our favor.

An older gentleman and his wife—or possibly his mistress—look like they just docked from a long cruise across the pond. He's wearing a bowling hat, and she fancies herself with a mink stole. They both stare at me with slack jaws as I approach the desk.

"Hello," I say to the concierge. "I was wondering if you had a room available?"

The concierge looks down his long, slim nose at me. His frown tells me everything I need to know—someone like me has no business rooming in his hotel. "Do you have a reservation?"

"No, not exactly. I was just hoping—"

He cuts me off with the wave of his hand. "You have to have a reservation. This is The Kaplan, we don't simply take people from the streets."

Cue the waterworks. The tears which hovered from plucking my nose hairs slide down my cheeks. My bottom lip quivers and I give a soft sniffle. "I understand," I tell the concierge. "He's going to kill me. I'm such an idiot," I mutter to myself, rubbing at the superglued gash on my forehead.

"Ma'am?"

I wipe away the tear, wincing when I touch the bruise from giving myself a black eye when we got pulled over. I completely forgot about that.

"If you're worried about your safety, I can call someone for you. The police, perhaps," the concierge offers.

"Keep your voice down, please," I beg, the words clogging in my throat. "The police can't help me. He is the police," I grate out, pointing at Henry.

A lanky bellman dressed in maroon, who looks old enough to be my grandfather, walks behind the desk and tosses something on the counter. "Oh come on, Sal, for once in your life, don't be a prick."

"Fine," Sal sighs, annoyed. "But all we have left is the honeymoon suite. If you can afford it, you can have it."

So much for Sal not being a jerk. "I can," I tell him, pulling out a roll of hundred-dollar bills.

Sal rolls his eyes as I pay for a week's stay. He makes up a couple of key cards and glowers at me the entire time. "Enjoy your stay."

I hand Henry the keys. "Honeymoon suite for the week."

"Impressive. How'd you manage to pull that off?"

"I have my ways," I tell him as we walk toward the elevator.

The man and woman who were next to me when I was manipulating the concierge, whisper to each other and give Henry a scathing side-eye glance.

Henry slides the key card through the lock. "Did you tell people I beat you?" His tone is so casual, it throws me off balance.

"What?" I ask, flipping on the lights and fiddling with the pillows—they're the perfect balance of firm and fluffy. I'll sleep well tonight for sure.

"Those people in the elevator were giving me dirty looks. What did you tell them?"

"This bathroom is huge," I call behind me. "It's got a shower with two shower heads and a jetted tub."

When I turn around, Henry is standing in the doorway watching me, his arms and ankles crossed. He looks seriously amused. "Did you tell them I beat you?" he asks again, but this time slower, louder, and succinct.

"Uh, yeah?" I squeak.

He laughs to himself with a shake of his head. "Not only are you gorgeous, but you're a fucking genius. Color me impressed."

He was impressed? Color me flabbergasted.

He steps into the bathroom and pulls off his shirt. "Now, how about we try out the shower, order some room service, and watch a movie?"

"That sounds wonderful," I tell him, yanking him by the fly of his jeans and pulling him flush against me.

His lips meet mine, and our tongues dance to the music of lust. Lots and lots of lust.

20

Henry

Charlotte was disappointed when I wouldn't take her virginity last night in the shower. Disappointment is an understatement, more like irate. She stomped out of the shower, dripping wet, and slipped on the tile. The woman is a walking catastrophe.

I thoroughly scanned her body with my eyes and hands. Charlotte is a damn fine, beautiful, lollipop of desire. Her creamy skin was silken and slick with water. It took every ounce of strength I had not to give in to temptation. She stared at me, pleading to give her what she wanted, but I didn't cave.

Why the hell am I so hesitant to give her something we both want? Introspection is painful, but if I was to be honest with myself, I think I'm nervous about the idea that I'm her first. It's a big responsibility. Her first time will be how she judges the act of sex for the rest of her adult life.

No woman has ever complained about my abilities in the bedroom. I pride myself on being a generous and gentle lover.

Well, not so gentle that I would lose my man-status over it, but I know how to take a woman where she wants to go.

At least, I think I do.

Now, I'm questioning every sexual encounter I've had. What if all of the women before were only trying to appease me, and it turns out I'm shit in bed?

This morning, I woke up on the couch, where I had been sentenced to sleep for the night. It surprised me how much I wanted to climb into the bed with Charlotte. Not because of the ultra-plush mattress, but because I craved Charlotte in my arms, her warmth against my chest. However, she was having none of that.

As we dine for breakfast in the restaurant downstairs, Charlotte is chatty and bubbly like I hadn't even pissed her off. Her hair is tied back in a bun at the nape of her neck, and she's wearing a light pink blouse and capris. I don't think she has ever looked so beautiful, even with the dark purple bruise developing beneath her eye.

"I was thinking," I say as I wipe my mouth with my napkin. "Since we're in the city, and we still have to figure out some leads, what if we do the tourist thing for the day?"

Charlotte's eyes light up like a child, and she claps her hands. "Oh my gosh, yes! I love it. What do you want to do first? The Statue of Liberty? The Empire State Building? Wall Street? There's so much we can do."

"How about we walk around Times Square first and then figure it out from there?"

"Times Square?" she asks. "I would've thought you'd had enough of that place yesterday."

"I don't want to drive through it, I want to visit it," I clarify.

She smiles, and it's infectious. "Wait a minute, is this your first time in New York?"

"Yeah."

She pushes away her plate of Belgium waffles, and there isn't a single crumb left. "It looks like I'm not the lone virgin at the table."

"Cute. So, what do you say?"

"Sounds like fun."

After we pay our bill at the restaurant, Charlotte and I embark on a walk toward Times Square. Eight blocks later, and the hustle of the city is on steroids.

Neon lights and jumbo screens illuminate the square. People from around the world cruise along the sidewalks, popping in and out of shops, talking fast, and walking faster.

"Wow," I breathe out, overwhelmed.

"Welcome to New York City," Charlotte says, grabbing my hand and pushing her way through the crowd.

We tread a couple more blocks until we are standing in front of the world-famous Ripley's Believe It or Not. We amble around, taking our time to look closely at potatoes with a strange likeness of famous people. Lucky for us, there is a giant Buddha statue and tons of other unbelievably fake stuff which costs my pension for a simple glimpse.

After Ripley's, we check out a few souvenir shops, and Charlotte and I walk out wearing matching "I Love NY" T-shirts. Then we go to lunch at Planet Hollywood, where I have the best chicken salad sandwich of my life.

"What do you want to do now?" Charlotte asks as she licks the side of an ice cream cone.

"How about Central Park?"

"Let's go," Charlotte squeals with delight.

We stroll along Fifth Avenue, passing Louis Vuitton, Chanel, and Tiffany's. Surprisingly, Tiffany's does serve breakfast. I bet you have to book a month in advance for a table.

When we get to Central Park, we climb the shale mounds and shrink to the size of munchkins as the skyscrapers rise above us.

I collect Charlotte in my arms and give her a soft kiss on the pulse below her ear. "This is incredible."

"If you're in search of extraordinary, then I have precisely the thing."

We carefully walk down the hill, and I grip Charlotte's hand tightly, trying my damnedest to prevent her from skittering down the shale. Once at the bottom, we stroll along until Charlotte finds a man holding a clipboard. She browses the options from the menu the man hands her and picks one, then we follow him to a horse-drawn carriage. I don't think I could have picked out a more appropriate way to spend the evening if I'd done it myself.

I climb in first and hold my hand out to help Charlotte up. The carriage pulls away, and Charlotte snuggles into the crook of my arm. As the horse prances through the park, we pass the Literary Mall and the Balto statue.

Charlotte leans across me to point to a fountain with an angel perched on top.

"That's Bethesda Fountain. It's the one from the beginning of *Friends,* except that one was filmed on a Hollywood set. But it doesn't make it any less magical."

The wind blows, and I get the faintest hint of her shampoo. Just like that, I'm hard.

We continue to ride through the park and enjoy the sites of the lake and Bow Bridge. Strawberry Fields is heartbreaking yet inspiring, as was John Lennon. Also, no strawberries. Charlotte laughs as she teases me for the corny joke. This from the woman who didn't know what a spank bank was. But that smile, that laugh has me bowled over.

"I have to admit, with everything that's happened," I tell Charlotte, turning to her, "these past few days have been interesting."

"Is that a good thing?"

"I think so. No, I know so. And even with the fire and the gator farm, it's you, cupcake, that's made it so great. You're amazing. The sweetest and bravest woman I've ever met."

She rests her hand on my chest and smiles up at me. "A lot of crazy things have happened. Things I never could have dreamed up. But you've been there with me, helping me navigate all this, and I'm so glad I blackmailed you into working for me."

I let out a laugh because I didn't see that coming. It's true, of course, but to hear Charlotte say the words are entirely different.

After the carriage ride, we head back to the hotel. What Charlotte doesn't know is that while she was ordering us Gyros from a street vendor, I was calling the hotel and making arrangements for something special. It wasn't easy. The concierge believes I'm a wife beater, thanks to Charlotte. Still, I don't think that bothered the man much. He seemed more irritated by the hassle. The illusion that I beat Charlotte to a bloody pulp is a convenient excuse. Despite his annoyance, the concierge agreed, if simply to get rid of me.

Charlotte opens the door to the honeymoon suite and gasps. "Did you do all of this?"

Candles, rose petals, champagne on ice, low instrumental music playing in the background.

"May I have this dance?" I ask, offering my hand.

Her smile is so big, so bright, it makes something shift inside me to know I'm the one who put that look on her beautiful face.

I pull her close to me, her breasts soft against my chest.

"No one has ever done anything like this for me before."

Forehead to forehead, nose to nose. My heart pounds in my chest. "I told you, your first time should be special. I hope I'm pulling it off."

"You have no idea," she says, bringing her lips to mine.

Her lips are silky and soft with a hint of feta from the Gyro we had a little while ago. And she tastes fantastic. She pulls away, taking a step back and dropping to her knees.

"What are you doing?" I'm not sure if she's going to propose or give me a blowjob. When she unzips my pants, I know it's not a proposal.

"I've never done this before, so you're going to have to teach me."

Fuck me.

My dick twitches at the idea of being the first cock to touch her lips. I shove my pants and underwear to my ankles. "You can start by putting the head in your mouth."

She gazes up at me with those beautiful green eyes and my dick in her mouth. I don't think I've ever seen anything so sexy.

"Suck a little and use your tongue." A shiver of pleasure courses down my spine. "Now, work your way up the shaft."

Her tongue swirls as she works my dick further between her lips. "Use your hand and start jerking my shaft while sucking on the head." As she does, I fight the urge to come.

Without guidance, she cups my balls in her hands and rolls them in her palm. The sensation is so exquisite, I'm going to finish before we start. Wanting to make this last, I pull my cock out.

"Am I doing something wrong?" she asks, her eyes wide as if I wounded her.

"Not at all, cupcake. If I didn't know better, I'd think this wasn't your first time. If you keep doing that, I don't think we're going to get very far." I swoop down and cradle her in my arms, carrying her to the bed.

Anticipation and excitement bubble over as we hurriedly remove our shirts. Our mouths are fused, our hands work over each other's bodies like the end of the world is about to happen, and we'll miss our chance.

"Slow down," I rasp. "We need to slow down." I kiss my way across her belly. "We have all night, no reason to rush this." I unbutton her jeans and unzip the fly, pulling off her pants and tossing them in a corner.

She's wearing soft-pink panties adorned with a little bow below her navel. Fuck, that's hot. I pull her panties to the side and dive right in, running my tongue along her cleft. Her hips raise off the bed as if she's shocked, but I secure her and swirl my tongue around her clit, flicking and sucking the delicate flesh.

She cries out, *"Henry."* Her head thrashes back and forth on the pillow.

I slide one finger into her wet, snug hole, thrusting in and out. Her pussy is so tight, I can't wait for it to strangle my cock. I insert a second finger, and she moans in pleasure as I continue to lave at her clit.

"Henry," she says in a breathy plea, "I want to feel you inside me."

I may be more nervous about taking her virginity than she is about losing it. I don't know a whole lot about the experience of popping a cherry from a woman's perspective. It's not the kind of thing a sister shares with her brother. I didn't have any close friends who were girls in high school who would ever confide in me something so sacred. The one thing I do know is that a girl entering womanhood—in the biblical sense—isn't the most pleasant of feelings, maybe even painful.

I lift my face from between her legs. "I don't want to hurt you."

"It'll be fine," she says as I climb back up her body. "It's a completely natural part of becoming a woman. It comes with the territory." She snatches my wallet off the nightstand and pulls the condom out. "Use it wisely."

If she's ready, then I'm ready. I rip the package with my teeth and take out the latex. While holding the tip, I roll it onto my dick.

Charlotte lays there and watches as I do it. "I don't know why, but that's hot."

"Glad you like it," I tell her as I plant one hand next to her head, "because you're about to become intimately acquainted with it."

I line my cock up with her entrance until right before I penetrate. "You're sure? There's no going back if you change your mind."

She rakes her fingers through the hair on my chest and wraps her legs around my waist. "I'm sure."

"It might hurt. Tell me if I'm hurting you."

She bites her lip in that adorable way and nods her head with agreement.

My heart is whacking in my chest. The monumental choice which has been made weighs heavy on me. On the other hand, if my cock could talk, it would be telling me I'm the pussy and deserve to fuck myself for the rest of my life.

I plow through my own anxiety and press into her channel, moving slow but steady. Inch by inch, I push in until I can't tell where I end and she begins. My dick is encased in a warm vice grip which I can feel all the way to the tips of my toes. My balls draw up, and I struggle not to blow my load.

"Are you okay?" I ask, looking down at her.

Her face is scrunched in pain. "I'm fine," she says on a quivering breath. "Are you?"

"Yeah. Do you want me to stop?"

She shakes her head. "No. Maybe, start moving."

I realize I've been hovering, my cock resting inside her. Not that I mind, it feels terrific. I pull back a little, and she whimpers.

"Are you sure?"

"Yes, I'm sure. It's getting better. Please, keep moving."

I push back inside, and as she requested, I keep my hips moving, trying to relax to give her the pleasure this moment deserves.

If there is sex in heaven, this has to be what it feels like. I lean in and kiss her, moving my hips in and out. "I've never felt anything like this."

She rubs her hand against the stubble on my cheek and closes her eyes, throwing her head back.

The look on her face and the grip she has on my dick encourages me to pick up speed. Every instinct screams at me to pound into her, hit her to the very end. I ignore the impulse and force myself to hold back, keeping my pace steady, and watch her as she comes.

Her arms stretch out in a winning gesture as she writhes beneath me. She wraps her arms around my shoulders and digs her nails into my back as she continues to cry out her pleasure.

I can't hold back any longer, and my hips piston into her

until I achieve my own climax. "*Fuck*," I holler, squeezing my eyes tight, going stiff as I hover over her.

When I open my eyes, I look down to see her smiling up at me.

"Wow. Thank you," Charlotte says, grinning.

"No, thank you," I tell her, kissing her red, swollen lips while giving a few more pumps of my hips. I roll off her and get out of bed. "Give me a minute."

In the bathroom, I remove the condom and find it speckled with blood. Upon further inspection, I'm speckled with blood. The evidence of Charlotte's virginity claiming me as much as I had claimed it.

Charlotte gives a soft knock on the bathroom door and pokes her head inside. "Everything, okay?"

"Yeah, yeah, of course."

"That's good. So, can I come in? I kind of have blood all over me."

I nod, and she strides in looking no different than an hour ago, except for the luminous glow of a satisfied woman.

"I also ordered some clean sheets from room service. Do you mind if I get a quick shower?" She waves at my crotch, pointing out the smudges of her lost virtue still on me. "We can go in together."

After our shower—a completely nonsexual shower—we find the bed has been remade and a tray of desserts waiting for us.

We lay in the clean, king-sized bed, snacking on cakes and chocolates, and watch Gilligan's Island,

The credits roll and my dick twitches as she licks frosting off her fingers.

"Are you having any pain?" I ask, mentally chiding myself for being a horny bastard.

Charlotte shrugs her shoulders. "Not really."

"Good thing," I laugh as I flip her beneath me.

She lets out a yelp as I pull the covers over us.

21

Charlotte

My bits and pieces are a little sore, but on the whole, it didn't hurt as much as I had expected. There was a tiny pinch, a smidge of burning, but considering it was my first time, I don't think it was too bad.

The experience itself was sublime. Henry was gentle, kind, and incredibly romantic. As downhearted as I was when he turned me down at his parents—and at the motel, and in the shower—I'm glad he wanted us to wait. He took the time to make it special, and I'll never forget it. I think a lot of women regret the experience of their first time. If he would have given in when I pushed, I think I might have regretted it too.

The flowers and candles were part of what made the night magical, but the sweetness he exuded when we were making love has marked my soul. The way he kept stopping to ask if I was okay, has me convinced he was more nervous taking my virginity than I was to give it. How on earth did I get so lucky to have his brother be indebted to my family?

Yesterday was filled with tourism, delicious food, and fabulous companionship. Today it's time to get down to business. We landed in The Big Apple to find out what happened to Charlie. We have mere days left in this hotel before I have to come up with another ridiculous story to extend our welcome. Considering Sal the Concierge's attitude toward us, I don't think it's likely he'll be accommodating.

"Charlie liked massage parlors?" Henry asks, the bell ringing when we enter Madame Rouge.

A Korean woman sits at the front desk, her long glossed nails flipping through a *Cat Fancy* magazine.

"Excuse me? He would like a massage," I announce, pointing at Henry.

Henry's eyes pop, and the woman at the counter gives a small nod and leaves the desk to disappear behind a fall of beaded curtains.

"Why am I the one getting the 'massage?'" Henry grits out, his cheeks flamed.

"Because you're the guy. It only makes sense."

We take a seat in a row of plastic chairs pushed against the wall, waiting for the woman to return.

Henry scrubs a hand over his face. "I'm a fucking cop," he reminds me. "If this place gets raided while I'm back there . . ." he trails off.

I don't need to hear the words to get what he's telling me. I pat him on the knee. "I understand. I'll fix it." The woman I had talked to a few minutes earlier reemerges and waves for Henry to follow.

"I'm sorry. I made a mistake. *We* need," I point a finger between Henry and me, "a couple's massage."

The woman gives a brilliant smile complete with dollar signs in her eyes. "Five-hundred dollar," she says in broken English. I pull the money out of a Kate Spage bag I bought from a corner vendor yesterday. It was either Kate Spage, Couch, or Michael Chores. The Kate Spage was super cute, the decision was easy.

The Korean woman snatches the money from my hand. "Plus tip."

I fish out another hundred dollars, and she snatches that from me too. "This way," she says, walking through the beads.

Henry and I follow her down a poorly lit hallway with several closed doors on either side. She shows us into a room with two massage tables and walks out, shutting the door behind her.

"This should be interesting," Henry says, leaning against one of the tables.

"Charlie used to visit this place every time we were in New York. I guess he liked the company," I say with a shrug.

"You know what they do here, right?"

"Yeah. They give massages."

Henry shakes his head and pinches the bridge of his nose. "No—"

The door creaks open, and two women come in wearing kimono-style robes.

"Hi," I greet, reaching out my hand to be friendly.

The women look at my outstretched arm, then at each other, finally landing on Henry. Henry drops his head in his hands with a groan of embarrassment.

"Naked," one of the girls says as she drops to her knees.

"Come again?"

"She wants us to get naked," Henry clarifies, bending at the waist to help the woman stand.

"Why?" Don't they give you privacy to change into a robe or get covered first? "Never mind, I don't want to know. Listen," I tell the two girls as I pull out a picture of my brother which I printed from the hotel lobby computer. "Have you seen this man?"

One girl cranes her neck to look past me and directly at Henry. "You cop?"

"No," Henry lies. "This is her brother Charlie. Have you seen him?"

They both nod, and one says, "Two week ago. Big Russia guy

come in and steal him."

The information makes sense. It's been precisely nine days and six hours since I felt the light go out with Charlie.

"Can you describe the Russian?" Henry asks. "You said he was big. Big how?" he asks, using his hands to measure. "Big tall or big wide?"

"Yeah," the girls say in unison.

"What color was his hair? Brown?" he points to his head, "or blond?" he lifts a few strands of the tips of one girl's poorly maintained dye job.

Both girls shake their heads, then point to me.

"Red? Red like this?" he asks as he picks up a bright red vase.

"No," one girl says, then picks up a bottle of massage oil with a browner shade of red on the label.

"Okay. Good. Did he have a beard or a mustache?" he asks, putting his index finger above his lip. I guess that's supposed to be the sign for a mustache in charades.

"No, no," the one with the blonde tips says, then she points to an eyebrow and slashes her finger across her brow.

"He has a scar?" Henry asks.

The girl nods vigorously at Henry's remark. "Thank you," Henry says, guiding them out of the room. He shuts the door behind them and walks to the massage table I'm sitting on.

He doesn't speak for several minutes. Judging by the wrinkles on his forehead, he's got a lot on his mind.

"What are you thinking about?"

"I can't explain the red hair, but your father had a scar over his right eye too."

"So what? I'm sure he wasn't the lone person in the world with a scar over his right eye. Besides, I hate to point out the obvious, but my father is dead. Has been for almost thirteen years." Lies, all lies. At some point, I'm going to have to tell Henry that my father is very much alive and well. To do so may put his life in even more jeopardy than it already is. I'm going to wait it out until I have no choice but to spill every little detail because, with any luck, that moment will never come. If the opportunity doesn't present itself, then Henry will remain safe.

Henry squints and shakes his head. "I know, but are you sure he's dead? They never found the body."

He's asking all the right questions but now is not the time. Not yet. "I hate it when people talk about my father as if he wasn't a man of flesh and blood," I tell him. "He was. And as bad as people believed him to be, he also had the biggest heart. He was kind and tender and, you'll never understand. But this much I can tell you, John Scalise is dead. I went to his funeral. And," I pause a moment for effect, "it was an open casket."

Henry's head reels back in surprise. "Then why don't the police reports say that? As far as the Miami PD is concerned, his death is still an open investigation."

"Because he was buried as John Sutton," I say, deflating and deflecting.

"I see," Henry says after a beat. "John Scalise wasn't his real name."

He has no idea how right, yet so wrong, he is. "I know, it seems silly, but the FBI was always looking into stuff on John Scalise, it gave my father and me and Charlie some anonymity. Nobody knows that except . . ."

And then it hits me.

"Except who?" Henry prods.

"Ray. Ray and Charlie. And me, of course."

"Not even your mom?"

"No, she was never invested enough to care."

He stands up and grabs my hand. "Well, we still have a lead. Those text messages Charlie sent you before . . ." He pauses. There's no polite way of saying that my brother died. "And what those girls were saying. Charlie was in deep with the Russians. Now we have to figure out where they're running their operations. And what beef they had with Charlie."

We walk out of the massage parlor hand in hand.

"And how do we find all that out?" I ask, referring to the Russians.

"I don't know, but we'll come up with something."

What was it about Madam Rouge's that Charlie liked so much? It didn't seem that great to me. "If they don't give massages, then what do they do?"

Henry smiles. "Your innocence is adorable," he says, dropping a kiss on my head. "It's a brothel."

I stop walking and yank Henry back toward me when I don't step along with him. "My brother slept with prostitutes?"

"So, it would seem."

22

Henry

Per Charlotte's suggestion, we picked up a couple of local newspapers. We watched the evening news to try and get a handle on where some of the higher crime areas of the city are located. The obvious burrows, like the Bronx and Harlem, are automatically on the radar, but we want something more specific. We've employed the computer in the hotel lobby, searching for biographical information for some of these neighborhoods.

First, we take the train to Brooklyn to visit Little Odessa. It's known for its large population of Russian immigrants. As we walk through the neighborhood, we look for signs of mobster hangouts. Restaurants, strip clubs, apparently paint by numbers stores—as I learned it is an activity they all seem to like to do. None of the restaurants or paint and drink places seemed shady enough to hide a mob boss's business.

However, the craft store seems like the most likely place, at least in Charlotte's opinion. As we walk in, the cashier glares at us. I have to give credit where credit is due, Charlotte might be on to something.

"Restaurants and strip clubs are too cliché. Everyone's seen *The Godfather*. It's not like that in real life," she tells me as we walk down the scrapbooking aisle.

"Let's say, for argument's sake, you're right. Behind this green door," I point toward the back of the store, "there's a group of men putting together a scrapbook. You bust through and have their full attention. Then what?"

"Good question. What do you recommend?" Charlotte flashes that adorable smile, and I have to remind myself I'm on the job at the moment.

"We've got two options. One, we walk in and have a look around. If anyone finds us, we look lost. Or the second, you tell them who you are and why you're here. Option one gives us some time to figure out what we're going to do, but it may get us nowhere. Option two will out you, perhaps prematurely."

"What if we split up? You can browse the woodwork section, and I can accidentally wander into the back room," she suggests.

"No way."

"If we go in there together, and they're in the middle of something, I can look all harmless and lost. It would be completely inconspicuous."

She has that harmless look down, that's for sure. "Not happening. Since I'm the one with the gun, I'll be the one who goes in there. If I run into trouble, I can do something about it."

She lets out a resigned sigh. "Fine."

While Charlotte wanders off toward the yarn, I try to look at stuff as if I have a plan in mind. A plan that doesn't include walking back in a stock room and raiding a mob meeting. I pick up a box for a model airplane and set it back down, then pick up something else, I don't know what it is because I set it down as three men step out from behind the green door. They're all short and stout like teapots, wearing leather jackets and Kanga hats. It seems the Russian mob has a dress code.

The men speak in Russian amongst themselves as they pass

me and walk toward the front by the cash register. I take my opportunity and sneak into the storage room. For a craft store stock room, I expected to see bins of fake flowers and glue guns, but instead, it's near empty except for a large table cluttered with beer bottles and cigar butts.

I search for anything out of the ordinary—which is almost impossible because there is nothing ordinary about this place. Then I come across a poorly lit office. Just as I'm about to walk in, two of the three Russians return to the table.

I crouch low and keep my ears open in case they say something which might be useful. After ten minutes, my legs are cramping, and my gun is digging a hole in one of my kidneys. And, of course, I don't speak Russian, so I don't understand a single fucking word these guys are saying.

Until someone else enters the room and greets them in English.

"Hey, what are you guys up to?" the guy asks.

Trying to stay out of sight is keeping me from getting a good view of the new person. All I can see is the back of his head and that he's wearing an army surplus jacket and jeans. Considering he isn't wearing the Russian wardrobe and he's speaking English with an American accent, leads me to believe he's more of an associate.

"We were talking about our clothes," one of the Russians answers, "for Saturday."

"Right," the American says, taking a seat. "You guys bringing dates?"

"Yes, definitely. She has great big," one of the Russians mimes a rack of impossibly large tits. "And she's a giver."

I roll my eyes. What a pig.

"Lots of women going to be there," the other Russian says. "Need to keep my options open."

That guy with his bald head and beer belly won't have a lot of options. He should definitely plan on finding a date if he wants to get lucky.

"Remember," the American says, "this is a classy event. Black tie only. No prostitutes. No druggies. Got it? The biggest names in the business are going to be there, we can't afford to fuck this up. There are a lot of opportunities to expand and network. I can't stress this enough."

The Russians mumble something, but they seem annoyed by the American's insistence.

The American swipes a cigar from the table and lights it up. "You guys better be on time. Eight o'clock at The Kaplan, or you'll regret it."

The American walks out the green door and back into the craft store. The Russian goons sit back, and one of them starts dealing cards.

The mission has been successful, and we now have a lead. The problem now is that I'm stuck here until these guys leave. How the fuck am I going to get out of here?

23

Charlotte

Henry got himself locked inside the craft shop while waiting for the Russians to leave. I'm glad he talked me out of being the one to go into the storage room. If it had been me, I definitely would have gotten caught because I would probably trip over a ball of yarn or a kitten that had no earthly business being there. I would have died, and I'm not ready to die yet. I've fought way too hard to stay alive only to turn around and die.

On the other hand, if the situation would have been reversed, I wouldn't have had to wait six hours for Henry to come up with a plan to get me out of there. All the doors were locked, and if I had tried to break in, it would generate too much attention. Except, as Henry pointed out later, my idea wasn't any less noticeable.

As I waited for the store to clear out, I devised a plan. It involved a rope and the back bumper of Henry's dad's car.

Yanking off the back door from the building might not have been my brightest idea. Perhaps I could have utilized the lock picking kit which Henry had in the glove compartment, but to be honest, none of that occurred to me.

It's because of that little stunt that I have found myself at a gun range in New Jersey learning how to fire a weapon.

"Tell me again why I have to learn to shoot?" The idea of a gun in my hand is nerve-wracking. No one with my high percentage of "accidents" has any business holding a weapon.

"Let me list all the reasons. First, there's the fact that the Russian mob is now on high alert because someone," Henry looks down at me, "decided it was a good idea to rip off the back door of their hideout. Then there's the thought that as the daughter of a mob boss, and currently the head of his empire, it seems natural that you would be gun savvy. And last, but not least, I won't be around to protect you forever. You need to be able to defend yourself."

My heart hurts because, as Henry pointed out, our time together is finite. This arrangement, what we have, it can't go on forever. Henry's a cop, and I deal in dirty businesses with the dirtiest people on earth.

"Alright," I say, pulling down my goggles. "Let's do this."

Henry smiles and hands me a Saturday Night Special. He wraps his arms around me and pulls me against his hard chest. His warm hands envelop mine as he guides my arms.

"Keep your feet planted on the ground and your elbows straight. There's a bit of a kick to it," Henry says, placing his finger over mine.

His breath is hot in my ear and way too distracting for me to be holding a gun.

"Level the gun to your sights and aim for your target. Keep your elbows straight." His finger presses against mine and, together, we pull the trigger.

Even with noise-canceling headphones, the bang reverberates through me, pushing me against Henry.

Henry is firm and controlled, taking the blow to steady him and me.

I turn around, excited, smiling, and jumping. "I did it. That was awesome!"

"Whoa, whoa, whoa. Watch where you're pointing that thing," Henry hollers, grabbing the top of the barrel and pressing my hand downward.

"Sorry," I giggle, too excited to take it as seriously as I should. "When can I shoot that one?" I ask, pointing to the gun Henry has holstered on his hip.

"Never. You're not ready for a Magnum. Too much power for someone so tiny. Besides, you need to master this one first," he says, pointing to the pocket pistol.

"Fine."

We spend the next hour practicing my aim. If I may say so myself, I'm getting pretty good at it.

After the gun range, we drive back into the city and go for lunch at Los Tacos to talk about what's next.

"Find out where the Russian's hideout is? Check. Learn to shoot a gun? Check. Find out the time and location of the fancy mob party? Check, check. Shopping for a black-tie event? No check," I tell Henry before I bite into my Carne Asada Quesadilla.

"You want to go shopping?" he asks, taking a sip of cola.

"It's not a matter of wanting to, it's a necessity. Don't you think?"

He smiles. "If the lady says so."

We hit Fifth Avenue in search of evening wear. After going in and out of several stores, we discover that finding a tailored suit at a moment's notice is next to impossible. That is until we try one last little boutique on the way back to the hotel.

"No one's going to have anything with notice this late. This fact has been proven seven times over," Henry grumbles as I pull him into the shop.

"Then an eighth won't hurt. Come on, you never know."

"Hello?" a short woman with cropped bright red hair greets us. She's tiny—like little people tiny. She's adorable wearing a cute vest covered with buttons.

"Hello?" I parrot back.

"Welcome, welcome," the woman says excitedly, grabbing me by the hand and pulling me further into the store. "I have the perfect thing for you."

"Great. But you see, I have a super fancy party to go to tomorrow night, and we," I point between Henry and me, "don't have anything to wear."

"Yes, yes." She skips up to Henry, pulling out a tape measure from the pocket of her vest. She runs the scored ribbon across Henry's arms and along his inseam. "I have precisely what you need."

"Come with me. Let's try some things on," the store lady says. She starts grabbing dresses off the rack and piling them into her arms. The gowns are so long, longer than her, and drag on the ground. She pushes me into the dressing room and shoves the garments in my arms. "Try these on," she says, slamming the door.

As I slip into the first gown, I overhear her ushering Henry in another direction. I can't help but giggle, she's just as hurried and harried with Henry as she was with me.

The first dress is silver, short, and flirty. Even though it's cute, it isn't quite right on me. I take it off and hang it on the hook for the "Nope" pile. Next is a black fit and flare with a beautiful hi-low that's too long for me. It's still charming, formal, and accents my favorite features, so, I start a new hook for "Maybe." I try on five more dresses and work up a sweat. Three in the "Maybe" pile and two in the newly dubbed "Not In This Lifetime."

There's a slight knock on the door. "How are you doing in there, dear?" the store lady asks.

A twirl in front of the mirror while wearing the last gown brings a smile to my face. "I think I found it," I sing, stepping out of the dressing room.

She covers her mouth. "This dress was made for you." She walks me in front of a full-length mirror a few feet from the dressing room and stands on the tips of her toes. She combs her fingers through my hair and twists it on top of my head.

"Stay just like this," she says, and I grab onto the twist as she scampers away. A few seconds later, she returns with a couple of items in her hands. She bends down and taps my ankle, and I lift my foot, then she does the same to the other. Once I'm in four-inch pumps, she kicks over a stool and stands on it from behind. She brings her arms around me and clasps a beautifully ornate necklace around my neck. "You look so beautiful," she says, her eyes shining brightly.

"Everything—"

Henry is stopped short as the store lady hops off the stool to intercept him. "No, no, no. You can't see her. Not yet."

"Okay, okay," Henry says with a light laugh under his breath, his hands held up in surrender.

"Did you have anything for Henry?" I ask the little lady.

"Yes. But you? You are a masterpiece."

A masterpiece? Now that's something I'd love to hear every day. "I'll take it."

—

Henry

The little woman at the boutique was crazy and reminded me of the gingerbread man with all her buttons. A gingerbread man, or woman, who found a great tuxedo that fit perfectly. The price was friendly too. It was something I could afford, but Charlotte refused to let me pay. She insisted it was her treat, spinning it as a business expense. When Charlotte asked if it could be a tax write-off, I laughed. I wasn't sure if she was being serious or not. Her sweetness confounds me.

While Charlotte's in the hotel salon getting all gussied up for tonight, I'm on my way to the dress shop to pick up our order. The gingerbread woman greets me as soon as I walk through the door. She had promised our purchases would be tailored and ready to go by noon.

"Welcome," she says, running up to me with three pins

sticking out from her lips. "Have a seat. I'll be right out with your stuff."

She hurries to the back and reemerges two minutes later with her arms full. Charlotte's dress and my tux are wrapped in white plastic, and she hands them to me. "No peeking," she says, "it's bad luck."

I'm pretty sure that only applies to wedding dresses, but who am I to question such a wise woman with a stick of chalk poking out of her hair? "Understood. And thank you for being so accommodating. I'm sure it wasn't easy to pull off with such short notice."

"Nonsense. I'm always ready to help a couple in love."

I choke on a breath. "We're just friends." With a few benefits.

She looks past her glasses with a twinkle in her eyes. "Of course," she says, smiling. "I hope you two have a wonderful time this evening." She walks away, leaving me standing there, questioning myself, questioning Charlotte.

How does Charlotte feel? Is she in love? That wouldn't be too surprising. Women have a tendency to equate intimacy with love, and I was her first. As I ponder a hundred thoughts, I walk back to the hotel and decide to stop in and pick up over-priced coffee to take back to Charlotte.

As I place my order, I take a seat in the bistro while I wait. I pick up a newspaper to occupy my mind when I'm approached by two men. One of them is freakishly tall and lanky, never making eye contact, looking around as if people are watching him. The other one is more average, my height maybe, wearing a cheap suit and a buzz cut.

"Can I help you?" I ask as the men stand in front of me, but don't bother to introduce themselves.

The first thought which comes to mind is that Charlotte and I have been discovered. However, these guys aren't giving me a Goodfellas vibe.

"Henry Cain?" the guy with the buzz cut asks.

I wrap my arm behind my back and put my hand on my gun,

disguising the action as sitting back in the booth. "I am."

Buzz-cut reaches into his suit jacket and discreetly flashes me his badge. "FBI."

I didn't see that coming. "Can I see that?" I gesture to the badge he tucked in his suit jacket.

He sighs and pulls it back out, handing it to me.

Upon closer inspection, it looks legit. Considering everything Charlotte and I have been through in the past week, I can't say I'm willing to have blind faith in the guy.

I turn around and tap the shoulder of a man sitting behind me. "Excuse me," I point to the phone he's using. Looking at porn in a coffee shop, classy. "Mind if I borrow your phone for a minute?"

Charlotte and I have been off-grid since the house fire, and it's been a smart move, in my opinion. Except right now when I could really use a phone.

The man quickly swipes away the contents of his internet browsing and hands me the phone.

"Thanks." I dial a number which I am far too familiar with— the FBI office in Miami.

The phone rings a few times, and an operator answers. "Yes, I have been approached by one of your agents, and I need to verify his badge number."

I rattle off the number, and the operator confirms that James McHale is, in fact, an agent for the Federal Bureau of Investigation. I slap the badge shut and hand it back to him. "What can I do for you, Jim?"

He glances around the bustling coffee shop. "Can we go somewhere private to talk?"

"Can't think of any place more private than this." I lean back in the booth and hand the phone back to the pervert behind me.

The tall one glares at me and then slides into the booth. Jim follows suit.

"Harry? Harry?" a barista calls out.

These places never get the names right. I raise my hand, and the barista drops off two to-go cups of coffee in front of me.

The tall guy looks out the window, and Jim speaks. "We've been tracking your movements since the fire in Coral Gables. A quick jaunt up to Fort Lauderdale to see your parents after taking a leave of absence from your job. Interestingly, you've had a woman with you this whole time."

He's telling me more than I would have expected from an FBI agent. "And what?" I ask. "I'm not allowed to go out of town with my girlfriend?"

"Of course you can. Except," Jim pauses, "she's not your girlfriend."

"Why do you say that?" Somehow, I feel like we're in opposite roles. He's the one spilling the beans, and I'm the one asking the questions. The FBI needs to revise its training program if this is what they're teaching.

"Because Charlotte Scalise is the daughter of a known mobster. And you've been hanging out with her."

There it is. "I see. Well, first of all, her name is Charlotte Sutton, and even if she were John Scalise's daughter, it wouldn't matter because he's dead. But let's stretch the truth a bit further and say they are related. It doesn't mean she'd have anything to do with whatever it is you're looking for."

"True," Jim acknowledges, "But, Charlotte Sutton is looking for Charlie Scalise. And we're looking for Charlie Scalise."

My stomach rolls. According to Charlotte, Charlie is dead. "What do you want with Charlie Scalise?" I realize I'm walking a fine line. They have me on the hook, and they know it.

Jim visibly relaxes and smiles. "Seems Charlie is looking for new interests that are far outside the usual repertoire of the Scalise Family."

"Care to be more specific?" I'm a cop, my curiosity can be a bitch to satisfy.

"Sex trafficking," Jim says.

I squeeze my eyes shut and rub my forehead, severely disappointed. Charlotte has gone to great lengths to keep me in the dark about what her family does. Now I understand why. "What do you want from me?"

"There's some sort of mobster's ball going on tonight," Jim says.

I glance over at the gown and tux nicely wrapped and wonder how close on our heels the FBI has been?

Jim digs in his jacket pocket again, and this time pulls out an envelope. "This is the invitation to get in."

Now, I'm kind of glad I was approached by them. An invitation would make entry much more manageable than sneaking in. As I've learned after spending all this time with Charlotte, she's not the most graceful person in the world.

I snatch the invitation out of Jim's hand. "What's the catch?"

"We want you wired. You're going to be running into a lot of people the FBI finds interesting. Even though we prefer you to follow Charlie, in case he doesn't show, there are a few other people we want you to talk to."

Charlie is dead, but obviously, this is not information in the hands of the FBI. I could agree to this farce of an operation. There's no harm since Charlie is dead. However, my instincts are screaming that nothing about this deal will go well. "No way."

"I understand," Jim says. "It's your decision. You have to do what you think is right." He slips out of the booth and straightens his shirt and jacket. "Of course, I don't know that your captain will feel as supportive when he finds out one of his officers is associating with a known crime family. But then again, maybe your career in law enforcement isn't as important to you as mine is to me."

That cuts deep. My career in the Miami PD is one of my proudest achievements. I swore to honor and uphold the law, and I don't know that my association with Charlotte delegitimizes my commitment. However, Agent McHale makes a valid point—it wouldn't look that way to my captain, or anyone else for that matter.

The moment has come to choose between Charlotte and

my career. Actually, it isn't even about my relationship with Charlotte. It's about saving my brother's life. Although knowing Charlotte like I do, I don't believe Brian would be harmed.

My life, my family, and my career will be over if I stay with Charlotte. If I don't do what McHale wants.

"Have a lovely evening. It'll be the last good time you have for a long, long while," Jim says.

"Wait," I call out, just as Jim and the tall guy begin to walk away.

"What about my brother? What will happen to him if I take this offer?"

24

Charlotte

My dress fits like a glove. The tiny lady at the boutique has phenomenal taste. The gown is sparkly with a subtle rainbow pattern of sequins, a low-cut neckline, and an even lower cut back. My short stature must have kept her up all night altering, to keep it from trailing on the floor.

The entire day was spent in the hotel spa, being pampered and primped. My fingers and toes are painted a beautiful rose pink, my legs waxed and buffed to a shine, and my hair flat ironed to rid any thought of a curl. I slip on the silver heels and assess myself in the mirror. It's sad, but for the first time in my life, I feel like a million bucks and look like it too.

I stride out of the bathroom with confidence, promising myself that tonight will be a success. A dream of high society and romance. True, the so-called high society will be the lowest of the low, but for a blip in my life, I will get to rub elbows with my peers, not only those within the Scalise Family network.

It's strange to look at it that way, but necessary. The Scalise

Family isn't comprised of upstanding values and ethics. Although I'm not certain of the ins and outs of the underground business at large, I know connections will need to be forged. Relationships which will undoubtedly be important in running the family business on my own. There is so much I need to learn. Most of all, I need to be seen. Seen as the head of the Scalise Family.

This event fell into our laps and provides immense opportunity. The first being to find out what happened to my brother. I will sacrifice everything in Charlie's name, even the business. The second, showing the world our family is strong and will not tolerate being double-crossed.

In the living area of the suite, I find Henry wearing a hole in the carpet as he paces back and forth, fiddling with his cuff. My heart pitter-patters as I drink him in. "Wow," I breathe out. His tuxedo is the inkiest of black and tailored to perfection.

I'm not sure if Henry heard my ragged breathing or naturally sensed I was there. When he turns around, his eyes flash with something indiscernible. Just as quickly, the unnamed emotion flits away, and lust fills his gaze. Complete and utter desire.

"You, you," he stammers as he approaches me, his arms extended. "You are a vision." He pulls me to his chest and nibbles at my neck.

I give him a half-hearted shove, wanting him to continue more than I want him to stop. "We can't. We have to get going."

He brushes his fingers down my arm and kisses a path to my breasts. "We can spare some time. We don't want to be the first ones there."

This is a persuasive argument. If we're the first to arrive, two people whom no one has ever met, we'll stick out.

He nips at the globe of my breast, and my logic becomes hazy. "Okay."

A wolfish grin fills his face. "I knew you'd see it my way."

Step by step, we dance toward the bed. He swings me out wide and then pulls me back to him, our hips swaying. One more swing outward, and I am artfully tossed on top of the bed.

I laugh at Henry's sudden playfulness, loving every bit of it. He grips my ankles, yanks me toward him, and rests my heels on his shoulders. His mouth trails from the top of my foot, down my leg, pushing my gown up as he goes.

"No panties?" he asks as he exposes my sex, blowing a breath of hot air over the tantalized flesh.

"Panty lines," I breathe out as his tongue slips between my folds.

He rims the entrance of my channel with a finger. "Look at me," he says, his voice thick and raspy. He lowers himself and glides his tongue along my seam, flicking my sensitive bud with fervor.

I glance between my legs to see the most beautiful man. My slickness covers his face and the deepest of desire is alight in his eyes.

"Have I ever told you what I thought when I first saw you?" he asks, his finger penetrating my sex.

I whimper. "No. What did you think?"

He inserts a second finger and rubs circles on my clit. "That I bet you made the most erotic face when you came." He lowers his head and nips at the inside of my thigh. "And how beautiful your pussy would look when you cream all over my fingers."

His filthy words set my entire body aflame.

"And how hard I would have to make you come to—"

He pushes his pants down his legs, flips me over onto my belly, and hauls my ass up in the air, pushing the dress up to my midsection. Without holding anything back, he thrusts into me then reaches around and resumes circling my clit with his fingers. "How hard I have to make you come to get you to swear."

My insides clench with an onslaught of pleasure. Every pore in my body prickles with the most intense sensation of bliss.

He smacks my ass, and the sting reverberates between my legs. Powerful fingers grab at the roots of my hair, my head tugging backward. Every little sensation flitters across my body as it builds to a release. *"Holy shit."*

He continues to thrust, riding the waves of my pleasure.

"God damn. Fuck my cunt. Shit that—Oh, God." My censor and any remnants of self-control are obliterated. "I'm coming so hard. *Fuck.*"

He roars his release, digging his fingers into my hips as he spills into me. I crane for a look at the beautiful man behind me. His head is thrown back, the cords in his neck prominent, his face red as a beet.

As he withdraws from my warmth, he lowers himself to the ground and runs his tongue along my cleft, rubbing the sore spot on my bottom. When his tongue makes contact with my sensitive bundle of flesh, I jolt forward with shock and land on my stomach.

My body is shaking, my vision blurry, and my brain a pile of goo. Henry made me swear and say the nastiest things to ever leave these lips. The insanity of it is mind-blowing. There's one thing left to do.

"Why are you laughing?" he asks, sitting on the bed next to me. His cock bobs between his legs, drenched in my arousal.

The sight of reality is bright and frightening, halting my laughter. "You didn't wear a condom."

25

Henry

There's no good reason as to why I fucked her bare. No way to convey it in a way which Charlotte will understand. All I can say is, "I'm sorry."

"You're sorry? You're sorry. That's all you've got?" She rolls off the bed and pushes her dress down. She stomps into the bathroom, and I follow her.

"What do you want me to say? That I did it on purpose? That I was looking to knock you up?" It hits me then that those responses might not be as far from the truth as they should be. There's a primal, carnal need to—I don't know—plant my seed. The idea percolates, and I know it's outrageous, but it might be right. There's no way in hell I'm going to try to explain that to her, she would never understand. Hell, I don't understand.

Charlotte violently runs a brush through her hair. "You haven't forgotten before. Why now when we have so much on the line? Now, we have to go down to the ballroom and play spy, and all I'll be able to think about is whether or not your sperm is worming its way into my egg."

I stand in the mirror next to her as she touches up her makeup, and I fix my bowtie. "There are over-the-counter remedies for that."

Her gaze meets mine in the mirror. Those chaste green eyes blaze with a fury I didn't think possible for Charlotte to possess.

"I don't know how to respond to that," she says, capping her lipstick. She storms out and grabs her purse. "Let's go."

The ride down in the elevator is torture. I want to apologize, again, but Charlotte isn't in the mindset of forgiveness. Instead, I grab her hand and give it a gentle squeeze. That squeeze is supposed to mean, I'm with you whatever you choose to do or not do. Her hand remains limp in my palm, not bothering to return the gesture.

"Where did you get the corsage?" she asks, speaking to me as we make our way past the reception area.

The corsage was Agent Jim McHale's bright idea. A red rose pinned to my lapel is equipped with a tiny camera. It doesn't have a live feed to a poorly disguised FBI van out front. Instead, it's voice-activated and records into a device hidden in my tux jacket. If I get into any trouble, I can flip a switch and it will go live, notifying McHale. A fail-safe of sorts. "The woman at the boutique gave it to me. She thought it would look nice with your dress."

I escort Charlotte to the doors of the ballroom, her hand tucked in my elbow. Sal the Concierge guards entry, accepting invitations from throngs of people as they enter the room. We wait patiently in line until we come to the podium.

Sal glares at me, then focuses on Charlotte. "I like your dress," he tells her, his asshole demeanor not cracking an inch.

Charlotte gives him a polite smile. "Thank you."

He swings his attention back to me and lifts his chin with superiority. "This is an invitation-only event."

I dig in my jacket and tug out the invitation McHale had given me. "Good thing we were invited then, isn't it?"

Charlotte's jaw drops as I hand Sal the envelope. He looks it over suspiciously and frowns. "Very well. Have a wonderful evening."

"Where did you get that?" Charlotte whispers as we enter the ballroom.

I don't know how to answer in a way that won't elicit more questions. So, I don't respond. Instead, I evade. I swing her onto the dance floor and pull her close to me. "Let's dance."

The room is elegant and suave. Unlike the classic twenties architecture of the hotel, the ballroom is modern with white furniture, and a svelte backdrop of white curtains lit with soft purple lighting. Decadent, to say the least. Socialites, mobsters, and the one percent are dressed to the nines like they are attending a State dinner. Some of the faces I recognize are from the news, others from the post office. A blend of bureaucracy, elitism, and special interests.

Charlotte falls in step with me as we glide across the dance floor. We swing wildly, working our way around other couples.

"Where did you learn to dance?" she asks. "You're amazing."

"My dad."

"Really? How did that go?"

"Well, I was about to go to prom and had no clue how to dance. My mom isn't the most feminine woman in the world, and my dad has a stronger maternal instinct. It's a weird dynamic, but it works for them. So, Dad and I practiced every night for a month. I learned all types, but I drew the line at swing dancing."

For the first time since our argument, Charlotte gives me a genuine smile. I hate myself that much more for upsetting her in the first place. "I'm sorry."

Her smile falters, and she lifts her hand, rubbing her palm against my cheek. "I know."

"Excuse me," a man says, interrupting us. "May I have this dance?"

"No." I don't want to let her go. I want to throw her over my shoulder and take her far away from this world.

"Darling," Charlotte says, swatting playfully at my chest. "We have a lifetime of dances. I think you can spare one for this gentleman."

The man is short and greasy. A true goodfella. Maybe Charlotte can get some information from this guy. I'm practically useless right now as my head reels from Charlotte's term of endearment and mention of "lifetime." For the purposes of our mission, I step aside and wave my acceptance.

The man sweeps her around the room, and from a distance, she seems to be having a pleasant time, laughing when he says something, letting his hand go a little too low on her back.

I want to murder him. If I have any hope of surviving the night, I need to walk away, keep my distance, and let Charlotte do what she needs to do.

"Well, hello, handsome." A tall brunette sidles up to me at the bar and grabs a glass of champagne. She's older, mid-forties maybe, but certainly takes care of herself. "I don't think we've had the pleasure."

"I'm from out of town." I order a glass of scotch on the rocks. I could use a drink right now.

"It's your first time?" she asks.

"Yeah. Do you come to these parties often?" I ask because I don't know what else to say. However, I've learned this isn't a once in a blue moon kind of event.

"I haven't in a long while. It isn't really my scene. The men can be ferocious. Especially once the bidding starts."

I choke on my scotch. "Bidding?"

She laughs. "Oh, honey, I know you can't be that innocent. You're in a room filled with the most dangerous men in the world."

"Of course. Yeah. I just didn't know it was a bidding process. How high do the bids usually go?" I ask, hoping like hell I've been able to cover my missteps.

"I don't know. On a slow night, a couple million. But if the girls are primo, well, then we're talking tens of millions."

My eyes immediately scan the room for Charlotte. "Well, it's been an enlightening conversation. Thank you for talking with me, Miss . . ."

"Mrs. Sutton," she answers, her smile gracious and entitled.

"Sutton? Is that your stage name?" I joke, trying to conceal the nerves vibrating through my body. I grab her hand and place a kiss on the back of her palm. This might be our break.

"No. Well, kind of. My husband, as paranoid as he is, insists on it. Anonymity is so hard to come by these days."

Charlotte had mentioned before that her father insisted on fake birth certificates for anonymity. That can't be a coincidence.

I look a little harder at the woman in front of me and search for any likeness to Charlotte or her brother Charlie, but I'm not seeing it. Maybe someone in Scalise's former employ took the great idea of using a common name to hide their identity. Except they weren't original enough to come up with their own name.

I survey the room again, looking for Charlotte, and still don't see her. My heart sinks to the pit of my stomach. "I'm sorry to cut this short, but I need to find my date," I tell Mrs. Sutton, a little annoyed I'm letting this opportunity slip by. But if Charlotte is in trouble . . . I can't go there right now.

"It was nice talking to you," she calls to my back as I walk away.

A few laps around the room and I'm praying Charlotte has simply blended in with the crowd, but I don't see her. Nor, do I spy the man she had been dancing with.

There are two exits out of the ballroom. One is guarded by bulky hitmen dressed in black suits, and the other is managed by Sal.

Sal is a complete tool, and I consider taking my chances with the hitmen, as opposed to dealing with the concierge. Not wanting to blow our cover too soon, I swallow my pride and make my way to Sal's podium.

"I'm sorry to bother you," I tell him, disdain rolls off him in waves. "But you didn't happen to see my date leave? I can't seem to find her anywhere."

"Perhaps, sir, she found someone who is man enough not to express his anger with his fists on her face."

I roll my eyes. I could almost kill Charlotte for giving this prick the impression I was beating her. "I didn't hit her," I grit out, "she's ridiculously clumsy."

"Did she fall down the stairs? Run into a door?"

"Did you see her or not?" My fingers itch with the urge to jab him in the throat.

He purses his lips as if he just sucked on a lemon. "No. Not that I would tell you if I did. But I didn't, so it doesn't matter."

Shit. I look around one more time, my heart beating ferociously in my chest, but I still don't see her. What I do see turns my blood cold. Four men dressed in designer tuxedos making their way through a back door. I hadn't noticed the exit earlier. It must have been hidden by one of the backdrops cascading from the ceiling. The men each have a highball in one hand and a stogie in the other as they walk and talk, laughing. Nothing about this can be good.

I temper my steps, the urge to run almost too powerful to ignore, but the last thing I need is to draw attention. As the door is about to close, I stick my hand in the jamb and sneak in. Behind the secret door is a dark hallway.

I follow the raucous laughter of the men down a stairwell. My people of interest come to a stop, and I hug the wall, hoping the darkness will hide me.

"You are in for a treat, my friend," one man says.

"I've waited my entire career for this invitation. From what I've heard, the selection keeps getting better."

The men once again start walking, and I watch as they pass through yet another door. The murmurs of excited voices fill the narrow hall. I give a three-second count and man up, pulling open a thick oak door.

It takes a moment for me to grab my bearings, and I realize I'm in some kind of auditorium, but fancier. Men and women gather around a stage, chatting amongst themselves like they're waiting for the curtain to rise at the opera.

Mrs. Sutton is sitting a few rows down from where I'm standing, and the opportunity couldn't have been better if it had fallen in my lap.

I slip into an empty seat next to her. "Hello again."

"I'm so glad you made it. I hope you have your checkbook ready. I heard the selection tonight is one for the books."

I pat my jacket pocket. "I'm always prepared."

She leans over and whispers, "I heard there's a violinist, a model, and a belly dancer. I love watching the men fighting each other. And these women will be worth the fight."

26

Charlotte

"Who are you?" I demand, the strength of my voice stronger than my conviction. I'm not ashamed to admit I am beyond scared. The man's grip on my arm is so tight I'm sure a bruise is already forming.

"Keep walking," he insists, pushing me down a dark hallway.

How did this go so wrong? One minute, I was being swept off my feet by Henry, and then I'm swept away from civilization in the next blink. "What do you want from me?" I ask, ripping my arm from his hold.

His grip falters, and he grabs a tighter hold, his nails digging into my flesh. A sharp jab pokes me in the side, dropping me to my knees.

He hauls me back up, his face so close to mine, I can smell the wine on his breath. "Shut the fuck up."

A knife in my side and a good old-fashioned threat is all the motivation I need to obey.

The walk is long, seemingly a hundred miles from The

Kaplan when we come to our apparent destination. The man shoves open a door, the hinges creaking like the Tin Man stuck in the rain. The knife in my side is withdrawn as he shoves me into the dark space, and I tumble, tripping over my heels.

The horror which surrounds me has already scarred me enough for ten lifetimes. I am in the middle of my own scary movie. The room is dank with iron-rot heavy in the air. But it's the huddled mass of at least twenty women in the corner that brings a moving picture to reality. The ages of women span the gamut, but most are on the younger side. Although it's hard to tell with dirt and grime camouflaging their faces. Their clothes are filthy, threadbare, and shredded.

The women gawk at me, and I return their shock. What else am I supposed to do? Nothing about this situation is normal. There is no How-To Manual for being kidnapped and shoved in a hole with other women. Then again, there is nothing even remotely conventional about my life, my upbringing, or my family. From a warped perspective, it almost seems fitting that I should find myself here.

I stand and swipe at the dirt on my knees when a young woman approaches.

"What's going on? What am I doing here?" I ask her, my voice shaky, and in desperate need of an answer.

Her eyes are sullen and sunken. Her body, which I'm sure was stunning once upon a time, appears to be wasting away. "I'm not sure you want to know the answer," she says with a barely perceptible French lilt.

"You're wrong," I tell her, "I do want to know. I need to know. Please."

Another young woman approaches. She looks as defeated as the one before. "It's your worst nightmare come true."

My stomach rolls. "What do you mean?"

"You know all those news programs talking about sex trafficking?"

I blink in response.

"It doesn't seem so real when it's on TV. It was just a trip to the mall. I go there all the time. All I needed was a new pair of shoes. I was supposed to start a new job the next day. I was so excited . . ." she trails off, staring at the ground. "They have signs in the restrooms at gas stations, giving a number to call if you're a victim of sex trafficking. A lot of good it does when you don't have access to a phone." She shakes her head and laughs humorlessly at the comment. "Never in my life could I have predicted this. If I would have known, maybe I would have appreciated the truly important things. The stuff I considered valuable means nothing when you don't have your freedom. I never imagined this would be my reality."

Her story doesn't register. I pick and pry as I focus on placing the pictures of the puzzle together in a way that makes sense. "You're saying I'm, what? Up for sale?" I ask, cutting the tale down to its purest form.

"It's true," says another woman stepping forward, her belly bloated like she swallowed a basketball.

The room begins to spin. The women meld together into a blob of tan and brown with specks of pink. "*No*," I scream. "No! No! No!" I run to the door and bang on it with desperation. "Help! Help!" The pitch of my screams pierces my own ears, burning my throat until it's raw.

"*Stop*," demands yet another female voice. "You're going to get us all in trouble. If they come in here—"

Her words are cut off when the door opens. A tall man in a Kanga hat steps in, and I immediately recognize him as one of the Russian men from the craft store. "Who's yelling in here?"

None of the women answer. Those who seemed friendly and helpful moments ago are now hiding in the corner. I'm standing in the middle of the room alone. I might as well be a neon sign flashing, "It Was Me!"

The Russian sighs his annoyance. "I should have known it would be you. I told Maxym you would be nothing but trouble." He reaches into his pocket and pulls out a small cylindrical object. Using his teeth, he pulls off the cap and spits it onto the floor.

It's a syringe.

Which he swiftly jabs into my neck.

I clap my hand to my neck and step back, shocked and out of sorts. I stumble toward the middle of the room as it revolves around me and fall to the floor. I gaze at the women who are a mere few feet from me until everything turns black.

When my eyes open again, I'm no longer in that little room. Instead, I'm lying on a couch. The decor is of a hotel suite. The furnishings and architecture are the same as my room in The Kaplan.

I sit up quickly, and the room gyrates, the effects of whatever that Russian gave still hanging around but wearing off. I wonder if it was all a terrible dream, maybe I had too much wine at dinner. Except, my last memories are not of dinner but vivid images of worn and weathered women. And the room I'm in is not the room I've been sharing with Henry.

Henry. Where is Henry? I survey the room with a new level of vigor. My brain, however, doesn't agree with my movement. My cranium feels like it is about to pop off to relieve the pressure between my ears.

"Settle down, bug," a voice says from behind. "It will wear off soon enough."

Every cell in my body frays at the pitch of the man's voice. A voice I know too well. Ignorance is bliss. I've never understood the meaning of that saying more than I do right now. I swallow hard, too frightened to look up, wishing with my whole heart that this is nothing but a bad dream.

Not yet having looked at the man's face, I know he is sitting in a chair adjacent to me. The scent of stale Cuban cigars permeates the air. His legs are crossed as he rolls his foot. His shoes are insanely shiny, and the one thing I can think about is the book about Ken Kesey. What's it called? Right, *The Electric Kool-Aid Acid Test* by Tom Wolfe. Tom Wolfe goes on about how the FBI could never blend in no matter how hip they dressed because their shoes were too shiny.

This man is not from the FBI or any government agency. He isn't here to save me. I'm certain he's the reason I was plucked from that dungeon, but it wasn't to spare me. Most likely, he wants the opportunity to take me down himself.

"Why are you here?" I ask, daring to tread into this swamp of uncertainty. My options are limited, and there is nowhere to go but forward.

"Maybe I missed you?" the man suggests.

My heart is filled with rage, betrayal, and confusion. I suck in a deep breath and gather all my strength and wits, taking the giant leap to look into the eyes of my captor. The eyes are the same as mine, but it's the aging face of my father which stares back at me.

It's been thirteen years since I've seen him. He's exactly how I remember, yet so much has changed. His once dark brown hair is streaked with silver, but the scar over his right eye is as dark and angry as ever. His frown is deep-set and prominent as if he hasn't smiled since the day he left. Maybe he hasn't? Perhaps the decision to leave his children behind was a torment I could never understand.

I'm not sure if I want to jump in his lap and sing nursery rhymes or shoot him where he sits. I'm not ready to forgive or forget. No matter his reasons, I must remember I was drugged and kidnapped under my father's authority.

What Charlie had texted me about the Russian's being a problem, that they were getting restless, I get it now. This man is no longer the father of my memories. He's become the monster I knew he was. I just didn't expect he would ever go so far as to try to destroy his own flesh and blood.

"What happened to Charlie?" I get straight to the point. I'm in the presence of a master manipulator, and the best way to keep my advantage is to stay focused.

He leans over and picks up a stubbed-out cigar from an

ashtray and I catch the glint of a small pistol on the end table. The gun calls to me, but I keep my eyes trained on my father.

"You and Charlie," he says, lighting the cigar and puffing on the end. "You two were thick as thieves. So close, it was almost unhealthy."

"We're twins. We shared a womb. Of course, we were close. Where is he?" I already know the answer, but I need to hear the words. However, if he says them, it will make it real, and I don't know how I will handle that. I like to think it will be with grace and decorum, but I won't hold myself to unrealistic expectations.

"Charlie had a tendency to get into trouble. You, bug, were the good one. Always did as you were told."

There is a myriad of emotions flitting through me, and I don't know what to do with them. A child's love is unbreakable, at least in my case. I'm not blind. I know John Scalise is one of the evilest men in the world. He has, and probably continues to, commit some of the most heinous and unimaginable crimes ever conceived.

Despite these truths, he's my father. The man who kissed my boo-boos all better. The guy who bounced me on his knee. He's been gone so long it's almost simpler to delude myself and recall the good memories.

"And I'm guessing you expect that of me right now," I say to his good girl comment.

"It would be nice."

"So, what? You expect me to drop all of this and tuck my tail between my legs and run home? Life as usual?"

"No, no. I would never expect you to forget everything. Instead, it seems I have an open position that needs to be filled."

"Charlie's job," I say, not needing to ask. There is no evidence that Charlie was working for my father. Still, the stars align in such a perfect way, it seems unlikely for there to be another scenario. Everything came to a head when Charlie arrived in New York. The Russians are in deep with this human trafficking business, and it's no coincidence that my father pulled me from the pit of despair. Charlie was working for my father, but my father is not working for or with the Russians. He is the Russians. There isn't an ounce of the old John Scalise left, it's all Vlad Petrovsky, head of the Russian crime family, now.

"He could never do as he was told, but you, you are my good girl."

"Tell me what happened to Charlie, and maybe I'll consider it." There is no way in Hades I would ever accept that position, but I want him to talk. I need to know where his head is at. I know my father, and as brutal as he may have been, his love for his children was pure and fierce. Something isn't adding up.

"I don't have to tell you because you already know," he answers.

"Darling," a woman sings as she walks into the room. She stops in her tracks when she sees me on the couch. "I didn't know we were expecting company."

"Just a business matter. It's almost settled," my father says as he strides over to her, giving her a kiss on the cheek. "Go ahead and warm up the bed. I'll be in shortly."

Acid roils in my stomach from his blatant display of affection. "Is that my new mommy?" I ask after the woman leaves.

My father laughs but doesn't answer. "So, what do you say, bug?" he asks, leaning against the arm of the couch.

"It seems like a lot of responsibility. I haven't had a ton of experience in this area of the business. I don't know if I would be a good fit."

"Nonsense. It's in the blood," my father says, taking another puff from his cigar.

Not enough in the blood to save Charlie. "I don't know. Can I think about it?"

"Of course. I wouldn't want you to regret anything. But don't take too long," my father says, pulling his phone out of his pocket.

He hands it to me, and the picture I see is enough to make

my blood run cold.

"One of my men sent me these. It seems Brian Cain only has enough oxygen to last another hour. And this," he says, swiping to another picture, "is your boyfriend working with the feds."

27

Henry

The auctioning of dozens of women opened my eyes. I thought this underground world only existed in movies starring Liam Neeson. Logically, I know it happens, but to see it in front of my face brought new understanding. As a cop, I've tracked some of this shit. However, I've never had the displeasure of sitting next to the men who buy other humans for their own gratification.

By the time the last woman stepped on stage, I was beyond relieved to find Charlotte wasn't on the auction block. The downside was that I didn't have a clue where she was or how to find her.

Then Mrs. Sutton invited me to her suite. When I asked her how her husband would feel about my presence, she laughed it off and said he would be too preoccupied with business to notice.

I went with my gut. What are the chances that another woman with the last name Sutton, would be in attendance at a human trafficking convention? I know Charlotte says she saw her father's body, and I don't doubt she believes it. However, a grieving child is going to see what they want, what they need, and what they're told to perceive.

Perhaps I'm off base, and John Scalise is buried. Maybe Charlotte is wrong, and Charlie wasn't murdered. Although, I'm more inclined to trust Charlotte's instincts than the notion of John Scalise being dead.

All those thoughts and unlikely scenarios are how I ended up naked in Mrs. Sutton's bed. Lady Luck must have smiled upon me because Mrs. Sutton had a few too many glasses of champagne and is now passed out next to me in drunken bliss. I had no clue how I was going to wiggle my way out of having sex with her when I followed her to her room, and I wouldn't have slept with her either. I'm a one-woman type of guy, Charlotte's man, and luckily for me, I don't have to try to figure it out. I hop out of bed and throw on my tux, leaving the bowtie to hang loose around my neck. Mrs. Sutton lets out a few little snores, and I creep out of the bedroom.

The hallway is short, with rooms on either side. I tip-toe to the end toward a set of double doors with light spilling from beneath. This must be the office where Mr. Sutton spends his time working. If I'm lucky, Charlotte is included in tonight's tasks.

I depress my ear against the door and listen, but I can't understand anything being said. It's a man's voice, grumbly and thick like he's smoked cigars since he was in diapers. Moments later, my stomach twists when I hear another person speak.

Charlotte's lyrical voice is all the confirmation I need. She wasn't auctioned off because she was never for sale. Charlotte Sutton was a pre-order.

I grab the gun from my waistband and secure it with both hands. Everything will change when I make my move. Good or bad, it will raise the stakes for someone. I clench my teeth so hard a molar cracks. I lift my foot and kick in the door, the wood splintering as I storm the room.

Charlotte is standing behind a man whose hands are raised in surrender. My heart swells with pride when I realize my adorable, clumsy cupcake is holding a gun to the man's temple.

Her beautiful green eyes are wild with rage. I lower my gun and tuck it in my pants. "Charlotte, cupcake, put the gun down."

"He should be dead, not Charlie."

I scrutinize the man. He's weathered with silver hair. The thick scar over his right eye confirms my previous suspicion. John Scalise is alive and well. I can't imagine the thoughts running through his head, realizing his daughter is prepared to take his life.

"I know," I tell her, keeping my tone calm and judgment-free, trying not to spook her.

"It wouldn't be murder, you know. John Scalise is technically already dead."

I thought it was rage I saw in her eyes, but I couldn't have been more wrong. It's the genetic impulse of a woman born and bred for organized crime. She's the one in control, she's ruthless, and she's ready to prove it to her father. My dick jerks and I'm not sure if I'm scared or turned on by her change in demeanor.

"Listen, cupcake, I'm not going to say I know how you feel because I don't. But what I do know is that the Charlotte I first met was so concerned with her brother that she blackmailed a police officer into finding the truth. Shit, I'm not making my point. The Charlotte I know trips over her own feet, sits in her library, snuggled up with dusty books, and reads all day. She is so sweet she doesn't know what it means to whack someone off. And, until tonight, I didn't think she even knew how to cuss."

Her cheeks pink-up, and I know it's because she's reliving what we did earlier. Now that I think about it, that might not be a good thing. I didn't use a condom, we had a big fight, and she's holding a gun. Hopefully, with everything going on, she's forgotten.

Her face pales, and I know I'm not that lucky. "What I'm saying is, the Charlotte I know, the Charlotte I love, isn't a murderer."

Charlotte blinks once, then twice. A few more seconds pass, and she blinks for a third time. She seems to be in shock, so I take tentative steps toward her, filching the gun from her hand.

"It's about fucking time," John Scalise grunts from his delicate position in his chair.

Charlotte stops mid-step and raises her hand to her father, striking him with a slap that makes my own cheek ache. "You can go back to being dead."

"Don't worry, he will," says Ray Thatch as he enters the room. "I'm sorry, bug, I didn't want you to find out like this."

"How did you want me to find out? It's not like you were going to tell me," she spits. "I told you I was worried about Charlie, and you knew the whole time. You lied to my face. The one person I trust most in this world, and you lied to me."

Ray twists his beard with his finger. "I'm sorry, bug," he says, walking to Charlotte and opening his arms for a hug.

She puts her hand up to stop him. "No. Stop. This is over."

Ray has the good sense to take a step back, and his face falls at her words.

"If I can't trust you, I can't keep you around. You're fired," Charlotte tells Ray. She hikes her thumb over her shoulder and points at John Scalise. "But, I believe Vlad has a job opening."

Vlad? John Scalise is Vlad Petrovsky? It's starting to make sense now, and I have a thousand questions, but I don't get to ask because Charlotte grabs my hand and rushes us out of the suite. No parting words for her father or Ray, no hugs goodbye. Nothing. I don't think she's even mad anymore—more like on a mission. She presses a button for the elevator, and I stand there like a dumbass having no clue what to say or do for her.

Charlotte taps the rose corsage on my jacket lapel with her fingertip. "How does this thing work? Do I just talk into it?"

I rub the back of my neck nervously. "I, um, you know about that, huh?"

"I might not be the worldliest, but I'm not stupid. Is it on or not?" Charlotte asks, her tone clipped with urgency.

I pull the box out of my jacket and flip a switch which gives us a direct line to McHale. "It should be good."

She pulls me to her by the collar of my coat. "If anyone with the FBI is listening, I need you to go to Pier forty-six. Brian Cain is being held captive underwater in a wet suit. He has less than thirty minutes of oxygen left."

The doors to the elevator open, and I stand rooted to the ground in shock. My brother's life hangs in the balance, and I'm useless. Somehow, Charlotte has become the knight in shining armor, and I am the damsel in distress.

"Come on," Charlotte yells. "We don't have much time."

Her stern tone takes me out of the fugue which had me lost in an imaginary world. A world where my brother had not been kidnapped by the father of the woman to whom I just confessed my love.

As the elevator descends, I turn to Charlotte. "When were you going to tell me that Vlad Petrovsky is your father?"

She wrinkles her nose as she explains. "I know, I should have told you sooner. I just didn't want you to get mixed up in any more of this mess than necessary. The thing is my father has always been with the Petrovsky Family. We only have a couple of minutes, so I'll give you the cliff notes version. Once upon a time in a galaxy far, far away—"

"Seriously?" I ask, raising an eyebrow.

"Fine. My father, Vlad, grew up in Moscow. My grandfather was the leader of the Petrovsky Family. He gave my father the best of everything. The nicest clothes, the best schools. He was set up for success. He was also the one person in his network to learn English. And with an American accent to boot. My grandfather had plans for his son. When my father was in his twenties, he was sent to America and instructed to infiltrate the Scalise Family.

"Anyway, my father assumed his new position and title as John Scalise and ran the business quite successfully for decades, until—"

"The Petrovsky's came calling. They wanted him to make good on his mission."

Some of this disaster is starting to make sense, but Charlotte's betrayal stings more than I expected. I was confident we'd developed a relationship of trust, love, and passion. I guess she doesn't feel the same way. It didn't escape my notice that she hasn't said she loves me too. I don't expect her to declare her undying love and devotion to me, but it would be nice.

The bell dings and the doors slide open. "We have to hurry," Charlotte presses, striding out, her walk turning to a jog as she hails a cab at the curb.

"Pier forty-six. There's a hundred-dollar tip if you can get us there in the next ten minutes," she tells the cabbie.

The driver gives her an enthusiastic nod. At three in the morning on a Sunday the traffic is light—someone up above is looking over us.

Images of my brother drowning invade my mind, and I squash it because there is nothing I can do at this moment. We're already doing everything we can, and the cops are on their way. All I can do is distract myself from thinking the worst. "You knew this whole time your father was alive, and you lied to me about it," I say, reeling from everything that has happened in the past ten minutes.

"And you've been working for the feds. It seems we both have our secrets."

"No, no, no. Don't you dare try and turn this around. I was approached by the feds this afternoon when I was picking up your dress. You've known about your father since the first time I asked. You even went so far as to tell me that you saw his dead body."

"What does it matter, huh?" Charlotte asks, her temper flaring. "It doesn't. My father is a dead part of my life. So what if I like to tell myself that he was an amazing man who was taken from me? There's no harm in that. Not all of us come from a traditional family." A tear slides down her cheek, and she crosses her arms sitting back in her seat.

I've gone from being on the right side of the argument to being so wrong, I don't know how to find my way back. How does she do that? "Shit. I'm sorry. You're right. I can't imagine what that's like. And I hate that a woman as incredible as you does know. You deserve so much better." I pull her into my side, tilting her face toward me, and wipe away her tears.

I lean in to brush my lips against her decadent mouth. Our tongues slide and tango, the heat of our argument fading away.

The car jolts to a stop, and Charlotte and I are flung into the backside of the front seats. I clench my eyes and shake my head as I figure out what happened. Before I can even say a word, Charlotte tosses a wad of cash at the cabbie.

"We're here," she says, hopping out of the car and running toward the pier.

"Charlotte, wait," I call out, chasing after her. Sirens scream in the background, becoming louder and closer with each step I gain.

Charlotte's arms raise up. A large slit in her dress which I hadn't noticed earlier becomes obvious like someone had a knife to her side. In the blink of an eye, and with perfect form, she dives into the water.

I jump in after Charlotte, my alignment far less impressive, and fight against the filth of the harbor to find her and Brian. I can't see a goddamn thing, the moonlight does nothing to help illuminate the water.

There for the grace of God, I see a flicker of light beneath me, then another. I swim harder and faster into the depths of the Hudson, chasing the pulsating glow until it rises above me.

I follow the flashes until I break the surface and find Charlotte ripping off a facemask from a body. All I can see are their heads as Charlotte struggles.

"Help me," she cries.

I scoop at the water with my arms and make my way to her.

She's cradling Brian in her arms. The lack of light and the water splashing against us make it difficult to tell if he's alive.

I can't imagine my life without my brother. The world will continue to turn, and everyone will simply go on with their daily lives as if nothing has changed. But everything will have changed for my family and me.

How will I tell my mother?

Brian's entire body jolts, and he gasps for a lungful of air and coughs.

"Thank fuck," I say, dropping my forehead to his. "You scared the shit out of us."

He gives me a weak smile. "Sorry about that, bro."

"Um, can you help me?" Charlotte asks, using that sweet tone I've come to adore. "He's kind of heavy."

"Oh, yeah." I grab onto Brian using a lifeguard hold, and the three of us make our way back to the pier.

Charlotte climbs up first and then reaches out to help Brian. I climb on last to make sure he doesn't fall back in the water. We manage to make it to a bocce court and collapse onto the grass, heaving for oxygen.

Finally, Brian says, "Cutting it kind of close, huh?"

"Don't thank me, thank Charlotte," I tell him.

Brian gives Charlotte a seductive smile, grabs her hand, and drops a kiss to the back of her palm. "Thank you. How can I ever repay you?"

I want to punch him in the balls and stake my claim, but Charlotte retorts before I get a chance.

"That'll be one-hundred and seventy-five thousand dollars," she tells him, and Brian's face falls flat.

I can't hold back the laugh. Brian knew he was in for a lot of problems with the Scalise Family, but he had no idea who Charlotte Sutton was, until now. "Brian, I'd like to introduce you to Charlotte Sutton."

"I know who she is, asshole. She was at Mom and Dad's last week, remember?"

"Yeah, but to you and them, she was a friend I was trying to help. Remember when I told you that someone from the Scalise Family propositioned me? Meet the queen pin."

Brian blows out a deep breath. "Holy shit. So Charlotte, you don't by any chance take payment plans?"

"Don't worry about it," Charlotte laughs. "Your debt has been repaid, thanks to your brother."

The police and fire departments arrive, and Charlotte and I have no desire to be anywhere near the scene when the questions start firing. We leave Brian on the bocce court after a brief goodbye and make our way back toward the hotel.

28

Charlotte

I don't know what persuaded me to run into the Hudson. I don't know what possessed me to hold a gun to my father's head. I certainly don't know what is prompting me to get into the Thunderbird with Henry as we make our way back to Miami.

Since we left Brian, I don't think I've spoken any words of substance to Henry. I've only communicated when he's asked questions. Even then, it was yes and no answers. I'm not sure how I feel after everything that's happened. All I want is to go home. The problem is, I no longer have a home to return to. Nowhere to live. No one missing me, awaiting my homecoming.

As we hit the highway, I lean the seat back and close my eyes, desperate for a nap.

"It's been a long night," Henry says, turning down the radio.

"Yeah."

"Are we going to talk about it?"

What I want to say is: Talk about what? How you planned to rat me out to the feds? Maybe we can discuss how we had sex without a condom? Most of all, I want to ask about his declaration of love. Instead, I say nothing and look out the window. Avoidance is the easier option.

A few hours later, Henry pulls into a motel parking lot. He shuts off the engine and turns in his seat to look at me. "I never did thank you for saving Brian. I've spent so much of my life trying to save him from himself, and I could never do it. And you? You jumped into the Hudson without a second thought of your own safety. And to top it all off, you wiped away his debt."

It isn't that simple, and he knows it. Brian's obligation was forgiven the moment Henry arrived at my front door. Henry could have called it quits anytime, and I still would have pardoned Brian for what he owes the family. I could tell him all of that, but I'm not talking to him at the moment.

Henry cracks open his door. "Anyway, thanks."

At the front desk, we check for a vacancy. The clerk asks if we need one room. As Henry says we do, I interrupt and declare the need for a second. Henry grunts his frustration, but his emotions don't bother me one bit. I have enough stuff to figure out at the moment.

The clerk's face strains with apprehension. No doubt, he would rather be anywhere other than in the middle of a domestic squabble.

Our rooms are next to each other. I'm not sure how convenient that is for me, but I know Henry considers it a win.

As I pull the keycard from the lock, Henry grabs me by the arm. "Hold on. I know you're mad. And I don't understand everything you're pissed about because I know it can't only be about the condom. But I hate the idea of us in separate rooms. We might have left your father and Ray in New York, but that doesn't mean you're safe." He pulls a gun from the side pocket of his duffle bag.

It's the same weapon I had pointed at my father just before Henry burst through the door. It was sitting on the side table next to my dad, calling to me. My chat with Father Dearest had been interrupted by a phone call. Some guy named Maxym was on the line. My father had wandered away to take the call out of earshot. That was when I saw my chance, and I embraced it.

Henry places the gun in my hand, wrapping my fingers around the grip and the barrel. "I've taught you how to shoot, kind of. Use it if you have to. I'm right next door if you need anything—and I mean anything. A hug, someone to watch TV with, an orgasm. I'm right here."

I take the gun and walk into my room and shut the door behind me without bothering to acknowledge anything Henry said. After a long hot shower where I could shed a hundred tears without judgment, I spread out on the bed.

And think.

At first, I try to think about nothing at all. Certainly not about my father, or the lies Ray has fed me. The sad thing is, nothing that happened with my family—or so-called family—is what's upsetting. All the dysfunction is par for the course in a family like mine. It's to be expected.

What's bothering me the most is whether or not I've mourned for Charlie the way I should. It's been less than twenty-four hours since I learned the truth about my brother. Then again, I already knew he was dead from the moment it happened. There's a pang in my chest. The guilt of not grieving my brother, my twin, is eating away at me. I curl up on the faded duvet and cry quiet tears for Charlie, but I know the best way to honor him is to find out what happened.

My father gave the impression he had his own son killed. I think back to all the beautiful memories of my childhood, and I simply don't buy it. John Scalise, or more accurately, Vlad Petrovsky, is not a perfect man. He's a monster. Of course he is, he's a dang mobster. What can anyone expect? It's a necessary part of the job. My father had to make hard choices. He followed through on egregious decisions in the name of the family.

Charlie and I were thick as thieves like my father said, but we were so different. My father was right, I was the good one, saving raccoons from certain death. Charlie tried to declaw our childhood cat. Charlie had an underlying hum of sickness to him which made him the perfect complement to the family business. I never had that.

I chew on my bottom lip, wondering—not for the first time—if I have what it takes to be at the top of the Scalise Family. When the moment comes, will I have the guts to make the genuinely nasty calls? I hope so.

To top it off, Henry's confession of love is niggling in the back of my mind. I feel terrible that he fell for someone like me. It has been proven time and time again that I beget nothing but misfortune. He has saved my life more times than any one person should. The one way I know how to repay him is by wiping his brother's debt clean.

Is that payment enough, though? Forgiving that debt was part of our deal in the first place. It was the genesis of how we came to be. That and the three-point-five million dollars which will be deposited into Henry's account two weeks from tomorrow.

The idea that Henry Cain loves me is so far out of my periphery it seems impossible. He might like my body, but to love me for me? I don't know about that. No matter how much I try to talk myself into or out of confessing I love him too, there's always one stopper. He's a police officer. His mother is a retired detective. Me? I'm the head of the Scalise crime family. Nothing good could come from our union.

Sure, there's the option of leaving it all behind. I've fired Ray, my house is a heap of ash. I could walk away scot-free. But I won't. No matter how good a girl I am, I'm also a businesswoman. As long as there is a demand for the goods, I will continue to supply them. That fact will remain a source of contention between Henry, his family, and me. It's part of who I am. It's the world I know. After losing everything in my life, I'm not willing to give up that little bit of comfort. Not only does it add stress to a potential relationship, but it also puts Henry and his entire family in danger—as evidenced by the kidnapping and near suffocation of Brian. There's one thing left to do.

After dressing, I visit the front desk and purchase a burner phone I'd noticed when Henry and I had checked in. My first call is to Ray. I'm not sure what is going on, but I know my father was telling me anything but the truth.

"Hello?" Ray answers

"Do you believe him?" There's no point or time for greetings. I'm on a burner, and I only have so long before Ray traces my location.

"Charlotte," he breathes. "Where are you? Are you okay? What the hell were you think—"

I cut him off. "It doesn't matter. I need the highlights about what's actually going on. I don't have much time."

"Don't believe a word your father told you. Something isn't right, I'm trying to figure it out. Your father is too. I need you to lie low and have faith in me. And bug? For what it's worth, I'm sorry."

The sadness in Ray's apology floats through the line. Maybe I've been too hard on him? He's never given me a reason not to trust him, and I was so quick to toss him to the curb, never considering his efforts behind the scenes. There is so much I don't know about this business, and a wise woman would have secured all her resources to help her navigate this treacherous trade. I am not that woman. Even though I have some regrets, it doesn't change my position or what I need to accomplish to move forward.

"I know," I tell him, hitting the end button immediately after I speak. Time's up.

The next phone call is a bit trickier and definitely carries more weight in terms of risk. Without risk, there is no reward— or something like that.

"McHale," Jim answers, his voice gruff with sleep.

I've known Jim for as long as I can remember. He sniffed around my house, hopeful for any sliver of evidence that would nail Ray and Charlie to the wall. He was hard to pay off at first, sticking to his morals. Even before Charlie died, I knew he was a problem I needed to take care of. Every person, no matter how dedicated they are to the law, has their price. Jim McHale's silence was purchased with irrefutable proof of his affair.

"I need a favor."

He barks out a laugh. "I think you've been given all the favors you're going to get."

"Listen, I know it was you who approached Henry yesterday. I hate to think you're backing out on our deal. Perhaps you need a little more incentive."

He clears his throat, and I know I have his full attention now.

"I think your wife will be devastated to see those photos of you and someone else in the throes of passion."

"Maybe I'll tell her about the affair. Then where's your leverage? You don't scare me, Charlotte. You're a nobody. You'll never have the strength or brutality of your dad, Ray, or Charlie. You might as well give up now."

"That's true. I'm still new to this whole thing. But wouldn't it be interesting if your wife found out about your boyfriend? Or, how about if your boyfriend's wife found out about you? Better yet, what if it was leaked to the press? What a scandal it would be. I can see the headline now: Republican Presidential Nominee having an affair with a piece of poo-poo FBI agent."

The line goes silent for several beats, and I know I've won this round.

"What do you want?" he seethes.

I fill him in on a few piddly demands, and he readily agrees. I like to think this is the most altruistic blackmail scheme I've ever cooked up.

After we hang up, I call and make arrangements for what will most likely be the most expensive cab ride of my life.

Bag in hand, I slip a note under Henry's door and meet the cab idling at the front of the building. This is the hardest thing I've ever done. I'm leaving Henry behind to pursue a life of crime and immense wealth. Also, to save him from the heartache which will follow if I let our relationship develop any further.

Sadly, I can't say the same for myself.

29

Henry

I'm a shell of a human being when I pull into the driveway of my parent's house in Fort Lauderdale. I can't believe Charlotte up and left. The one thing to tell me how she felt was a torn-off sheet of motel paper stuck in my door jamb with the word "Sorry" scribbled on it. No signature, no declaration of love, nothing. One word. That's all she had to say for herself.

Aside from her note, she left me one other gift. A swarm of police cars and the FBI. Jim McHale and the tall guy to be precise. McHale was smug as ever wearing his FBI windbreaker and aviators. I was on my knees, my hands behind my head, and a dozen guns pointed at me. I spent eighteen hours in a jail cell in Podunk, USA, as I was interrogated.

McHale was on a fishing expedition, asking me what I learned at the mobster's ball. His questions were weak and suspicious. I'd bet my bottom dollar the Scalise Family has something on him, and he was stalling. To what end, I don't know, and I didn't give a flying fuck.

By the time they released me, my chest was aching so badly, there was a tingle racing down my left arm. I briefly thought I was in the middle of a heart attack but decided it was more likely the pain of a broken heart.

When the chips are down, an opportunity can present itself in the form of a highway billboard advertising a shooting range. Discharging my firearm to burn off steam is bad practice. What the hell, it seems everything I do is bad practice nowadays—why should this be any different? Shooting the shit out of a faceless paper man helped dull the ache of my heart and the jolting pain searing down my arm.

"You look like shit," Dad says as I walk into the kitchen. One glance from me and his head rears back. "You okay?"

Am I okay? Hell, I don't know. "Yeah," I tell him, shrugging off my tux jacket and peeling off my shoes. I leave them in a pile in the middle of the kitchen, not caring enough to clean up after myself.

I go upstairs and take a shower, but keep it brief because it isn't until the water hits my skin that I realize the last time I was in this shower was with her. Taking all my anger out on the shower curtain, I yank it back, and the rod falls to the ground.

I don't give a fuck. Like my clothes in the kitchen, I don't bother to fix the shower curtain either.

I wrap a towel around my waist and walk into my bedroom. What should greet me? A messy bed trapped in time. Eleven days ago, to be precise since I shared my childhood room with her.

The bed is so inviting I can't help but crawl under the cover and rub my face in the pillow she had used. It smells like my mom's shampoo and the unique sexy scent which is all Charlotte.

Now I feel weird about the hard-on that's happening under my towel.

Fuck it. This is the last thing I have of the woman who stole my heart and then ripped it to shreds.

"Hey," a soft voice says, rapping lightly on my bedroom door.

"You alright?"

My eyes open, and I look around. The sun is low, and I realize I must have fallen asleep. My sister stands at the threshold, concern crinkling her brow. I don't have it in me to deal with her, so I cover my head with a pillow, preferring to go back to sleep for the rest of my life. "Leave me alone."

Bea yanks the pillow away and sits next to me on the bed. "It's going to take a lot more than showing me your ass to get me to run."

I look up at her. Then at my ass. The towel must have come off while I was sleeping.

"Shut up," I tell her, covering myself with the blanket.

"Do you want to talk about it?"

I rip the pillow from her arms and smash it over my head. "*No*," I shout through the mattress.

"How's your friend? Is she doing okay?"

"Probably." I hate that I'm sulking, but I can't help it. All my emotions are at the surface like a hormonal fifteen-year-old.

The bed shifts and the pillow is once again yanked off my head. I sit up, ready to protest, but am stopped short when a pair of boxers are tossed in my face.

"Get your shit together," Bea says, using her trained voice of authority. "Mom just got off the phone and says she needs to talk to you."

I don't move, boxers still dangling.

"Now." The door slams shut as Bea leaves.

What the fuck? I am not in the mood to deal with Mom and her obsession right now. Bev Cain is irrationally obsessed with my love life. She was convinced Charlotte was "the one." A part of me wants to believe Mom is right. The other part of me thinks I'm a dumbass for even considering fantasies like true love.

Regardless, I have to face the music. Mom isn't going to let me out of this house until she has the opportunity to pry apart and dissect every part of mine and Charlotte's failed relationship.

After I dress, I head downstairs to find Mom and Dad

sitting on the couch in the living room. They're staring at me expectantly, and I have no clue what they want me to say.

"What?" I grind out, raising my hands in the air.

Mom and Dad are sitting on the couch like they did when I was seventeen trying to sneak in after curfew.

Mom points to the recliner across from her. "Sit."

There's no room for argument when it comes to dealing with Bev Cain, so I do as I'm told.

"Tell us what happened," Dad says, his words heavy with worry.

"You can't let a little fight get in the way," Mom advises. "The two of you are meant to be together. I can feel it in my soul."

If she had an inkling of how far down the rabbit hole I've fallen, she wouldn't be saying that. Mom knows Charlotte was in trouble, and her house burned to the ground. "You have no idea what you're saying, Mom. It isn't that simple."

Mom points her finger at me. "No. It is that simple. Love is simple. The people we love are complicated, and that's what makes it so complex. But, you have to fight for her. You two have something special, and it doesn't come along but once in a lifetime. Don't let her slip through your fingers."

I'm a police officer, I've had extensive training in crisis management and de-escalation techniques, yet I can't seem to contain my anger. I stand and stare down at my parents. "No. You don't understand. I'm a cop, and she's the head of a fucking crime family. We're oil and water, we don't mix. We can't be together. I respect and enforce the law, she breaks the law and profits from it. It doesn't get much different than that. This isn't a little fight. Some sort of miscommunication. This is the difference between right and wrong."

Dad stares up at me, his jaw set hard. "Sit. Down."

Never in my life have I yelled at my parents, and the look on Dad's face has me ready to run for my life.

"Good," Mom says when I obey. "I hope you feel better now. And yes, I'm aware of who Charlotte is."

I open my mouth, ready to fire a hundred questions at her, but she puts her hand up.

"Let me speak. I know who Charlotte is. And I know she's running the Scalise Family. But that doesn't matter to me. Answer me this. Do you love her?"

I want to say no. No, I don't love Charlotte. I don't love the way she says all the wrong things. The way she trips over her own feet. The way she smells like me after a night of making love. All of that would be a lie. Lying to myself or to Mom would be futile. "More than my own life."

Mom nods her head as if she expected that to be my answer. All the stuff she was spewing about love moments ago was her fishing for confirmation. She's a crafty woman. It's no wonder she was such a damn good detective.

"That's all that matters. Don't worry about the details that will work themselves out with time. You'll know what you need to do to make it work when the time comes. Now, tell me how you met a woman in her position."

I give my parents the high points and conveniently leave out the blackmail part, but I totally throw Brian under the bus. He almost freaking died because of his carelessness. Now, he must incur the wrath of Bev Cain.

"He *what?*" Mom screeches. "How much? What did he do?" She bolts from the couch and stomps to the staircase. "Brian Edgar Cain, you get your ass down here *right* this second."

Brian bounds down the stairs, already hunched over in defeat. "Uh, yeah?"

"How did you become indebted to the Scalise Family?" Dad asks as if he wants to know the stats of a Rays game or something.

Charlotte never told me what Brian did to bring this all about. At the time, I didn't want to know, but my curiosity is getting the better of me.

Brian scratches his arm with nervousness. "I thought it would be easy money. They needed someone to run a shipment to the Keys. At the time, I owed my bookie for some bad bets. It seemed easy enough. Drive a box truck south and drop it off. But, I pulled over at a rest stop to take a leak and left the keys in the ignition. When I came out, the truck was gone. I wasn't about to search out Simon and tell him I fucked up. He would've put a bullet in my skull in a heartbeat."

"Who's Simon?" Dad asks, rubbing the stubble along his jaw.

"Simon is some guy my bookie knew. He hooked me up with him, so I could pay back the money I owed."

Simon? Charlotte has never mentioned a man named Simon. "What did he look like?"

"I don't know. Average height, average build. I think he used to be in the Army or something. He always wore this raggedy army surplus jacket." Brian cocks his head, then looks back at me. "And he had this gnarly-looking mole above his lip."

My mind plays on a reel with the description Brian gave. The mole. I know who that is. Well, not exactly. I now know that the man who was in charge when the men stormed the Scalise compound and burned it down goes by the name Simon.

The army surplus jacket is another good clue. The American guy at the craft store talking with the Russians also wore the same type of coat. I didn't get a look at the guy's face, but it could definitely be the same man.

Another piece of the puzzle falls into place, but there's still more I need to figure out. "What were you transporting? Drugs, weapons?"

Brian shrugs his shoulders. "I don't know. It was weird, though. The radio was broken, and there was no way to hook up my phone. It was quiet the whole way, except every now and then I could swear I heard crying. Figured it was my imagination."

Fuck.

"Why didn't you tell me this shit earlier?" I bellow, pinning Brian against the wall.

His face turns red, anger boiling to the surface. "You didn't want to know," he reminds me, his jaw ticking as he speaks.

I don't have time to deal with this right now. I have to get to Charlotte. I let go of Brian and take the stairs two at a time, rushing to get my stuff.

As I shove clothes into a large bag, Mom knocks hesitantly on the open door. "I know you're in a hurry, but there's something else I need to talk to you about."

"'Hurry' is an understatement. Charlotte has no idea how much danger she's in," I huff, shoving my dirty tux into a bag.

After the info I received from Brian, it all started to come together. The man, Simon, is a mole. A mole with a big nasty tumor on his face. Who put him in that position, I'm not sure. Ray Thatch can't be ruled out quite yet. Ray may have saved Charlotte's life when she met with Vlad Petrovsky, but it doesn't mean he's on our side. Her side, not ours.

As for the mystery man Simon, I have a theory. Someone, whether Ray Thatch, Vlad, or someone else I don't know, has Simon doing their dirty work. Brian just happened to stumble into an "opportunity of a lifetime" and transported the Petrovsky's new business venture—human beings. Simon is doing all the bidding, infiltrating the Scalise Family, expanding the Petrovsky's business down the coast. Lord knows Miami is the perfect market.

Not to mention that Simon was the man who ran the operation to burn down the compound. I almost wonder if Charlotte's father isn't trying to take back what once belonged to him. If that's the case, then he ordered a hit on his own daughter. What kind of sick fuck does that?

"Yes, she does," Mom says. "You're the one who doesn't have a clue."

I stop packing and turn to look at her. "What do you know that I don't?" I ask, and I'm perilously close to losing my shit. She needs to quit holding out on me.

"I just got off the phone with one of my contacts from the ATF. I called him after you first brought Charlotte here. Don't get me wrong, I like her, and I want you two together. My friend called because he's concerned about some movement he's seeing. Several big names in organized crime are on the move and converging in Miami. He's preparing for the worst. There's about to be a war in Charlotte's world."

I snatch my duffle bag off the bed and run downstairs. Mom follows me but can't quite keep up. When I get into the garage, I dig through all the cabinets. "Where are the keys?" I ask Mom when she catches up.

"Which keys?"

"To the gun safe."

Mom points to the opposite wall of where I'm searching. "The top right drawer. Take everything, including the other key."

I pull out a Glock G19, a Colt Defender, and a Wesson Specialist. "What other key?"

"The one taped to the ceiling of the safe."

I look up, and sure as shit, there's a key secured with duct tape. "What's this go to?"

"The storage locker. You'll find everything you need there."

As angry as I was with Mom earlier, my heart fills with pure love. I wrap my arms around her and squeeze hard while giving her a sloppy kiss on the cheek. "You're the best mom in the world."

I grab the keys to my car, and one quick drive later I'm in the parking lot of a Public Storage. Mom was right. Everything I could ever want is in a self-storage unit in Miami's Little Haiti. It's not the nicest neighborhood, but what it lacks in safety it almost makes up for with its amazing Haitian culture.

The building was closed for the night, so I had to work a little magic with my lock picking kit. When I opened the locker, I thought I had died and gone to heaven.

I run my hand along a multitude of assault rifles—AK-103's, M-16's, and G36's. Uzi and MP5 submachine guns. Grenade launchers, tactical and combat knives, and Kevlar vests.

Holy shit, Mom's been holding out on me.

I gather up as much in my arms as I can and load up the

trunk. On my second round, I spy the impossible. "No," I mutter to myself, excitement and fire coursing through my veins. "A fucking flame thrower? Mom, I don't think I ever gave you the credit you deserved."

Two more rounds and my trunk is loaded with more weapons and ammo than I'd ever seen outside the ammunitions locker at the station.

30

Charlotte

Disney World is the happiest place on earth. I needed a little happiness in my life. Everything is crumbling around me, and I've never been to the Magic Kingdom. So, that is what Vince, my cab driver, and I did for an entire day. A hug from Snow White melted my worries away. A dance with Tigger rejuvenated my spirit. The mouse ears on my head helped me to embrace the child I used to be and accept the woman I've become.

After a day at the park, I made one last pit stop and purchased a new burner phone. I had tossed the other one out the window somewhere along I-95 the day before. When living a life of crime while blackmailing an FBI agent, precautions must be taken.

There is one specific phone number in the mobster's Rolodex which will forever remain unchanged. It had been instilled in me since the day my father left Charlie and me orphaned to the care of the help. Like the drills for the safe room, memorizing this number was a safeguard. One ring is all it requires, and the head of every major family in the Miami district is notified. Within 24-hours, the powers that be, which now includes me, will be meeting at a pre-determined location to discuss the next step in my plan.

Over a thousand dollars and one Disney World admission later, I am back in Miami. More specifically, in front of the charred remains of the only home I've ever known. The entire property is abandoned, exactly like me. I have no one left in my life. No parents, my brother is dead. I fired Ray and ditched Henry. There is no one left in this world for me. Would anyone even notice if I fell off the face of the earth? Maybe Amara, but I can't contact her either—it's too dangerous, and I would die before I would let anything happen to her.

I walk the perimeter and stand before the rubble which was one floor below my father's office. Remnants of my former life lie half–burnt or incinerated. An ember of red sticks out, the leftover of the Picasso painting which used to hang on the wall. A glint of silver catches my eye as I scan the remains. I step through the debris, almost tripping, and pluck the item from the ash. With a gentle touch, I dust it off, and soot covers my hand. It's the picture of my brother and me with John Scalise.

It was such a happy time. Innocence long lost. My heart stutters as memories come flooding back. I want to latch onto those thoughts for as long as possible. Life was so easy back then, and I didn't have the foresight to embrace my good fortune. A life of luxury and advantage that has turned sour. A sob breaks free, and tears slide down my cheeks. The picture falls into the rubble, and I drop to my knees, the anguish of everything lost is too much to bear.

"Charlotte?"

My name is called, but I can barely hear it through my grief.

"Cupcake? Are you okay?" Henry asks, bending next to me.

I want to answer, I want to look at his handsome face and believe everything will be okay, but I don't have the strength. There is no way I will be able to hold my composure. "Yeah." I wipe at my eyes. "I'm fine."

"Bullshit," Henry breathes as he stands. He wraps an arm around my waist and hauls me to my feet, pressing my face against his chest. "You don't have to do this alone, you know? I'm here. Whatever you need, I'm here."

His words are a balm to my wounded heart. They're exactly what I need to hear even if it isn't true. I cry again, but this time gut-wrenching sobs put my breakdown moments ago to complete and utter shame. I cry so hard, I fall short of wailing.

Henry murmurs gentle words of acceptance. His encouragement makes me cry harder. I crush myself against him, needing him with every cell in my body. Sacrificing him was the hardest thing I'd ever done, but I can't pull him into this mess. He has a life, a future. A future that can't include me.

"Hey, hey," he says, tipping my chin up to look at him. "It's okay. I've got you."

I nod because I desperately want him to have me. I don't have the strength I need to walk away from him right now. I wish I were stronger, but I'm not.

"Let me take you home."

I search his eyes, and I see home. Home is with Henry. Henry is my home. "Okay."

We don't speak on the drive. There are a hundred things which need to be discussed. Still, I'm not ready to discuss the hurdles of our relationship and our future. Our hands are laced together for the whole ride, and from time to time, Henry lifts our joined hands and kisses my sooty fingers.

"Do you mind if I get a shower?" I ask once we arrive at his place. The ash and sweat from the day mixed with my breakdown feels like weight I can wash away, unlike other problems.

"Absolutely. I'll grab your stuff from the car."

After my shower, I find my bag sitting on the bed in Henry's bedroom. I change into a pair of shorts and a T-shirt and wander out to the living room.

"Henry?" I call out, but no answer. I check the kitchen, but he isn't there either. Instead of snooping, like I did the last time I was in this house, I sit on the oversized recliner and turn on the television. I flip through channels until I find a movie that interests me and kick my feet up.

"Dinner's ready," Henry says, brushing a kiss across my forehead.

My eyes are crusty from sleep. I must have passed out while watching . . . What was I watching?

"I'm sorry," I tell Henry. I must have dozed off. I caught a brief nap on the cab ride to Disney World and haven't had a decent night's sleep since before the mobster's ball. "I didn't mean to fall asleep on you."

"I didn't want to wake you. You looked so peaceful," Henry says, oven mitts on his hands.

I follow him to the kitchen where he's pulling a casserole dish out of the oven. He sets it on a hot pad on the table which is complete with flowers, candles, and a bottle of wine.

"I'm not the best cook, but I make a mean tuna casserole," he says as he pulls out a chair for me.

"It smells wonderful, thank you." I scoop a serving onto his plate and then some onto mine as he pours the wine.

He settles across from me. "We need to talk."

I don't know if I want to do this right now. I'm exhausted, and I don't believe I can be direct yet tactful. As much as I would rather avoid this conversation, I can't. "We do."

"I didn't appreciate you leaving me a note to break this," he waves between us, "off. I deserve better than that."

"You do. Absolutely, you do. I . . ." How do I explain this to him? "I chickened out. I'm sorry." I take a bite of casserole. It's simple with cheese and peas, yet delicious. "This mess—my life, my family—this isn't what you signed up for. You have your entire future ahead of you. If we see this thing," I mimic him and wave my hand between us, "through, your life will irrevocably change. Your career will be over. Your family? Your mom is a retired detective. This can't work."

"Don't I have a say in this? You're so worried about my life, my future, but you forget it's my choice. A part of me broke when I found that note."

Is he out of his mind? His whole life will go down the drain if he follows me through the sewers. "I won't let you do this. The price you'll pay is too much. Your family will disown you."

He smiles around a mouthful. "No, they won't."

"You don't know that."

"Actually, I do. I've already spoken to my mom. It seems you've charmed her like you've charmed me. She knows who you are. She knows your history."

I've been outed. How long until the SWAT team, the FBI, NSA, and God knows who else surrounds the house? My mouth hangs open, chewed food on display. As soon as I realize it, I snap my mouth shut, swallow, and finish my glass of wine in one gulp. "She knows?"

Fear and shock must be written all over my face because Henry covers my hand with his. "It's okay," he promises. "She wants us to be together. She thinks you're the one for me. And I don't disagree."

I love him more than I ever thought I could love one person. My heart, my soul belongs to him, but I have yet to speak the words. "What are you saying?"

He rounds the table until he's standing next to me. He gazes down, his eyes soft, holding a hand out. I take it and rise to meet his stare.

"It means, my sweet Charlotte, that I love you. And I'm willing to do whatever it takes, give up everything I have to be with you."

I want to say the words back, but he deserves better than the life he would have with me. "You don't know what you're saying," I plead. "You can't give everything up for me. It isn't fair."

He cups my jaw and runs his nose along my cheek. "What isn't fair is spending one more night without you. I need you, cupcake."

I need him so much. I press my mouth against his. Craving his flavor, I sweep my tongue across the bow of his lip.

He growls, his want vibrating through him, pulling me against him and crashing his mouth to mine. His hips jut against me, his cock contained by his jeans.

"You can have me. I'm all yours. I love you." The admission liberates me of any inhibition. I pull down my shorts and hop on the table, lying back and spreading my legs.

A smile ghosts across his stunning face. "You've made a meal of yourself."

"Yes. Now, feast on me." I've never been a seductress. Heck, I was a virgin until this man, but I want more than anything to feel his tongue against my most intimate parts.

"As you wish." His head dips between my legs, and he runs his tongue along my slit. A gentle finger follows up as he laves at my bud.

My hands fly to my breast, my nipples peaking against the cotton of my T-shirt. Henry's silky hair tickles the inside of my thigh, and I think I'm ready to lose my mind.

"Henry," I cry, trying to hold back my release. I'm not ready yet. I want this to last.

His teeth scrape against my folds while he pushes a finger inside my entrance. "It's okay, cupcake, let go. I want to taste you. I want to lick up every drop you have to give."

He draws the bundle of nerves into his mouth, and I'm helpless to stop the runaway train of my climax. My back bows and I thrust my center against his face. The stubble of his jaw is a match to a flame.

"Fuck, you're gorgeous," he says, removing his fingers from my channel. He pulls a condom from his pocket and shucks his jeans down his legs.

My orgasm continues to wrack through me as he plunges deep into my tight center. I choke out a breath, unable to withstand the searing pleasure of him filling me.

"Fuck, you feel so good. I'll never get enough," Henry says, pulling me upward and crashing his mouth against mine.

A tremor washes over me as another release pulses through my body. Henry's thrusts increase in speed, his tempo erratic. The veins in his neck bulge, and I lick and nip at his neck as he roars his rapture.

31

Henry

Charlotte spent the entire night in my arms. After several rounds of making love, she passed out from exhaustion. I don't blame her, she's had a busy few days. I'm not sure what she's been up to since she left the motel that night. Nor do I know her plans for the future. What I do know is that I am a part of that future regardless of how things shake out.

"Would you like some pancakes?" I ask Charlotte as she pads out to the kitchen, her hair a mess from sleep.

A grin of satisfaction spreads across her face, and I love knowing I'm the one who satisfied her.

"That sounds great." Charlotte grabs my cup of coffee and takes a sip, her face turning sour as she gags.

I can't hold back my smile. "Would you prefer a cup of tea?" I ask, remembering she prefers tea or juice over coffee in the morning.

"Yes, please," she answers, setting the cup down.

"I don't have any green tea. Will Orange Pekoe work?"

"Anything is better than coffee." She digs around in the cabinet as I whip up the batter for pancakes.

"Why don't you like coffee? Is it too bitter?"

She sets a cast-iron pan on the stove and flicks on the burner. "The smell of coffee is amazing. Invigorating even. I've tried a million times to like the nectar of the gods, but I can never get past the taste."

"Maybe creamer would help," I suggest as I pour a ladle-full of creamy mix onto the preheated pan.

She shakes her head. "You know that deep-down-coffee-taste every coffee drink has? The one which can't be covered up? That's the part I don't like," she tells me, swinging the spatula in my direction for emphasis.

We work together in harmony as I cook sausage links, and she griddles a towering stack of pancakes. She sips from her tea and forks some food onto her plate.

"So, what's on the agenda today?" I have no clue what she has planned. I wanted to ask her a thousand times last night but didn't want to ruin the mood. I'd just confessed that I am head over heels in love with her. I needed her to trust me so we can work through this together.

She chews on a bite of pancake, then takes her time cutting up her food. She's stalling. Still, I wait. Hurrying her along will do nothing for us. Once her plate is clean and her teacup empty, she sits back in her chair and rests her hands on a bloated abdomen.

She pats her belly as it gurgles. "About that. Listen, I know you want to be a part of this. And I admire that. But, I've had a lot of time to think, and I believe it's best if you stay here."

I take a sip of my coffee and raise an eyebrow at her. She's a tough cookie, that's for sure. "I don't think so."

Her face reddens, and her gaze narrows. "You don't have a choice. Things are about to get ugly. So ugly, even I don't want to be a part of this. And I'm the one spurring it on. Those men you met at the Painting Palette? They're kittens compared to the people I've contacted."

I pick up our plates and walk them to the sink. "All the more reason you need me there. You can't do this alone. I'm more than prepared to help you any way I can."

She laughs at my offer, and I take a profound hit to my pride. I grab her by the hand and walk her to the garage.

"I don't know what you think you can show me to change my mind because I won't bend on this," she tells me as I flick on the light.

As the room illuminates, her words trail off as she takes in the stockpile of weapons in the middle of the garage. "Is that a flame thrower?"

I chuckle at her surprise. "Yeah."

She walks around the space, checking everything out. "Grenades?"

"Yup."

"Where did you get all this stuff?"

I shove my hands in my pockets and rock on my heels. "My mom," I tell her, pride swelling in my chest. "She gave me a key to a storage locker. Said I might need a few things."

"Wow. I guess your mom really is on board with this whole illegal business thing."

"I wouldn't go quite that far," I wrap my arms around her waist and pull her back to my chest. "She's on board with me being with the woman I love."

She lets out a deep sigh and turns around. Her green eyes staring up at me. She rubs the tip of her nose against mine and presses a gentle kiss to my mouth.

I want to lay her on the floor and make love to her. Again. I can't get enough of this woman. My hands travel down her back to her ass, and I give a firm squeeze, the supple flesh stirring my cock to life.

"Again?" She asks with a laugh as I press my hard-on against her belly.

"I can't help it. You drive me crazy, cupcake."

She moans as I run my tongue along the column of her throat. "Why do you call me 'cupcake'?"

"Because the first time I saw you, I thought you were adorable, and I wanted nothing more than to know how you tasted."

"The consensus?"

"Even sweeter than I imagined." My hand travels down her shorts, while the other works its way to her breasts. As I access her warm center, I'm pleased to discover she's already soaked for me.

"We can't," she whispers, but it's a half-hearted plea.

"Sure we can."

"Not if you want to know the plan," she counters. "I have to leave in thirty minutes for a meeting."

I drop my forehead to hers and groan with disappointment. "You're sure?"

"A hundred percent."

"Damn."

"Come on," she says, grabbing my hand and pulling me into the house.

We sit on the sofa, my erection still thick, and refusing to go away as I stare at her peaked nipples. "So," I clear my throat, "what's the plan?"

"On my way back to Miami, I made contact with business partners." She says "partners" like they trade real estate or something, not drugs, weapons, and humans. "What my father's doing is wrong. I know I'm not in the most altruistic business or anything—"

I snort, and she gives me a disapproving look. "Sorry."

"Anyway, we aren't the best people, but human trafficking is a no-go. No one the Scalise Family is affiliated with dabbles in such abhorrent business. It's because of this that I've called a meeting. Today. Everyone who is anyone will be there."

What? Okay, I know, I was ready for anything, but this? Not so much. I figured it would be like Rambo versus . . . anyone. Not an entire crime syndicate. "So what, you're going to war? Some

Godfather type of shit?"

She shakes her head as she considers my question. "Not necessarily. Maybe? I don't know. I'm sure we'll strive for a peaceful solution. But we need to expect the worst."

Mom told me her connections were expecting a war, but it's different to hear the words from Charlotte. By the nervous look on my cupcake's face, I doubt peace is possible.

"I'm not certain what ideas the other guys will come up with, but I don't think we're going to find a diplomatic way around this," Charlotte says. "I understand if this isn't something you're up for. I want to protect you. I told you it was going to get ugly. We haven't even gotten to the ugly part yet, and you look like you're having second thoughts."

Last night I promised to stand by her. That I would do whatever it takes. Now? Now, it's become all too real.

—

Charlotte

Everything I've done—leaving him at the motel, sending McHale in to interrogate him—has been to keep him as far away from this as possible. Last night, he wanted nothing more than to stand by my side. Now the moment has come, and he's having doubts.

"It's okay," I soothe, patting his knee. "This is a big deal. Being associated with me will forever alter your life. I understand if you've changed your mind. If I could, I would too. This is you're out. Take it now or forever hold your piece. There is no going back."

He winces at my words as if I've hit a nerve. "I'm not backing out. It's just a lot to take in. Give me a minute."

He leans into the sofa and turns on the TV. We don't have time for this, I need to leave in less than fifteen minutes if I want to make it on time. Tardiness is kind of frowned upon. Still, I'll give him a couple more minutes to process his decision.

"Can't we run away to a deserted island?" he asks, laying his head on my lap.

I run my fingers through his silky brown hair. "That would be easier. But I can't do that. If I don't stand up and do something, who knows how many women and children will be auctioned off for God knows what purpose."

He bolts upright. "Good point. Let's go."

As we drive down the highway, he peppers me with questions. I think his mom may have looked a little too far into my background.

"What is your first memory with your dad?"

I shrug my shoulder. "I don't know." I think back as far as I can. So many of my memories are ones I've chosen, blocking out all the scary and bad things my child-like mind couldn't interpret. "Me, my dad, and Charlie were coloring in books, lying on our tummies as the news broadcasted on the television. Some old guy on the news talking about economic collapse." There, that one wasn't too bad.

"That's sweet," Henry says, changing lanes. "How old were you?"

"Five or six, maybe? I'm not sure." He's dancing around a subject, and I think I know what he's searching for. "Just spit it out, Henry. What do you want to know?"

Henry makes a hard right onto the side of the road, gravel skipping behind the tires from the rigid brake. Car horns blare as they swerve around us after the sudden lane change.

He shoves the gearshift into park and the car jerks. He turns in his seat and stares me down.

"What is the matter with you? You had all the time in the world to pump me for information yesterday and this morning. I told you when we were at your house to speak up or shut up. Why all of a sudden are you desperate for the money shot?"

He whoops out a guffaw as he holds his stomach, his face turning almost purple.

The heat of my anger rushes from the tips of my toes and up my neck. "What? What are you laughing at? Nothing about this is funny."

"No, no. Of course it's not. It's just that you said," Henry laughs some more. His chuckle wanes, and he collects himself. He takes a deep breath and speaks, but the smile on his face remains. "I know it's not funny. I'm sorry. What I was trying to ask was what happened that your father decided to go back to the Petrovsky's?

"When Charlie and I turned sixteen, Ray sat us down and explained what happened the night my father left. He said the Petrovsky's had wanted my father to get into some dark business and my father refused. That sparked a war between my father and his brother. His brother, who I never once heard my father mention, was the second in command, below my grandfather. My grandfather was in his late seventies and still running the family but was considering some new ventures."

"Human trafficking," Henry suggests.

"Most likely," I say. "So the story goes, my father had to make a decision. Risk his children's lives to save the Scalise Family or run the Petrovsky's. Ray claimed my father knew we would be safer with Ray. That, if he stayed, the Petrovsky's would always be after us. The best way to protect us was to fake his death and take over his own family's business.

Henry scrubs the stubble on his jaw. "Now that he's been running the Russian family for so long, I guess sex slavery doesn't seem so dark to him anymore."

"I don't buy it. My father sacrificed everything because he wouldn't sink that low. Including taking out his own father. It's inconceivable that he would change his mind. But what do I know? Until last Saturday, I haven't seen the man in thirteen years. I guess people change."

Even as I say it, I don't believe it. The truth is staring me in the face, but my unwillingness to accept doesn't change the facts.

Henry takes a moment as he absorbs the colossal info dump I laid out. "Most of it makes sense, but something still feels off.

I can't quite put my finger on it."

Him and me both.

Henry checks the traffic and merges onto the highway. As I direct him on which exit to take, he turns to me and asks the one question I haven't even considered. "Whatever happened to your uncle?"

"I have no idea."

32

Henry

Charlotte directs me onto a few back roads where it feels like we are a million miles from civilization. My temporary cell phone doesn't even work out here. There is no one to hear screams for help, no backup, nothing. The last time we met with the other heads of family, I didn't have so many reservations. Maybe I was hyped on adrenaline, convinced I could take on the world and save the princess at the same time. So much has happened, so many things have changed. My entire worldview has shifted. That, and I'm helplessly in love with Charlotte. Maybe that's the difference. Before, I wanted to square my brother's debt—and maybe bang Charlotte too if the opportunity arose—but now I have a lot more skin in the game.

"Where are we?" I ask Charlotte as we get out of the car. We're parked in a dusty gravel lot filled with armored vehicles situated in front of what appears to be a palatial-style greenhouse. The glass building is gigantic, the sun streaming in. It's beautiful and inspiring. It's probably a plantation for marijuana or something.

The area is densely populated with gators, which would be a pretty strong deterrent from theft, in my humble opinion.

"Scalise Greenhouse," Charlotte replies, flipping her sunglasses on top of her head. She points to the West. "And over there is Gertrude's Gator Farm."

We walk through massive glass doors and traverse the masses of flowers and shrubbery, the air sweet with lavender.

"Do you own the Gator Farm too?" I ask, stepping over a hose running along the floor.

"Yeah. It's good business," is all Charlotte says as she slips an apron around her neck. "Just like last time, you need to hang with the other security guys. Make yourself comfortable. Get to know them, become friends. If you want to be a part of my world, forging alliances is the first step."

My ego takes a hit at her words. She's right, of course, but it doesn't mean I have to like it. I want to be with her, sitting at the big kid's table. I have just as much, if not more, to lose. Hanging back and letting the grown-ups do the talking isn't sitting well with me. I approach a group of men who all look like they were cut from granite, topped off with buzz cuts and tight shirts. Aside from the hair, I think I'm going to fit in without much trouble.

"You're the new guy with the Scalise's, right?" A tall man with a stone jaw ambles up to me, his hand outstretched. "I think we met at the Painting Palate a few weeks ago."

I recognize him as Francisco Diaz's head of security. I shake his hand. "Yeah, Henry. Nice to meet you."

"Alberto, it's a pleasure. Come, sit with us. We're about to break out a game of Texas Hold'em. You in?"

"Sounds great." I follow him to an area off to the side from where the hotshots are sitting.

I keep one eye trained on Charlotte at all times and watch as she smiles, shaking hands with her associates—and I use the term loosely. These people may have converged for one common goal, but only so much as it impacts them or their wallets. I remember something Charlotte said to me, *a gentleman will attend the wedding and dance with the bride, then whack-off the father in the bathroom.* The memory has me smiling to myself. My sweet, naive queen pin.

The men fawn over Charlotte as they kiss her cheek and hug her a little too long for my liking. I recognize a few of the men she's meeting—all the same ones from the last time. Then there are a few others I can't quite place. From time to time, I've seen videos or pictures of them on the news. However, there was nothing concrete as to what they deal in. Come to think of it, I'm still not sure what all the Scalise Family is into. I make a mental note to ask Charlotte about it on the drive back to my place. Initially, I didn't want to know the damage to her family, preferring to remain ignorant. Now that I've all but jumped into the deep end, I think it's time I find out what Charlotte will be peddling.

"Henry, I'd like you to meet Shane, Caleb, Armando, Sven, Scottie, and Buck."

I shake hands with all the men. "What about them?" I ask, pointing my thumb to several men walking the perimeter of the greenhouse.

"Them?" Alberto says, "They don't play well with others," he laughs, and the other card players also laugh as Sven deals the cards.

"Good enough for me," I mumble, pulling up a crate to sit on and join the game.

As the game rolls, I continue to watch Charlotte and am taken aback when she works to fill pots with dirt.

"What are they doing?" I ask Buck.

Buck looks up and gives a boyish smile. "They're gardening. They pot plants and have them delivered to nursing homes. Helps to cheer up the old people."

"This whole mobster thing isn't at all like the movies." At The Painting Palate, the world's deadliest men painted poor reproductions of famous portraits and sipped wine. It still blows my mind.

Armando snickers at my comment. "Not everything is like the movies. But some things are spot on."

"Are you going to hold 'em or fold 'em?" Caleb jabs Buck.

Buck throws in a pile of chips. "I'll see your five and raise you twenty."

"Too rich for my blood," Sven calls, as do the rest of us.

Caleb takes the pot with a full house, and Buck mutters a string of expletives under his breath.

"You think that customs agent is going to make it?" Scottie asks, sweeping the place with his gaze.

"What customs agent?" As far as I know, the only people invited were the heads of certain families. "Why would they invite him?"

Armando shrugs his shoulder. "I overheard one of the guys walking around that Petrovsky invited some man who was managing the ports for them."

"Petrovsky? I hadn't heard anything about him attending." I toss in a couple of chips and try to keep a typical poise, but my insides are stirring with fury and fear.

I'm not sure how Charlotte feels about her father, I think she's on the fence about him. What child wants to believe the worst in their parent? No matter Charlotte's position, I don't trust Vlad Petrovsky any farther than I can throw him.

"Not that Petrovsky," Scottie answers. "The other one—Maxym. It seems Vlad sent his brother in his stead."

The missing piece of the puzzle is right here in this room. In the car we were both curious as to what happened to her uncle, now we know. The man is sitting across a table from his niece, potting plants.

The front door of the greenhouse opens, and every armed personnel stands in response, drawing their weapon—myself included.

"Relax," Armondo says as he sits back down. "It's just Simon, the customs agent I was telling you about."

33

Charlotte

"Charlotte, I wish I could say I'm glad to see you. But, under the circumstances..." Jimmy "The Wonder Boy," Bevino says. His words linger as he embraces me in a hug that lasts a few seconds past appropriate.

Jimmy is the boss of the Bevino Family, ruling over Brooklyn. Racketeering is their game, and they're major league players. Having them on our side is paramount to winning the war which is about to be waged.

"I know. I wish it were with better news as well," I tell Jimmy as I step out of his embrace.

Some of the men I'm associating with, I've known my entire life, but there are quite a few I've never met. The emergency number is used to contact our allies. Although I was given the information to assemble them, I've been kept far enough away from the action not to know everyone.

Jimmy gives me the run-down of who's in attendance. One of the bosses on the other side of the flowers, catches my attention because he's staring at me. His beady eyes make my skin crawl. He's brooding, with dark red hair and a barely perceptible scar over his right eye—just like my father.

"Who's that," I ask Jimmy with the jut of my chin.

Jimmy frowns. "That's Maxym Something-or-other. Some prick from Russia. I've met him once. He gives off bad vibes."

At least I'm not the only one getting the creeper feels from this Maxym guy. I don't have too much time, I need to get this meeting underway. I have no idea how long it will be before the first shipment of women arrives in Miami. I'm guessing not too long since the auction was five days ago. I have days, maybe hours to get this plan worked out.

"Gentleman," I call out to rouse their attention. "If you would, please browse the flowers, pick the top five which strike your fancy, and meet at the round table. There are pots and dirt at your ready. Pick diligently. Remember these flower arrangements will be sent to nursing homes all across the city. They will brighten the lives of the generations who have given so much for us to be here today."

The men do as they're bid, careful to select the perfect plant. These tough guys look ridiculous as they gather around the table, sliding on gardening gloves. Even more preposterous when they begin digging with spades to marshal their gifts to the community. My heart swells with pride for my fellow mobsters that we should all enjoy something so domesticated, the men chattering and laughing as they pot and plot.

"Some of you are aware that my dear brother, Charlie, has passed," I announce as I remove a Colorado Blue Columbine with the utmost care. "Since the former John Scalise has switched sides and assumed his birthright with the Petrovsky's, I am adopting my brother's role. Jane Scalise, if you please," I declare with a chuckle.

Not a word is spoken as I proclaim my position at the head of the family. I'm the sole female in this entire greenhouse, and I have these men's full respect regardless. I must be doing something right.

"The reason I've called this meeting is that I've learned some disturbing news." I swallow the lump in my throat. This is the moment that will change everything. "I know we're not in the noblest of professions."

Jimmy Bevino, Ove Lindholm of Sweden, and Carlo Messina let out a small chuckle at my little joke.

"But I like to think we have a moral code of conduct. Sure, it can be stretched thin, but there are some lines we will not cross."

"Could you be more specific, Mademoiselle?" Cédric Baugé of Paris asks.

"Human trafficking. I suspect for sex slavery, but as long as someone is willing to pay the price, the reason is of no real consequence."

The men at the table gasp with shock.

"Who is it that is committing this atrocity?" Benedikt Raddatz of Berlin asks.

"Vlad Petrovsky. My father."

The men throw down their spades, knocking over their pots as the outrage spreads like a virus.

I hate that I've thrown my father to the wolves. That I, a mobster's daughter, have ratted him out. Despite my reservations on whether or not my father is complicit, I have to look at the facts.

No one but the former John Scalise would have the in-depth knowledge of the Miami market to be able to deploy illegal goods so swiftly. No one but Vlad Petrovsky would have his own flesh and blood kidnapped and thrown in a dungeon. I would like to also blame my father for the death of Charlie, but no matter what way I slice the cake, it doesn't cut evenly enough that I buy into that accusation.

"I know. I know," I holler over the crowd. "The problem at hand is that my father seems to be looking to expand his business down the coast, from New York to Miami. Lord only knows where it will go from there. That's why I've called this meeting. I don't possess the experience that you gentleman have. And although I have some thoughts on what should be done, it's my duty to inform you all and solicit your thoughts on the matter."

"Y'all need to get your shit straight," Tyrel Ross of New Orleans announces. "This is some serious shit. I ain't no angel, but every man or woman has the right to choose the course of their own lives. Ain't no fuckin' Russian gonna fuck with my business."

Maxym stands and flaps his arms up and down like a bird. "Friends, please. Let us settle down. Getting riled will not help the situation. I have a contact within U.S. Customs, who I have been working closely with. He took care of a problem a few weeks ago for me, and I believe he can help now."

A man walks through the doors of the greenhouse, and every security man draws their weapon, including Henry.

"Here he is now," Maxym cheers.

Each security man looks to their respective boss for the nod to lower their guns. One by one, they all do. Except Henry.

Henry's face is hard, his gun poised and at the ready. I can feel the tension rolling off him from a hundred feet away.

"Charlotte, everyone, I would like to introduce you to my friend Simon."

Simon makes the rounds and shakes hands with some of the deadliest men on the planet. I can't get a good look at his face, but his stature is brawny and tough, dressed in a pair of relax-cut jeans and a camouflage army jacket.

When Simon reaches me, the sun shines through the glass ceiling, almost blinding me. I can't quite see his face, but his profile seems familiar. I've seen him somewhere, but I can't put my finger on it.

"Pleasure to meet you," Simon says, giving a slight bow at the waist.

"Yes, um, yeah," I stutter as dread fills my gut. "Nice to meet you too."

My gaze flicks to Henry, in search of some clue as to what's happening. Henry sits on his crate and keeps his gun perched on his knee beneath the table. Whatever is going on, I have to play nice before this falls apart and someone gets hurt.

Or dead.

"Why don't you join us," I suggest. "Pick out some flowers to plant. They're all being donated to a good cause."

Simon chuckles with a shake of his head and mutters, "Since when do crime lords give back to the community?"

Maxym resumes his potting. "Simon has been instrumental in allowing us to continue our business at the port."

"How is that?" Ove inquires as he separates the petals of some red Geraniums.

"It is true that many officers have been reassigned at the port. But my friend has been a constant," Maxym says, pointing his thumb toward Simon. "Thanks to him, the feds are off our scent. The newest shipment is due to arrive via a contracted cruise line. A new beginning is on the horizon. And we stand to make a lot of money."

The cruise lines. Everything falls into place like leaves in autumn fall to the ground. My father is using the cruise lines to transport his new cargo—humans. My skin itches with nerves, and I urgently want to have a pow-wow with Henry. Still, I can't lose my grip in front of these men, or my reputation will crumble before it's even built.

"He was working for the Scalise's, running shipments to their destinations until the right opportunity presented itself," Maxym finishes.

Working for us? I don't remember anyone named Simon on our payroll at any time in my adult life. I might not have rubbed elbows with the who's who of the underground world, but I sure as heck knew who was working for my family. Simon isn't one of them.

Simon situates himself next to Maxym with an array of

begonias, marigolds, and Touch-Me-Nots. When he looks up at me, I get a good view of his face. What I see steals my breath.

A mole. Just above Simon's lip. It's big and black and maybe cancerous. He should have that looked at. The mole explains why Henry is on high alert, his finger on the trigger.

I clear my throat to tamp down my nerves. "Thank you, Simon, for all you've done to ensure our business continues as usual."

The words are like acid on my tongue. To thank the man who burned down my home and tried to kill me is far beyond my ability to comprehend.

"Hey, are you okay?" Jimmy asks, whispering in my ear. "You're white as a ghost."

I'm fighting to be brave, but apparently doing a poor job if Jimmy notices.

"Yeah, Charlotte," Simon chimes in. His voice is thick and grates against my eardrums. "What's wrong? You act like you've seen the devil or something."

The glint in his eyes tells me he's baiting me. He wants a reaction. To show me he's the master and holds the power. He's no one's master, and I am the one with the most power in this room. Now, if I can convince my bladder of that because I think I'm about to pee my pants.

What would Ray do if he were here?

No. What would Charlie do?

Scratch that, it doesn't matter because they aren't here, and I am. So what would Jane Scalise do?

She would kick ass. "I agree, Simon. The devil is in this room. And it's not you. Gentlemen," I say, addressing my new colleagues. "I'm afraid we have a traitor amongst us."

The attention of every person in the room is on me, and it's terrifying.

There's no going back now. "Excuse me Maxym, but your friend here is a problem," I say addressing the man named Maxym.

He smiles, but it doesn't reach his eyes. "Maxym? Is that any way to address your uncle, my dear, by his first name? Where I come from it shows a lack of respect."

The blood drains from my face and rushes straight to my stomach. I'm not sure if I want to pass out or puke. I never knew my uncle's name, and now that I get a closer look, I can see a slight resemblance to my father. Maybe they have different mothers? Aside from the sharp Slavic nose, broad shoulders, and coincidental matching scar, there isn't much to suggest Maxym and my father are related. I force the knowledge to the back of my mind. It's time to be the Jane Scalise my family needs me to be.

"Respect? That's rich because no respectable man would commit the sin you did, Uncle Maxym," I say, keeping my tone even and void of emotion.

Maxym clears the guilt from his throat. "I'm not sure what you're talking about."

"Did you think no one would notice you ordered a hit on your nephew?"

"You're being ridiculous," Maxym says, glancing around the room as if trying to convince my colleagues I'm crazy.

I spread the soil around the flowers in my pot. "Let me tell you what I think. I think you saw an opportunity when Charlie showed up in New York."

"That's an interesting story, Charlotte, but there isn't an ounce of truth in it."

"You're right. You probably didn't have the guts to do it." I goad.

Maxym sniggers and I know I've got him. "I did it once. I'll do it again."

I know I spurred this on but, boy oh boy do words hurt. "What did you just say?" I stand and plant both hands on the table in front of me, faking every ounce of bravado.

"You are a minor inconvenience, Charlotte. Charlie was the real threat. You are a mere thorn in my side."

"My friend," Francisco Diaz speaks and steps beside me. "I think you underestimate our allegiance. We are family. Dysfunctional? Yes. But, family nonetheless. Most of us have known each other for decades. You have been with this network for what, three months? Who do you think we're going to trust? You, or sweet Charlotte, whom I've known since her christening? You do not hold any power in this room. And are severely outnumbered."

All the bodyguards stand and raise their guns, pointing them in Maxym and Simon's direction.

Maxym raises his hands in defense. "So it would seem. But there is something more powerful than guns."

Carlo Messina steps forward. "And what would that be?"

"Information," Maxym answers.

"Information?" I ask. "Fine. How about you tell everyone here what happened to Charlie? He was the successor to the Scalise Family, and I don't think anyone here appreciates you snuffing out his life." A tear streaks down my cheek, and I hate the sudden display of weakness.

I have no desire to learn the circumstances of my twin brother's death. I suppose some people believe closure is obtained by details. I am not one of those people. The trauma of losing Charlie is enough on its own merits.

A hoard of guns remains directed at Maxym and Simon. I scan the room and assess everyone's position, but more importantly, search for Henry. Where is he? I'm not sure what he's up to because what could be more important than what is happening right now? What I do know is that I need to stall.

"He was a slippery young man. A real speedster," Maxym answers. "A simple cut to his brake lines was all it took. That and the cyanide-laced energy drink he had as he was driving."

My throat constricts, and there isn't enough air. The pain of knowing how my brother died brings about visions of Charlie foaming at the mouth, gasping for air as he speeds toward his death.

"But it is the secrets that you hold which are the most intriguing," Maxym prods. "I think everyone in this room would like to know the truth. The truth that they have been betrayed. By you, *Jane* Scalise." He says my title name as a joke followed by a chuckle.

For all intents and purposes, the name "Jane Scalise" was a joke. The accusation he's throwing is not funny in the least.

"What are you talking about?" There is nothing in my life I'm hiding. My story is an open book, and several of the men here today know everything worth knowing. Whatever information he has, it's either blown out of proportion or completely fabricated.

Okey, an Appalachian moonshine runner with bare feet and no last name, steps forward. "Explain yourself, boy."

"She has brought a police officer into our midst."

Except that.

The weapons which were drawn fall to the sides of every bodyguard in the room. The protection I felt is gone in the blink of an eye.

"You better explain yourself, Petrovsky," Finlay McCabe grates out, "and quick."

My heart swells with relief as the final pieces fall together, and I realize my father is not the monster he tried to portray. Instead, all this carnage was caused by Maxym.

Maxym continues. "It seems her bodyguard is one of Miami's finest in blue. And to top it off, his mother is a retired homicide detective. I have it on good authority that his mother has made contact with some U.S. agencies. How is your friend Agent McHale doing, Charlotte?"

This is bad, bad, bad. Worse than I ever could have imagined. Where on God's green earth is Henry? "He's doing fine. And I won't let this accusation discredit me or my loyalty. Every person in here has some connection to the law. We wouldn't be able to function without their cooperation. I won't let Maxym skew the truth for his benefit."

"Is it true?" Jimmy asks. "Is your bodyguard a cop?"

The rest of the men murmur their incredulity. I don't need to hear what they're saying to know I'm losing their faith and trust.

"It's true," I admit to the crowd. "My bodyguard is a police officer. I had to seek outside help after Charlie died. I didn't know who to trust. I was worried—and rightfully so—that I was next on the list."

"Bloody hell," McCabe mutters, scrubbing a hand over his face. "This is a real feckin' mess."

Movement in the opposite corner of the greenhouse catches my eye, and I realize it's Henry. He's crouched low, hiding behind several potted palms. He spies me looking at him and raises a finger to his lips, telling me to keep quiet. He's up to something, and I can only hope he has a plan to get us out of this mess with our lives and limbs intact.

I turn my back to Uncle Maxym and give Finlay my full attention. "I know. I'm sorry. I didn't know what else to do. I didn't even trust Ray. I was on my own, and I had to find a way to survive."

An arm wraps around my waist and pulls me backward. A loud yelp tears from my throat, and the bodyguards raise their weapons once again.

"Everyone, get back, or I swear to God I'll slit her pretty little throat," Simon's husky voice pierces my ear while the tip of his knife pierces my neck.

"Please don't do this," I beg Simon as my associates take several steps away from me.

"Shut up," Simon spits, his hot breath blowing over my ear. "I'm getting tired of you, you know that? You've been nothing but a pain in my ass. It's time to roll the fucking credits on this show."

34

Henry

Crouched behind a potted palm, I watch as everything changes. One minute, I'm playing cards, the next Simon has arrived as the guest of honor to Charlotte's newly discovered uncle, and all hell has broken loose.

As Charlotte turns to McCabe and begs for forgiveness and understanding, Simon reaches into his pocket. A glint of metal refracts from the sunlight beaming through the glass ceiling. It's a knife, and it's huge—like Crocodile Dundee huge. There's no time to assess, it's pure instinct and muscle memory to guide my actions. I jump from my position and run toward Charlotte, McCabe, and Simon. As the blade presses against Charlotte's neck, my heart plummets to my feet with fear.

The toughest men in the world are in this greenhouse, and the ones dressed to the nines take a step back from Charlotte. Every fucking one of them is a coward. I don't care what Simon demands, they need to be men and help her. Their henchmen, on the other hand, are armed and at the ready with their guns pointed toward Simon and Charlotte.

Simon's mouth rests against Charlotte's ear as he whispers something. The idea that his breath has touched a single fucking inch of her beautiful body spouts flares of anger through my veins.

"Put your goddamn guns down," Simon screams. The veins in his neck bulge, the mole above his lip reddens with anger. Can moles do that?

All the members of security do as he says. Logically, I know it's the wise choice, but I've never been a lemming so, why start now? My gut has navigated Charlotte and me through each disaster we've encountered, and I refuse to change course.

"Not gonna happen," I tell Simon, my gun still raised.

Charlotte cries out as Simon pushes the tip of the knife further into her flesh. Blood trickles down her throat, and I can't help but second guess my instincts. "Fine," I concede, lowering my weapon and tucking it into the waistband of my pants. I raise my hands. "What do you want? You kill her, you die. What's your plan here, Simon?"

"My plan?" Simon asks. "My plan is to get what I'm owed. Your uncle made a promise to me and I intend to get what I was promised. I'm going to be the next John Scalise," he tells Charlotte.

Charlotte laughs but there isn't a bit of humor in it. "You want to be the head of the family? Do you have any idea what you're asking? It's not glamorous. It's a lonely and isolated existence."

The heads of other families all seem to murmur their agreement.

"I had to send my children to boarding school to keep them safe from my world," Ove chimes in. "My relationship with them will never be what it should because of my business. It is a sacrifice my entire family had to make."

"I never had a family because I valued my business more than anything else," Francisco Diaz says.

What the hell? Am I in some kind of group therapy for

mobsters?

"I don't give a fuck," Simon says, pushing the knife further into Charlotte's skin.

Charlotte cries out and tries to pull away, but Simon yanks her back to him.

"You know what? Fuck it. Give me twenty mil—" his words are abruptly cut as pink mist sprays the air. Simon falls to the ground and Charlotte dashes toward me.

Her hair and face are covered in blood as I fold her into my arms. My hands roam over her shaking body, assessing for any more injuries.

"Are you okay?" I ask, my throat tight.

She nods as she hides her face in my chest.

A man with a beard long enough to touch his belt strikes up a conversation with Carlo Messina, asking what happened. It's a good question. A loud cough echoes through the space, and everyone turns in tandem to the awning perched at the far side of the greenhouse. There stands Ray Thatch with a sniper rifle.

"Oh my gosh," Charlotte says, covering her mouth with shock. "Ray?"

She lets go of me and jogs to the other side of the building, meeting Ray at the bottom of the steps. I follow closely behind.

Charlotte wraps her arms around Ray and hugs him. "How did you know we'd be here?"

Ray raises an eyebrow and pulls out a burner phone. "You called," he says as if it's obvious.

I suppose it is obvious. Charlotte said she had to call one number to alert the entire mobster network to gather for an emergency meeting. Ray Thatch ran the Scalise Family for years, so it's not surprising that he would have been notified too.

Tears well in her eyes. "I'm so glad I did."

I offer a hand to Ray, hoping he will let bygones be bygones. I'm not so sure a crime family is of the forgiving sort, but it's worth a try. "Thank you."

For the first time since I've met him, Ray gives a genuine

smile. It's unnatural and extremely awkward, but I'll take it.

"No. Thank you, officer," he winks. "Thank you for protecting Charlotte during these uncertain times. Mr. Petrovsky appreciates your service."

It might be his way of graciously asking me to leave, but I refuse to take the hint.

"What happened? Why is Maxym Petrovsky gunning for Charlotte?" I ask Ray as we walk toward the crowd.

Ray shoves his hands in his pants. "How do any wars start? A family feud," he answers simply. "Years ago, Vlad had to make a choice. It was the lives of his children or the Scalise Family's interests. He chose his kids as any good father would. His father demanded he return to the family, or he would hand the reins over to Maxym. His brother had a chip on his shoulder and a sadistic nature. Charlotte's grandfather was serious enough that he branded Maxym like he had Vlad. A red-hot knife to the brow."

Ray's words strike straight to my heart, and I think back to the rocky relationship between Brian and me. Like Maxym, Brian has always been a fuckup. The significant difference is that Brian couldn't hurt a fly. My appreciation for my brother has soared with a little perspective, courtesy of Ray Thatch.

"Vlad knew if he didn't heed his father's call, it would be a blood bath," Ray continues. "It almost was, too. He stormed the Scalise compound, killed seventeen men. Vlad didn't have a choice, he took the helm of the Petrovsky business in New York. He tried to satisfy his brother's sickening appetite with being second in command. I think he thought it would keep Maxym close where Vlad could keep an eye on him. When Charlie went missing, we all knew Maxym was up to no good. When Charlotte showed up at The Kaplan, we knew your uncle was going to make a move. You two were monitored for your entire stay in New York.

"When pictures of you working with the feds and your brother being dropped into the Hudson were sent to Vlad,

Maxym's motives became clear. He would take out anyone who got in his way of taking over both families. Charlie was his first target, then Charlotte and last would be Vlad."

Ray turns to Charlotte, his face solemn with regret. "Everything we did was to protect you. Your father wanted you as far away from New York as possible until he found your uncle and neutralized him. Even if it meant you hated him for the rest of your life. Maxym slipped through our fingers, and we couldn't find him until you called. Your uncle was on the call list, along with the other men in this room. We knew he would strike here. He could take you out and convince the others to do the same to your father. Two birds, one stone."

"If Vlad loves Charlotte so much, why isn't he here?" I ask, imagining the abandonment Charlotte must feel after hearing Ray's account.

"When the time is right, he'll visit," Ray says as we meet up with the pack on the other side of the greenhouse.

Gagged, tied to a chair, Maxym is sporting a black eye, swollen lips, and three missing fingers.

I take in a deep breath as I try to comprehend the sight. "You guys don't waste time, do you?"

Tyrel Ross from New Orleans chuckles. Pruning shears dangle from his fingers with blood dribbling from the tip. "I'm in my element, what can I say?"

I fight the smile which tugs at my lips but lose. These men are a completely different breed. As much as I love Charlotte, I can't help but wonder if she's cut out for the position she's fought so hard to keep. The head of a crime family isn't all money and glory. It's manipulation and gory. She's smart, sexy, and sweet. Too sweet for this life. Too sweet for this position.

Maxym's cries are muffled by the gag as Tyrel clips off another finger. Charlotte and Ray stare at the scene before us completely unaffected.

"What do you want to do with him?" Ray asks Charlotte.

Everyone turns their attention to Charlotte. Maxym's eyes

plead for mercy.

"Cut out his tongue, then feed him to the gators in the back," Charlotte orders, her chin held high.

She turns to me and clasps my hand. "How about we go home, get cleaned up, and then I'll let you treat me to a nice dinner on the town."

My thumb grazes her cheek and smudges the blood droplets, which still have yet to dry. I am in total awe of this woman. She was sprayed with brain matter, then ordered the death of a man, and now she's talking about a night out. Any concerns I had about her ability to handle the job have evaporated.

The rest of the world would do well to stay on Jane Scalise's good side. She isn't as sweet and innocent as she looks.

Epilogue

Charlotte

I'm not too proud to pat myself on the back. I did well today. My first official act as the head of the Scalise Family prevented a multi-organization crime war. Henry was happy to avoid the chaos which would come with a battle but was disheartened he didn't get to use any grenades or the flame thrower. I promised him we would take a trip to a plot of land farther inland and spend a day blowing watermelons and scarecrows to kingdom come. Secretly, I'm excited to play with the flame thrower myself, but I should probably buy a flame-retardant jumpsuit first.

I've been running on adrenaline for what feels like weeks, and the reality that I'm the boss of the family is still hard to wrap my mind around. A month ago, I was a completely different person than today. Henry and I have survived so much, and we have both emerged into a new world of understanding. Understanding that nothing is the way we thought it was. Understanding that not all bad guys are equal—although I already knew that. Understanding that Henry and I are stronger together than apart.

The first time I stepped into Henry's home, I was plagued with self-doubt. I wasn't sure I possessed the strength needed to fill Charlie or my father's shoes. However, it was surprisingly easy to sentence Maxym Petrovsky, my uncle, to death by hungry alligators. I didn't even flinch. Aside from now, I haven't thought about it once since it happened. Then again, it could be that I'm wrapped up in the strong arms of the most amazing man in the world.

"Are you sure you want to do this?" I ask Henry as we dance across the floor of one of Miami's newest night clubs. My entire life, I have been sheltered. As I learn a new version of the world, the first thing I wanted to do was be my age and hit a nightclub.

Techno pounds in the background. People jumping, flailing like their hair is on fire as the music inspires them to move. Henry and I sway back and forth like Sinatra is crooning.

"You mean about my job?" Henry pulls me tighter against him, the silk of the silver dress caressing my nipples into points. He kisses me on the cheek. "As it turns out, I have some pretty strong connections with this private business I know of. And the boss owes me a favor or two," he says with a delicious smirk.

He's too cute for his own good. "I don't know about that. I heard going private doesn't pay too well."

"I'm not in it for the money. My new boss is sexy as fuck. I'll take payment in sexual favors." His hand slides down my back and over my bottom, a finger grazing above my thigh. "Naughty girl," he says as his hand travels further up my dress. "No panties."

"No panties, indeed. What are you going to do about it? Will you squander this opportunity?"

The crotch of his pants nudges at my belly. He runs his nose along my neck. "Not a chance."

He grabs my hand and pushes through the crowd until we come to a darkened alcove by the restrooms. Our lips fuse together with anticipation and excitement as he roughly turns me around, pressing me against the wall. He hikes my dress up, and the zipper of his pants notches against my buttocks.

"You're so fucking wet," he breathes into my ear as he runs one finger through my slickness.

"That's what you do to me," I pant.

He pushes my hair to the side and nibbles along the nape of my neck. A thousand pinpricks skitter across my skin. Chatter, laughter, the drumming beat of the background is drowned out by arousal.

His thick shaft fills me. "And this is what you do to me."

The cold sensation of the wall seeps through my dress and teases the pert buds of my breasts with each thrust of Henry's hips. I can feel the latex of the condom. As much as I wish we could make love with nothing between us, I'm also relieved that he took precautions.

"I gotta take a piss," some guy calls out as he passes us.

My mind reels back to reality while Henry has his wicked way with me in the middle of a nightclub. "Henry, people can see us," I say between moans, the head of his penis hitting my deepest spot.

Henry reaches around my front and strums my clit. "That's part of the thrill. But, don't worry, cupcake, no one can see us from here. I'll always protect you."

His words whirl in my head as my belly tightens, the need for release building. Henry tugs on my ear with his teeth, and I fall apart, choking back a scream of satisfaction.

"Shit. That's it," Henry whispers in my ear, his tempo becoming erratic as he chases his orgasm. "Fuck, you're milking my dick."

His filthy words and thickening length spur on a second release as he continues to manipulate my clit. My knees are weak, and I can barely hold myself up. Thankfully, I don't need to because Henry has me pressed hard against the wall as he pounds into me.

He lets out a long groan as he comes, his hand dropping from between my legs. "Holy shit. That was . . ."

"Yeah," I sigh. There are no words.

Henry steps back and pulls out of me, straightening my dress as I turn around to look at him. "You look like you just had sex in a dark hallway," I quip, brushing his hair off his face.

He lets out a laugh as he tries to catch his breath. "Stands to reason. Something to check off my bucket list."

"You've never had sex in public?" I ask as we make our way back to the table where we were sitting.

He pulls the chair out for me. My feet dangle, and I can't help but kick them around. In the shadows of the alcove, I felt like a sex goddess. Now, with my heels barely grazing the ground, I'm back to feeling like a child.

The heated look Henry gives as he settles across from me, makes me feel marginally better. I am anything but a child to him.

The waitress appears, and I order a bottle of Cristal. "We're celebrating."

Henry looks at the wine list, and his eyes practically bug out of his head. "We are. But cupcake, I can't quite afford that. It's like fifteen grand a bottle."

"It's okay."

"No, it's not. I promised to take you out tonight. If you buy it, that's you taking me out. Let a man have some pride."

I smile inwardly. "Have you checked your bank account recently?"

"No. I haven't been working," Henry answers but then squints his eyes as he thinks a little harder. "Charlotte. I can't accept—"

"You can, and you will. I told you I would make it worth your time. I paid for your services, and you provided the protection. Brian's debt is clean."

Henry pulls out his phone, and his eyebrows shoot up to his hairline. "I can't . . . it's too . . . wow." He sits back in his seat and runs a hand over his face. "Is it safe for this much money to suddenly show up in my account? Won't it raise red flags or something?"

Probably. "Don't worry. It turns out you made a few good investments in the past month that paid off. You pulled out instead of risking the profits."

He laughs. "Do I wanna know how you made that happen?"

"Doubtful. Your cop-brain is in overdrive. You're going to want to work on that if you're going to be working for the Scalise Family."

He grabs my hand and grazes a gentle kiss on top. "Not just the Scalise Family. Jane Scalise—Queen Pin."

—

Henry

The past few months have been better than I could have ever imagined. Charlotte and I have worked side by side as we attempt to reassemble the Scalise organization. Never in my wildest dreams would I have expected to be the second in command of a crime family. I had dedicated my entire life to protecting others and upholding the laws of our city, state, and country. If someone had told me last year that I would be where I am today, I would have laughed in their face. The entire idea is ridiculous. Yet here I am, next to the most amazing woman I've ever met, helping her run her empire.

"Do you think you'll ever get tired of me?" Charlotte asks as she stirs together a batch of potato salad.

I pull her against me and run my nose along her neck, inhaling her intoxicating scent. "Impossible."

"Get a room," Brian says as he stalks in the back door.

My whole family is visiting for the afternoon. Dad is grilling on the deck while mom strolls along the beach.

"This entire house is my room," I remind him.

"Whatever," he says as he walks down the hall.

"This entire house is *our* room," Charlotte corrects.

246 | JACQUELYN MARKER

I drop a kiss on her nose. *"Our* room."

Her beautiful green eyes stare up at me, and I wonder how a bastard like me could get so lucky. My fingers skim the spaghetti strap of her dress. "I like this dress on you. But I'd like it better crumpled on the floor."

"Would you now?" she teases. "Maybe you shouldn't have invited the entire Cain family over if you wanted to spend the day in bed. Speaking of, where's Bea? I thought she was coming."

I look at my watch. "She should be here any minute. She worked the night shift and said she would drive down after a couple of hours of sleep."

As if on cue, the doorbell rings. "That must be her," I say, begrudgingly leaving Charlotte behind.

When I pull open the door, my heart drops to my feet and bounces back up to my throat. "Mr. Petrovsky, what can I do for you?"

Shoulders back, stance wide, and chin held high, he answers. "I'm here to see my daughter."

His posture oozes intimidation. I don't care who he is, he's not going to intimidate me. He may not have been the man attempting to assassinate his daughter, but I still don't trust him.

I mimic his stance and hold my ground, wishing like hell my gun wasn't locked in the safe. "I don't think that's a good idea."

"Don't make this harder than it has to be. I have moved Heaven and Earth to protect my bug. Please, do the honorable thing, and let me see her."

The anguish in his eyes strikes right at my heart. He was forced to leave his children behind, then lost his son, and almost lost his daughter. I would be a real fucking prick to deny him. Not to mention, if Charlotte found out I had turned him away, I don't think she would forgive me.

I step to the side and open the door the rest of the way. Petrovsky walks in followed by two personal bodyguards. One with a neck as wide as his shoulders, the other with tattoos covering every inch of exposed skin.

"Is everything okay?" Charlotte stops in her tracks, a dishtowel dangling from her hands when she lays eyes on her father.

She seems to pull herself together after a moment and moves forward a few steps before catching her foot on the corner of the area rug. Her entire body plunges forward, the towel flying out of her hands as she skids across the tile floor.

When she comes to a full stop, she's directly in front of her father, staring at his shoes. "Hello, Daddy."

Petrovsky smiles with amusement, and it's the oddest thing I've seen in my life. "Hello, bug."

Charlotte works to stand, and I rush to her side to help, but No-Neck beats me to it. He hooks an arm around Charlotte's waist and pulls her upright.

The guy may be trying to be helpful. Maybe it's expected of him, and he knows if he lets his boss's daughter stay on the floor unattended, he'll be buried in the foundation of a new building. No matter his reason, I hate him touching her.

"Are you okay?" I ask Charlotte as I not so discreetly heave the beastly bodyguard away.

Charlotte snorts an embarrassed laugh. "Yeah, I'm fine." She turns her attention to Petrovsky. "Daddy, what are you doing here?"

Her father takes a look around, and I know he's judging my modest home. He probably doesn't think it's good enough for his daughter.

Petrovsky clears his throat. "I know we didn't part on the best of terms. And, I wanted to make amends."

I huff my disgust. I don't believe a word Petrovsky is spewing. He may not have been the bad guy, but he isn't a good one either. I realize how hypocritical the thought is since I gave up my shield to join the other side, but it doesn't change how I feel.

"Have a seat," Charlotte says to her father as she fluffs throw pillows on the couch.

Petrovsky wrinkles his nose with disgust but accepts Charlotte's invitation and sits next to her. "Like I said, I wanted to make amends. You have found yourself an honorable young man," he says, pointing to me. "And, I can tell you are working to make a new life for yourself. From what I've heard, you've made a lot of progress restoring the family business."

Charlotte and I have spent the past six months rebuilding the Scalise Family brand and fighting tooth and nail to take it back to its former glory. I never understood precisely what they did in the crime world. As I've recruited security and runners, I've learned more about organized crime than any cop should. The Scalise Family is not a family, per se. More like a company. The CEO passes the baton to his next of kin until someone runs a coup, and the tradition continues. Their dealings are mostly transactional, I'm not even sure they could be classified as illegal. They don't procure, sell, or trade any black-market commodities. They're more like mediators. However, the circles they work within are filled with the most dangerous people in the world. That, in and of itself, is the family's most valuable asset.

"We have," Charlotte agrees with her father as she smiles at me.

"You have a lovely home, Henry Cain," Petrovsky says, and I'm shocked to receive any type of compliment. "But—"

There's always a *but*.

"I think," Petrovsky continues, "my daughter, and her legacy, will require a little more."

"There's nothing wrong with—"

Vlad cuts me off. "No, of course not. There is nothing wrong with your home. But in this business, you will need a home with certain amenities." He sets a paper on the coffee table in front of him. "The Petrovsky Family would like to gift you a new home."

Charlotte leaps into her father's arms. "Daddy, you shouldn't have."

"I wanted to," he answers. "I understand if we must part

ways. Not all businesses mix. But, I do hope maybe someday, we might find some common ground which would benefit both sides."

Charlotte smiles at his words. Warmth and love between them are undeniable. It's hard for me to understand how she could so easily forgive him after everything that happened in New York, but that's a problem between the two of them.

Petrovsky stands and makes his way to the front door, his goons following on his heels. He turns to me and offers his hand. I accept, begrudgingly, and he pulls me into a hug. "You are a good man, and one day we will be family. But if you hurt her, I will kill you."

My blood runs cold as he releases me. I've been threatened more times in my life than I care to count, but I've never felt the conviction the way I did when Petrovsky said it.

Charlotte walks her father out to a car that idles at the curb in front of the house. I know I should wait for Charlotte to look at the deed on the table, but my curiosity gets the better of me. I unfold the paper and scan the words, then reread it because there is no way this can be right.

Holy shit.

"What's wrong?" Charlotte asks, walking up and wrapping her arms around me, resting her head on my chest. "You look like you're about to throw up."

"Your father bought us an island."

She laughs. "Welcome to the life."

Acknowledgments

Writing this story was a whirlwind filled with research and plenty of craziness in my home life. I am beyond grateful for my friends and family who supported me through it all. Thank you, Beth Yurosko, for helping me talk out my ideas. Craig Nix, you're keen eye for detail saved me more times than I can count. My mom definitely deserves a shout-out for being so supportive, even though the story is a bit naughty. Kaley and Seth, thank you for leaving me alone, so this mama could pursue her passion. Of course, I can't forget my puppies, Fitz and Cooper, for hanging with me in my office for hours at a time while I pounded on the keyboard. I wouldn't have been able to do it without my amazing editor, Kylee—you're amazing. Most of all, a huge thanks to you, my dear reader; you're the reason I do this.

About the Author

Jacquelyn Marker is the mother of two amazing children and a full-time nurse. She lives in Indiana with her adorable mix breed dog who is obsessed with playing fetch and a mischievous corgi that completes her soul. Jacquelyn enjoys bringing love and laughter into the lives of everyone around her. Blending the absurd with passion, Jacquelyn specializes in bringing a new angle to the romance genre.

CPSIA information can be obtained
at www.ICGtesting.com
Printed in the USA
FSHW010030110122
87506FS

9 781942 856993